VENCEREMOS

a novel by
HOWARD WAXMAN

⌘

VENCEREMOS

© **Howard Waxman 2011**

ISBN: 978-1-936447-60-2

All rights reserved. No part of this book may be reproduced in any form or by any electronic or mechanical means, including information storage and retrieval systems, without permission in writing from the author, except by a reviewer, who may quote brief passages in review.

Designed by Maine Authors Publishing, Rockland, Maine
www.maineauthorspublishing.com

Cover painting: *Cutting Sugar Cane*, by Ferdinando Tacconi, used by permission of Look and Learn, Ltd.

– For Lisa –
Take these broken wings and learn to fly

A Brief Word about Fiction and Fact…

Venceremos is a work of fiction. A fundamental element of the plot is a massive explosion in a townhouse in Greenwich Village. This event, which takes place in the fall of 1969 in the novel, is obviously based on the actual townhouse explosion that took place in May 1970 on W. 11th Street. My fictional version of the event is not meant in anyway to be about that actual event but is instead an effort to use that terrible and sad moment for its dramatic value. My descriptions of the life and people in that house in the months before the explosion reflect my experiences and observations from the same moment in time among people of the same age and perspective but in other houses on other streets in other cities. In no way do I mean to suggest any connection between the real explosion and anyone involved in the real Venceremos Brigade or for that matter any Americans in Cuba at that time.

…and About the Title

Venceremos is Spanish for, depending on the translator, "We Shall Win," "We Will Triumph," or "We Will Overcome." It has long been a rallying cry for South American revolutionaries. In our time it is most closely associated with Che Guevara.

ACKNOWLEDGEMENTS

Thanks to the many friends who read *Venceremos* as it progressed through several "final" drafts and who contributed—in addition to their encouragement—thoughtful comments about my writing as well as insights into the Cuba and America of 40 years ago. Each reader's contribution inevitably led to the next "final" draft.

Two printed sources were especially important. The first of these was *Cuban Journal* (Zoland Books, 2000) by the poet Joel Sloman who chronicled his experience in the Second Brigade in a diary format that provided me with a timeline for my story as well as many images to inspire my imagination.

The other key source was *Venceremos Brigade* (Simon and Schuster, 1971, eds. Sandra Levinson and Carol Brightman), a compilation of letters, diary entries, and other writings by many Brigade members that evoke the feelings, attitudes, and concerns of many on the Left at that particular time as well as providing more detail on the Brigade experience.

And special thanks to the team at Maine Authors Publishing—Cheryl, David, Genie, and Jane—for their tremendous support and encouragement.

In this age, which believes that there is a short cut to everything, the greatest lesson to be learned is that the most difficult way, in the long run, is the easiest.

—Henry Miller

PART I
Canada

- One –

This was back in 1970 when I went from wounded hero to deserter and headed up to Canada so as to stay out of prison. I was traveling with Sheri Cooper, who was set on joining a commune on Vancouver Island where some friends of hers from the Haight had gone on before.

I'd met Sheri in Golden Gate Park right after I arrived in San Francisco from New York via Chicago, Madison, Wisconsin, Denver, and a few other towns. I'd been watching a theater group do some antiwar skits on a little stage they'd set up. The bits were funny but at the same time scary in how they caught the craziness that was the war.

I wondered if seeing the skit before I was drafted would have prompted me to do more to stay out of the service. Probably not. I knew it was possible to resist the draft—I mean, Mohammad Ali had done it all over the front pages and the back pages of the *News* and the *Post*, so it wasn't a secret. But he had had the guts to stand up and take the punishment and I didn't. He was the Champ and gave it all up. I had nothing to lose and still couldn't do it.

As I was walking away after the show thinking about where I was going to lay my weary head I heard a woman's voice calling out, "Bill! Hey, Bill!" Since my name is Jay, it made no sense to look around. But I knew she meant me and I looked. She was in the crowd that had been watching the show and waved me over. I said my name was Jay and I didn't think we had ever met. She told me we never had but that she had felt a very strong vibe when I walked by and couldn't let me pass on by without calling out to me. The fact that I turned was proof that the vibe between us was real.

We hung out for the next few weeks, heading down to Big Sur on the weekends, sleeping out on the beach, making love in the rain, and generally having a fine time. Sheri was a big girl and warm and soft, and she folded herself around me like a thick quilt. It was exactly what I needed from the world. I think I made her happy, too. At least she said I did.

Sheri had a day job but had given notice and was getting ready for her move to Vancouver. I explained my fugitive situation, but to her, that was just further confirmation that we were supposed to meet and that it was her purpose to get me out of the country. I was more than happy to believe it was true … and anyhow, it worked out that way.

The commune was fairly copasetic. People actually worked. A lot of communes were just an excuse to lie around and get stoned until the money ran out. But this place, Pacific Breeze, was serious. The leader, Bob Zamchek, aka Ori, was an anal-compulsive former Eagle Scout who understood he had paradise for the taking. He was going to make sure it worked. Determined as he was, he was also the sweetest guy in the world and the happiest in his work that I had ever known—except possibly for some wigged-out Special Forces guys back in Vietnam who were in heaven because they got to kill people as part of their job description.

The commune grew fruits and vegetables, and there were small but thriving herds of cows and goats and sheep. The main business, though, was the vineyard, which was still new but being coaxed along with a great deal of tender loving care. I don't recall how many acres the whole place was, but I remember being impressed. Of course, I was a city boy, so anything bigger than a city block would have impressed me.

When we got to the commune, Sheri officially changed her name to Wildflower. I should have changed my name since I was on the lam, but what did it matter? The Canadians knew who I was but didn't care. The Army knew *where* I was but couldn't do anything to me if the Canadians wouldn't help.

Except for Vietnam, I hadn't been out of the country before. In fact, except for Vietnam, I had hardly ever been out of New York before. There was no question but that I missed the city and my life there. But I knew that what I'd had was gone. Friends had moved on or were dead, and I was on the outs with my family because of my being a deserter. I could still speak to my mom, but my dad wanted nothing to do with me.

He was a genuine hero, from World War II. He'd saved his whole platoon, holding off an enemy attack while the other guys made it back to cover. I was supposed to be a hero, but what I had done was just kill a lot of Vietnamese while the rest of my platoon ran. I'd have run, too, if I'd known they had all taken off, but I was out on the end of the line and no one had bothered to tell me we were cutting out.

My father knew his brothers-in-arms were hauling ass, but he stayed on the line anyway. He got wounded, got a medal and points, and got to come home when the rest of his unit was sent to Japan. I got wounded and got a medal and the Army gave me special leave to go home for R&R. They made a mistake. Once I got stateside, I was never ever going back to that jungle.

My dad had finally gotten to be proud of me instead of pissed off at me, which was what he usually was, and I had snatched it away from him. His son the hero had become his son the deserter. We got to yelling at each other about it and he told me to turn myself in and take my punishment. It was the last thing he said to me.

As much as I hated disappointing him yet again, I couldn't deal with the twenty years in prison I'd be facing for having taken off. Maybe it would have been fewer than that, maybe more, but whatever it was, it just wasn't anything I could do. A year in Vietnam had taught me a lot about my limitations.

So I stayed on the commune and tried to figure out a way to make things right without making my life more of a mess than it already was. While I pondered, I took care of the goats, helped out in the vineyard, ran errands, and generally made myself as useful as I could be, even though I wasn't officially a member. You had to buy shares to be a real member. (As I mentioned, this was a serious place.) Most of the people at Pacific Breeze had done that, using money earned by dealing drugs or from legitimate day jobs or by cashing in the trust funds their grandpas had left them.

I didn't have any money, but even if I did I wouldn't have joined. The members, even those as young as me, had all passed through their restless years but I was still in mine. It's no good pretending to settle down when your home is somewhere else. For me, Pacific Breeze was just a good place to be at that moment when my options were so few.

Curling up each night with Wildflower was good, too. But that was coming to an end. I could see that she and Ori were giving each other the eye. Everyone was cool, no pressure, no hurry, but cool only goes so far when a man and a woman need to get together. Sheri and I weren't in love and no one's heart was going to be broken. We had become instant great friends who had found each other at just the right moment. Now it was more a matter of where I was going to sleep when the time came to change partners. And that time was near. Maybe it was even past.

- Two -

With Wildflower and Ori wanting to get together, what I should do next was becoming more critical. I could have stayed. We were all friends, and it wasn't unusual for people to change partners without anyone having a trauma. This may sound like a lot of hippie crap today, but that's how it was. Of course, there were plenty of times when people were broken up when a lover left them for another, especially a friend. It certainly happened to me more than once (one time by sisters, Abbie then Ginnie Newman, one right after the other). All I'm saying is that a lot of the mythology of the sixties was based on reality. Often enough, we were as groovy as advertised.

That a switch was coming was obvious to all, and there were a few young women who were waiting to comfort me upon my impending loss. They, like me, were not members, just transients on the great hippie highway that stretched around the globe, working on the farm in exchange for room and board. I was envious of their freedom to move on. I could travel from one end of Canada to the other, which I figured was my next move, but once I reached the Atlantic, I couldn't see what was next except to turn around and head back west or to the far north while they could continue on to Paris, Istanbul, Katmandu, and beyond.

Then everything changed.

It was a Monday. I went into town to pick up the commune mail and a few things at the general store. The post office in Cowichan Bay was small, and there was usually only one person at work there except when the mail was being sorted out for delivery by the two carriers. This day it was Maggie the postmistress there by herself except for the two mugs lounging near the front door.

They were both dressed in seersucker suits, which seemed totally odd for February, even though the weather was mild and totally odd was not unusual on Vancouver Island. One was tall and bald with a thick mustache to compensate for his bare head. The other was short with sharp features but spongy skin. He wore a porkpie hat. They looked ridiculous but also deadly. They gave off an air of not caring. They wouldn't care if they hurt you, and they wouldn't care either if you hurt them. Pain was for sissies. They were beyond pain.

Maggie was trying to ignore them, but it was clear they were making her nervous, hanging out looking at the notices on the bulletin board and staring out the front window. They made me nervous as soon as I saw them. There was no question in my mind but that they were there for me. They weren't Army but definitely some kind of government agents. Maybe FBI, maybe CIA, maybe something so secret no one even knew about it.

I wanted to turn and run right out the door, jump in the commune pickup, peel out, and just go as fast and as far as I could until there was no more gas, then get out and run until my sneakers fell apart. If I ran, neither of them could catch me. I could tell that just looking at them. I was fast on my feet in those days. But I could also tell by looking at them that they wouldn't hesitate to put a bullet in my back.

As much time as it took these thoughts to go through my mind was as much time as they needed to close in on me.

"Jay Cardinale?" said Short One.

"Yeah." I couldn't say much. I was scared shitless. It was the most scared I'd been since coming back from the war. The most scared I'd been since Dau Tieng, when it looked like we were all going to die.

"Could you spare a few minutes?" said Short One. "For a little conversation?"

I knew he knew how scared I was. It didn't take much to see it if you knew about these things.

"Sure. Yeah. What's up?"

"There's some people want to talk to you. They're waiting over at the diner. If you don't mind …"

The diner? This was unexpected. I figured they were going to take me for a ride. The diner was across the street. Was it a trick? I didn't move. Tall One spoke.

"Come on, bud. This won't take long."

I looked at Maggie. Was she the last friendly face I'd ever see?

"I just need to get the mail."

I went to the counter. I didn't know Maggie really well. I'd only come into the post office to get the mail maybe a half dozen times since coming to the commune. We made small talk about the weather, sports, and farming. I felt she was worried about me, but I was sure right at that moment that she was worried more about herself and would be much happier if we all left before the shooting started.

"Hi, Maggie."

"Jay."

"You have the mail for Pacific Breeze?"

"Right here."

She had it ready and handed it to me. I put it in a bag I'd brought with me just for that purpose.

"Great. Well, gotta run. See ya."

I wanted her to press the button under the counter that would make the cops come. Then I realized I was thinking of a bank. This was the post office. I had to get a grip.

I went to the door and the seersuckers followed me out.

We crossed the street toward the diner.

"Why were you waiting in the post office?"

"Because you were coming for the mail," said Short One.

"But how did you know that?"

"We asked."

"Asked who?"

"People."

Jeez, I thought. Had they been to the commune? Had they ever come at night and stood over me while I was sleeping? Why was I thinking things like that? They were here now and they had me, so what did it matter how or when whatever else had happened.

There was a big shiny black Lincoln parked in front of the diner and we were heading toward it. They were going to take me for a ride, after all. My legs were getting wobbly. I was too scared to be embarrassed.

"I want a muffin," I said.

"What?" said Tall One.

"A muffin. At the diner. A Saskatoon berry muffin."

"A what-berry?"

"Saskatoon. They grow here."

"Sure. I'll have one, too."

How will you have one, I thought, since we're not going to the diner?

Except we were. We went right past the Lincoln and into the diner. Tall One held the door then followed in behind me and Short One.

I liked the diner. They had good coffee and great muffins, especially the Saskatoon berry. The place wasn't too crowded. Breakfast was over and lunch hadn't started. I recognized some of the faces at the counter from my other trips to town, but I hadn't been around enough for anyone to offer a greeting. The only friendly gesture came from a man in the booth at the far corner, waving for us to join him. I figured he was the man who wanted to talk to me. He looked familiar, fiftyish, handsome, but I couldn't place him.

A woman sat facing him in the booth. The back of her head looked great, her light brown hair glowing all the way across the diner, growing brighter as we walked to the table. It radiated health as if it had been brushed firmly for a long time by a specialist whose only task was to make hair shine.

We were at the table and the man stood and held out his hand to me. "Ed McWilliams," he said as we shook hands. "This is my wife, Lauren." She looked up and gave me the slightest nod. Her face glowed. Not the same as her hair, but still a glow.

I should have recognized them. I'd been in their home and seen their pictures in almost every room. The pictures didn't do them justice. It took seeing them in person to realize how healthy rich they looked, sporting the kind of grooming that lots of money can buy. Not just the effort and products of grooming, but money to buy the time needed if it were really going to show.

I looked at McWilliams's hand as we shook and I thought about my father's hands, the black cracks in his skin that never went away, and the nails, always splintered and dirty from working out in the weather, no matter the effort he put in to keep them clean.

"Please," said McWilliams, gesturing toward the booth seat he'd just vacated. "Sit."

I slid in. He sat down next to his wife. The seersuckers stopped at the counter and took up a pair of stools. McWilliams never looked at them.

I had shaved and showered that morning and put on a clean shirt wanting not to embarrass the commune when I went into town by looking like a cliché hippie. But now, looking at the two McWilliamses, I felt like God's own hippie. When was the last time I'd had a real haircut?

"Would you like a cup of coffee? Have you had breakfast? They have terrific muffins here."

"Um…" was all I managed to get out before the waitress arrived. I'd been in the diner before and the service wasn't bad, but it wasn't in overdrive, either. Yet even though McWilliams hadn't gestured, the waitress seemed somehow to have come in response to his desire that she be there. I wondered if he had been throwing money around from the moment he stepped in the door, or if it was only the feeling that he *might* if everyone there proved worthy.

The waitress—I was pretty sure her name was Joanie—smiled down at me as if she had just found Jesus. "What can I get for you?"

"Just coffee," I said.

"Have a muffin," said McWilliams. "Saskatoon berry. They're great."

There were no plates on the table, just the coffee cups that he and his wife were drinking from. If either had had a muffin earlier, the dishes had already been cleared. Or did he just know, even without the actual experience, that the Saskatoon berry muffins were special?

"Sure," I said. "That'll be great."

"Great," repeated the waitress, her smile getting even bigger in defiance of all the laws of nature. As she moved away from the table, I said, "I'm sorry about Edward. He was a good guy."

It was easy to say. Eddie McWilliams *was* a good guy. In fact, he was sort of a great guy. Most rich kid radicals like Eddie had cut off ties with their parents, even when their parents were liberals. Eddie's parents were very conservative (maybe ultraconservative would be more accurate) with lots of government connections and business ties to the war machine. Yet Eddie remained in touch with them, was respectful and loving. At least he was until the last days before the explosion that blew their New York City townhouse to pieces. Before that, he was intent on persuading them they had to change their ways. In retrospect, Eddie was a saint.

I got to know him while I was avoiding the Army's request that I return to Vietnam. He was working at a draft counseling center in the Village. We had some long talks, and when I needed to disappear, he hid me in his parents' house while we worked on a strategy for getting me out of the country. Through Eddie, I got to know a lot of the Movement kids. His house was a popular hangout that summer while his parents were in Europe, where his dad was supposedly making all kinds of evil arms deals. There were lots of drugs, lots of music, lots of arguing, and lots of sex. Looking at his parents now, I realized I'd probably messed up the sheets on their bed a dozen times or more.

"He wrote us about you," said McWilliams. About me being in their bed? I wondered. "He said you were very brave and also thoughtful and responsible. Very mature for your age."

I guessed he hadn't written about the bed.

"Well, he was all of those things, too" I said. "That's for sure. It's a terrible loss."

It was. Eddie was the kind of guy who you'd want to see as president someday. Maybe that's why he was dead already. Get the really good ones out of the way early.

"You knew Roger, too, didn't you?" said McWilliams. "The one who made the bomb?"

"I met him. A couple of times." I was lying, but it seemed the right thing to do. They might stop being so nice if they knew how much time I'd really spent with Roger.

"Did you know about the bombs?" said Mrs. McWilliams. She put it as a question, but it sounded like an accusation. Like, "Of course you knew about the bombs, you lying piece of cowardly deserter shit. And I know you knew about them and you're just as guilty as Roger."

Of course, I did know about the bombs. That's why I left. I didn't want to be anywhere near a bomb or a gun (they had plenty of those there, too) or a knife or a firecracker or, for that matter, anyone raising their voice. It was my own personal Peace Movement.

I had told Eddie the bomb stuff was all crazy. And he knew it, too. But Roger was one of those Svengalis that thrive in troubled times, and he had Eddie, as well as plenty of others, under a spell. It was the romantic spell of revolution, of the good fight, of Liberté, Égalité, Fraternité. We all got dewy-eyed when we heard the words. I still get that way. But the dew in my eyes didn't keep me from looking for the door.

Eddie couldn't go. He was home. Of course, Eddie was already a believer. But he had been committed to nonviolence until Roger turned him at the end.

So I lied to Mrs. McWilliams, to Lauren. "No," I said. "I was kind of an outsider. I was looking for help, you know, some advice about what to do. I wasn't actually part of the group." A true lie. I wasn't part of the group, but I wasn't exactly an outsider.

"Really?" she said.

I suddenly wanted to know why they were here. Seeing them, the grieving parents, had disarmed me after the initial panic with the seersuckers. I was ready for trouble and then here were these clean, wealthy people and life was suddenly coffee and muffins.

"Here you go," said Joanie, serving me my coffee and muffin. "Enjoy!"

As soon as she was away from the booth, McWilliams said, "You were in the group and you spent a lot of time with Roger."

He spoke in a matter-of-fact fashion, not accusatory, not angry. Just letting me know I was an asshole with a muffin. I didn't even try to argue. So much for my sensitivity to their feelings.

"Are you in touch with him now?" he said.

"No, I don't have anything to do with him."

"But you know where he is, don't you? You know he's in Cuba."

"Sure, it's not a secret. He went there after the explosion."

"And you haven't been in touch with him since he went there?"

"Look, I did spend time with Roger and I did know about the bombs. But I was gone before they blew everything up. And I was gone because I knew he was trouble and I didn't want to be there. And now I don't want to be here."

I slid out of the booth dragging my mail bag with me. The seersuckers got up from the counter, blocking the way out. My stomach was doing flip-flops. McWilliams put his hand on my arm.

"Please sit down, Jay. We're not done."

It seemed so ridiculous. It was daytime. We were in a public place with people around. People drinking coffee and eating muffins. People reading the newspaper or their mail. People talking about fishing. But

I was in a living nightmare with two beautiful rich people who hated me for killing their son, even though I didn't do it, and two thugs who looked ready to cut me into little pieces and then kill me.

"Sit," said McWilliams. "We have an offer for you."

"An offer? What kind of offer?"

"A good offer. Please. Sit."

I slid back in the booth. The seersuckers went back to their coffee.

"What do you want from me?"

Lauren spoke. "It's very simple. We want you to go to Cuba. We want you to go there, find Roger, and kill him."

I thought I must be delirious. Maybe someone on the commune had dropped some acid in my coffee that morning and I was tripping and didn't know it. Maybe none of this was happening. I really wanted it to be that or something like that. But I'd tripped enough to know the difference between the acid world and the real world. This was real.

"He killed my son," said Lauren. "He murdered him."

"It was an accident. A terrible accident—"

"No," she said. "It was murder. He killed him on purpose. It's the truth. I know it."

I wasn't going to argue with her. I took a bite of my muffin. Good as ever. I smiled as I chewed, thinking the smile would hold them off until I could think of a way to escape. I swallowed. My mind was blank.

I heard myself say, "I have to get back to the commune. I have the mail."

Well, it's true, I thought. They'll have to let me go. The mail must go through.

I started out of the booth again and the seersuckers swiveled on their stools to face me. This time they didn't even bother to get up. They knew I wasn't through yet.

"Hear us out," said McWilliams. "It's the least you can do." No, I thought, the least I can do is curl up in a fetal position and stay that way until you leave.

"For Eddie," said Lauren.

Oh, jeez, I thought, the dead boy's mom asks you to stay, and even though she wants you to kill someone, you have to listen. *That* was the least I could do. I took another bite of the muffin.

Lauren took over the conversation now, explaining their plan. "We want you to join the Venceremos Brigade. You know what that is, right? Americans going to Cuba to help with the sugar harvest? They're leaving for Havana next week and we can get you in. The fellow who lives next door to our place in Connecticut is quite the liberal, and if we tell him about you, the famous hero deserter wanting to go to Cuba, we are certain he can make it happen."

She went through the details with a calm but proud eagerness that made me feel like I was on the decorations committee for the Harvest Moon Ball at the country club and Lauren was in charge, and Gee, Madge, this is going to be the best ball ever!

I chewed and she talked. Roughly, it came down to this: Their neighbor in Connecticut (next door to their country house, the one that didn't get blown up like their city house) would pull some strings in the antiwar movement and throw some money around to get me into the Brigade. I'd go down to Cuba, run into Roger at some welcoming ceremony or some other place like a clubhouse where all the American exiles hung out, pick up the ties that bind, get closer and closer, and, when the right moment came, I'd kill him. They had a poison for me to slip into his coffee. It would look like he had a heart attack. No one would know I did it. And when the Brigade was finished chopping sugarcane, I'd simply come back with the others. That was it, more or less, and wasn't it a splendid plan? Madge would have been proud.

But I wasn't Madge. I had no pride.

"Um," I said.

They waited for more. I forced myself to focus.

"Um, Mrs. McWilliams, Mr. McWilliams, I liked Eddie. I liked him a lot. And I think Roger's really scum. But I can't do this."

"Why not?" she said.

"I can't just go and kill someone."

"But you've killed before," said Lauren. "You killed a lot of people. You got medals for doing it."

"That was war. And I didn't want to kill anyone then. I was trying to stay alive."

"But this will be safe. I explained it."

I realized she truly believed that it would be as simple for me to do as it was for her to describe. I wouldn't get anywhere trying to argue details with her. I looked to her husband to see if he also believed that it would be simple or if there might be a chance of reasoning with him.

"You think it will be safe?"

"We wouldn't ask you to do it if we didn't think so," he said.

He was lying. But he wasn't going to disagree with his wife in front of me. Probably not when they were alone, either. She needed to believe that Roger could be killed. She was clinging to it and he wasn't going to upset her with a reality check. He wanted to make her happy. Whatever happened to me was irrelevant.

"Of course," he continued, "we're going to make it worth your while."

"I don't think—"

He cut me off. "Would you like to go home, Jay? See your parents, get your life going again? I bet you would."

And suddenly we were there, what it was all about.

"We have friends, Jay. The most powerful friends you can imagine. You could be pardoned. You could go back to the States."

"Mr. McWilliams, I know you have a lot of friends in the government. Eddie talked a lot about that. But a pardon? I don't think—"

He reached inside his blazer and brought out an envelope and handed it to me. I opened it and took out the letter it held. It was my pardon, signed by the president.

"Wow."

"Wow, indeed," said McWilliams.

"But won't there be questions? I mean, I'm a well-known deserter."

"A ruse to disguise your courageous undercover work tracking down subversives for your government."

"So everyone's gonna think I'm a rat."

"They'll think you're a hero," said Lauren.

"They? They who?" I said.

"Your father," said McWilliams. "From what I understand he's rather upset with you. Do this thing for us, and you can be a hero again. His hero."

Wow, I thought. These guys are good. I suddenly thought of the book *1984*. One of the things that stuck with me from when I read it in high school was how they knew the guy's innermost fears. He would do anything they wanted once he understood they were inside his head.

"We never got to say goodbye to Eddie," said Lauren, her voice beginning to rise. She couldn't hold it back any longer. Her face became distorted and tears filled her eyes. "I never got to say goodbye to my boy!"

She made a horrible sobbing cry and tried to stand, shoving the table up against me as she jerked upwards. McWilliams got his arms around her and kept her in place. The people in the diner turned to look. The seersuckers stood up and everyone went back to their own business. The seersuckers sat.

Lauren sobbed and McWilliams patted her shoulder.

"I know, darling. I know."

I didn't know what to do. The table had me trapped in my seat, but I didn't want to push it back while she was crying. After a minute, she got control of herself.

"We need you, Jay," said McWilliams.

"I have to think."

I was just stalling and I knew it and they knew it. They had played me just right.

McWilliams reached out for the pardon. I held onto it for a moment, then let him take it from my hands. It wasn't as if the seersuckers were going to let me leave with it. He tucked it back inside his blazer. His hand came back out holding a business card. There was nothing on it but a phone number.

"Call us," he said.

We were done. McWilliams slid out of the booth and stepped back to make room for Mrs. McWilliams, who slid out right behind him.

She looked down at me as she stood. "Call us soon."

They walked to the door. The seersuckers got up and walked out behind them. As he left, Tall One flashed me the peace sign, then turned his hand down, pointing his index finger and snapping his thumb down like the hammer of a gun. I heard the Lincoln start up and drive away.

- Three -

The commune truck was back at the post office, but I turned the other way and went up the street to the gas station. There was a phone booth there, outside by the bathroom. I called the operator and placed a collect call to Brooklyn.

My mother answered before the first ring had finished, her familiar suspicious voice whispering a wary greeting, ready to hang up should it turn out that it was Satan on the other end of the line ready to snake his evil way through the line and grab her by the throat. Dolly Cardinale was not going to be caught off guard.

"Hello?"

"Ma, it's me."

She accepted the call.

"Oh, baby, is it really you?"

"Yeah, Ma, it's really me. No kidding."

"Where are you?"

"I'm still in Canada, Ma."

"Oh. Okay. You sound so close, I thought maybe you was home."

"No, Ma, not yet. Listen, how are you?"

"How am I? The same as always."

"How's Daddy? Is he feeling any better?"

When I left New York, my dad had been laid up for a week with the flu, and, according to my mother, had been complaining about feeling bad ever since.

"Your father is a joke. All he does is complain. His back hurts, his legs hurt, his arms hurt. I tell him, 'Go bowling, then you'll know why you hurt.'"

"Did he go to the doctor, Ma?"

"He won't see the doctor. He hates doctors. You know that."

"I know, I know."

"Jay, don't tell him I told you, but he hasn't gone to work now for two weeks."

"How would I tell him that since he won't speak to me?"

Two weeks. He'd missed a couple of weeks before I left New York. For Lou Cardinale to skip work, he had to feel like dog shit. It shook me up, but I didn't want to scare her.

"It's winter, Ma. He's just achy."

"It's more than that, Jay. Jay, I'm scared."

"Is he there?"

"He's taking a nap."

A nap. My father never took a nap in his life. Now *I* was getting scared.

"Look, Ma, tell Uncle Frank to talk to him about the doctor."

"All right. We'll try again."

"Again?"

"He talked to him already. They had a fight."

"Okay, Ma. Well, keep trying."

"When are you coming home, Jay? I could use a hand here."

"Soon as I can, Ma. Soon as I can."

"I love you, Jay."

"Love you, too, Ma."

I hung up but stayed in the booth for a minute thinking about my father. I wondered how much of what was going on with him was because of me.

- Four -

Ori and Wildflower hurried out to the truck when I got back to the commune.

"Oh, man, we were so worried," said Ori.

"Maggie called. She said a couple of guys kidnapped you," said Wildflower.

Maggie had called. That made me feel good.

"We didn't want to call the cops. In case, you know, it was nothing," said Ori.

I told them what had happened.

"So, what are you gonna do?" said Ori.

We had gone into Ori's office in the old farmhouse that had been on the property when he purchased the first parcel of land that became Pacific Breeze. From the office, there was a wonderful view of the new vineyard, a view that usually filled me with more hope than I typically held for myself or the world. I stared at it now and it was like an engine that wouldn't catch. It sputtered and heaved and refused to turn over.

"I don't know. I am open to suggestions."

No one said anything for several moments. The three of us sat and stared out at the vineyard and at each other, at the floor and the ceiling, at our hands and our navels. We stared at the insides of our eyelids.

Then Ori spoke.

"We oughta go up Mount Tzuhalem. Very spiritual place. A place to go for answers."

I had no idea what he was talking about.

"Where is it?"

"Just north of town. You see it from just about everywhere."

I knew the place he meant. It never occurred to me it had a name. It was just "the mountain north of town." Maybe that's what Tzuhalem meant in Indian.

"What do we do?"

"We'll hike up. There's a trail and a great view from the top. The valley, the bay. Everything will make sense."

"I think it's a great idea," said Wildflower.

"Well," I said, "it can't hurt."

I spent the rest of the day with the goats. Wildflower slept with me that night. We didn't make love, but she kept me warm.

The next morning we got an early start. It was chilly and clear. A sparkling day. Ori had an old Jeep that he had bought real cheap and fixed up himself, auto mechanics being one of his many real-life merit badges, and we took that instead of the commune truck. He'd done a super job, putting in lots of customized details, most notably the best springs he could find so that the ride was smoother than in any Jeep on the planet. He called the Jeep "Java," and I think he loved it about as much as he loved Pacific Breeze.

Ori had made some peanut-butter-and-raisin sandwiches on bread baked right there on the commune and had packed little bags of trail mix, a thermos of coffee, a jug of water, a flask of brandy, and a baggie with a few joints. He had a first aid kit, small but complete, and, just in case, a police whistle that could be heard over great distances. He also had half a roll of toilet paper and a flashlight. He carried most of the gear in a backpack. I carried the water. Wildflower carried her camera, an old Nikon that weighed half a ton but took great pictures. She didn't hang onto a lot of treasures, but the Nikon was one.

We drove to the trailhead just north of the town, past the stone church. The hike was easy at first but got steep toward the top, and we had to scramble up some tricky outcroppings. I was never a Boy Scout or much of a camper or outdoorsman. My contacts with nature came mostly from swimming in the ocean at Coney Island and standing at the rail of the fishing boats that went out from Sheepshead Bay. But Army training had done me good, and even though it had been several months since I'd been in the field, not to mention having a bayonet stuck in me, I was able to hold my own.

We reached a meadow surrounded by gnarly trees that spread sideways as much as they grew tall. Ori said they were Garry oaks. He could have told me they were rubber trees and I'd have said okay. He named all the flowers growing there, too—blue camas, spring gold, shooting stars, and more. Yet another merit badge. It would have been annoying, but he had mastered the art of sharing information like this without being overbearing about it. It just made him more lovable. I looked at Wildflower as she was looking at him and knew without a doubt how happy they were going to be together.

We continued to climb and came up to a big white cross.

"A little further," said Ori. "There's a good place to stretch out."

In a few minutes we were there. The view was, as promised, spectacular. The water of the bay shone in the sunlight and the valley glowed. Long patches of snow reflected the light so sharply it made us blink. Wildflower took a few pictures with the big Nikon while Ori and I cleared away some fallen branches to make a good clean place to sit.

We leaned back against the cliff face, staring out at the panorama, and let the sun warm us. There was no breeze, and at this time of the year no insects to speak of. Ori opened his knapsack, reached into an inside pocket, and came up with a joint and a small box of matches. Waterproof, of course.

"A reward for a job well done," he said, lighting up.

We passed the smoke around, took a slug of brandy, and ate our sandwiches. After a while, Ori dozed off, snoring gently. The soft rasping melded with all the other sounds of nature. Wildflower sat beside him and stroked his hair. We smiled at each other then went back to staring out at the beauty of it all.

I tried figuring out what I was seeing, where things were, roads and farms and ponds. If I could do that, if I could find landmarks, then I could put myself in the picture, figure out my place between the bright blue sky above and the world below. But there was nothing to figure out. I was where I was, and right then, at the moment, outside of time and not needing to be anywhere else or doing anything else.

In time, of course, that peace evaporated, but it was good and helpful while it was there, renewing, repairing, so that when time drew me back into its realm, I didn't feel so lost.

There was a substantial part of the joint left and I lighted it, took a toke, and stretched my hand out to Wildflower. She declined. I smoked some more by myself. My thoughts drifted back to New York and Eddie's house and Roger.

In the couple of months I'd crashed at Eddie's house, I don't think I ever had a kindly thought toward Roger. He annoyed me from the first moment I met him. That happens with people who are just too fucking full of themselves.

He was the kind of guy who took over a room. Part of Roger's ability to grab attention was his size. It wasn't that he was tall; in fact, we were about the same height. But there was something *long* about him made him seem much taller than he was. His face was long, too, with a long jaw, and he had a beard. The beard was short, but even so, it helped to accentuate the length of his face and his big jaw.

He always wore the same outfit. Not the same clothes, but the same layout, a long-sleeved white shirt with the cuffs rolled up a couple of turns, charcoal wool pants (trousers, as he referred to them) that were part of a suit whose jacket was never seen, and an unbuttoned vest. He must have had a dozen vests and wore a different one every day, then started over with the first one.

Also, while almost everyone else wore sneakers, Roger always wore a pair of heavy boots he said he'd picked up in London. I don't remember him taking them off ever, even late at night when those of us still in the house were in our bare feet. I thought he wanted to be ready to kick the shit out of someone if a fight broke out.

While he always kept his shoes on, he had glasses that he only wore some of the time. At first I thought they were reading glasses, since he didn't always have them on. But then I realized he often read without them and wore them at other times when he wasn't reading. I suspected they were clear glass and he just used them for effect. I tried to swipe them a couple of times to make sure, but never could.

A couple of girls had said to me that Roger and I looked alike, except for his beard, but I could never see it myself. I thought he was handsome. Not movie-star handsome, but his features were all good and they fit together. His eyes were big and he used them dramatically, staring intently into the eyes of whoever he was talking to. It annoyed me when he did it with me, but I realized a lot of the young girls found it appealing. It made them think he was really interested in what they had to say. He was really interested in getting in their pants, but it wouldn't have worked if he'd stared at their crotches.

The eyes were a big thing with him, but the really big thing was his voice. He had one of those Orson Welles voices that could be very soft yet very clear so you could hear it across the room. And then he could open up with it and blast you out of your chair. He'd save that up until he was deep into an argument with some poor sucker who was making a case for sit-ins or big demonstrations or peace marches, and then he would let go and roar that what was needed was violent action by real revolutionaries who weren't afraid of putting their asses on the line to shut down the war machine. He would invoke Che and Lenin and Ho Chi Minh like they were standing right behind him, looking over his shoulder at the pacifist scum shriveling into a ball under the heat of righteous anger blasting out of Roger's mouth.

One other thing I remembered about Roger was that he chain-smoked. We all smoked a lot, but he did the real thing, lighting one cigarette after another from the ash of the one he was just finishing. And while everyone else had pretty much switched to Marlboros or some other filter brand, Roger stayed with Luckies. I remember thinking he only did it so no one would ask him for a smoke.

But Roger was not above smoking other people's cigarettes, even filters, when he ran out. And he wasn't above swiping cigarettes. One time, a couple of French filmmakers, in the States to do a documentary on American radicals, came through the house. They were smoking Gauloises, and even the filter smokers had to try one. The Frenchies didn't seem to mind passing their packs around. I guessed this had happened to them everywhere they went and they were used to it. I thought they were like the GIs in World War II movies who handed out cigarettes to the civilians they'd just liberated, winning their hearts and minds instantly. My platoon had tried that in Vietnam after we would enter a village. The villagers took the cigarettes but kept their hearts and minds.

Once the Frenchies realized they'd be dispensing smokes wherever they went, they had stocked up. I noticed a carton of Gauloises sticking out of one of their knapsacks. Roger noticed it, too, because when no one was looking (except me, which he didn't know), he grabbed the carton, emptied half the packs into his own backpack, then put the carton back so the Frenchies wouldn't realize they'd been ripped off until they got to their next stop.

Roger smoked up a storm with his Luckies, but hardly ever smoked dope. I couldn't recall a time when he got high. I did remember that sometimes he would pass a joint on without taking a toke, and I also remembered seeing him put a joint to his lips but not really smoke it. I had thought at the time that for all his bluster he was one of those people who are afraid of losing control, that he had probably gotten high when he was younger and did some really stupid shit and wanted to make sure that never happened again. It was not all that common, but I'd known others who did the same. I thought about commenting on it, as a dig, since I didn't really like him, but I held back, waiting for a time when I would really want to zing him. That time never came.

I thought about the last encounter I'd had with Roger, just before I took off. He came up to the room where I was packing my bag.

"It's a shame you have to go," he said. "I really hoped we'd get to work together."

"Work together?"

"On the revolution."

"Oh."

"Odd, but somehow I feel that we will, that it's meant to be. You've got what it takes."

"To do what?"

"Get the job done."

"What job? What the fuck are you talking about?"

"Just that. You're on the ball. Steady as a rock. The only one here who is."

"Yeah? What about Eddie?"

"Oh, sure. Eddie's okay. But you've been tested."

You oughta be tested, I thought. But I didn't say it. I wanted to slip away without any more trouble.

So I slipped away, and Eddie was dead and Roger was in Cuba. And now I could slip back in. It was, after all, very simple. I could take a life and get mine back. Roger's life versus my life. One for one. Roger's life for my life and for Eddie's life. One for two. Eddie's parents mourned him and wanted revenge. My parents mourned me, in a roundabout kind of way, and I desperately needed to square things with my dad. Would anyone mourn Roger? Would anyone miss him? Did anyone care for him or love him?

Roger's parents were dead, or so he had told me once upon a time. Back in New York he had had his followers, but they had probably gone on to other gurus after Roger made his explosive getaway. There were some, no doubt, who would think kindly of him, especially some of the women, and others who would come to think "good riddance."

Had he gathered new Trilbys in Cuba? The competition there would be stiff, given the cult of Che and the living presence of Fidel. Roger was good at being a big fish in the small pond that was Eddie's circle of would-be revolutionaries. Had Roger been able to find a matching circumstance in Cuba? Were there people there who would miss him? And did it make any difference to me?

I realized the smoke had me following threads that didn't matter. My decision had nothing to do with what Roger worshipers might want. It had to do with what I wanted and whether I could kill to get it. Lauren McWilliams thought I could. She thought I was some kind of Ranger or Green Beret type with special assassination skills.

But I was just a GI who had fought to stay alive. It was an instinct, not a defense. Killing Roger to save myself was indefensible. Living in exile, making my dad hate me, was my lot for the choices I'd made, for the things I'd done.

A pardon, if it was real, would fix it all. I could go home. I'd be a hero again. "His hero," as McWilliams had pointed out. If it was real. The McWilliams house was loaded with pictures of Eddie's dad with the current president, as well as with President Johnson and even with Kennedy. There were pictures of him with all kinds of congressmen and senators, and even some with Vietnamese big shots I recognized from the news when I was over there. He was the real McCoy as far as being connected, so there was every chance the pardon was good. It made me sick in a way to think it could be so easy. And then I remembered that it wouldn't be easy at all.

- Five -

After a while, the sun began to hide behind an increasing number of passing clouds, the breeze picked up, and Ori shook himself awake. It was time to go. We had another swig off the flask, then made sure we left nothing behind to scar the mountain. Before we left, Wildflower took some more pictures of the vista, now gray under the gathering clouds. Then she set the camera on a rock, set the timer, and scrambled back to stand between me and Ori when the shutter snapped. Then we headed back down the mountain to the Jeep.

I looked so sour, neither of them asked me anything about what I'd decided or even *if* I had decided. I wasn't being very nice to them. These were my friends and I was acting like a brat. When we got down to the Jeep, I broke my silence and thanked Ori for taking me to the mountain.

"Did it help?" he asked.

"Yeah. I'm gonna tell them no."

"It's a tough call, man. But, for whatever it's worth, I think you're making the right choice."

Wildflower didn't say anything, so I asked her what she thought.

"I don't know. You shouldn't kill anyone, that's for sure. But you should be able to go home."

"Well," I said, "we'll just have to keep working on that."

I spread my arms and the two of them came to me and we hugged together. Then we got in the Jeep and went back to Pacific Breeze. As soon as we got there, I called the number McWilliams gave me. I didn't want to wait and let the confusion back in.

"Mr. McWilliams, it's Jay Cardinale."

"Hello, Jay. Have you done your thinking?"

"Yes, sir. I'm afraid I have to say no."

He was silent for a moment.

"Jay, are you sure? Do you need more time?"

"No, sir. I wish I could say yes. I wish I could help you and go back to the States and all that. But I can't do what you asked."

He was silent again, this time for longer. I wasn't sure after a while if he was even still there. I was wondering if I was supposed to hang up, when he spoke again.

"I must say I'm disappointed, Jay. Very disappointed."

"Yes, sir. So am I. But I can't. I thought it through, I really did, but that's all there is to it."

"I'm sure. Well, we will just have to see what happens next, won't we?"

"Um, sure."

I didn't really understand what he meant, but I didn't want to talk to him anymore.

"Goodbye for now, Jay."

This time he definitely hung up.

- Six -

About 3 A.M. the next morning, Ori's Jeep blew up. The explosion woke everyone on the commune and we all went running out to see what had happened. Several people, including Wildflower, had the sense to grab the fire extinguishers Ori had thoughtfully installed in every building, and they surrounded the burning vehicle, spraying away until the flames died out.

We stood around the smoldering remains of Java talking about what could have happened. Some of the guys went on about loose fuel lines and shorts in the electrical system and how something like that couldn't be helped. It was their way of comforting Ori, who stood off to one side fighting back his tears. He really loved that Jeep.

I didn't take part in the speculation. I didn't dare say what I was thinking.

- Seven -

I was out at the far end of the vineyard, on my knees repairing some torn grow tubes around the young vines. Probably birds trying to pick their way in had torn the tubes. The sun was high and the air warm. It reminded me of sunny days in winter when we would be on the boardwalk in Coney Island or Brighton Beach, sitting on a bench, back up against the buildings, out of the wind, at peace with the universe. I didn't think I would be at the commune much longer, but for the moment I was completely and wholly there and it was good.

Some movement caught the corner of my eye. I looked up to see the two seersuckers coming quickly down the lane along the row of vines where I was working. They looked exactly the same as when I'd last seen them at the diner just two days before. When they saw that I'd spotted them, Tall One even made the same shooting gesture with his hand. No peace sign this time.

I had that sick feeling again, as when I had first met them in the post office, that they were going to hurt me, and that they were hurrying forward, eager to begin inflicting pain. They were about fifty yards away. I got to my feet and started to run. I knew it was stupid, I knew I was going to have to deal with them sooner or later, but seeing them there, in that place of tranquility, was too much. I got to the end of the lane and turned right and ran down about five more lanes then turned right again, heading back toward the farm. I don't know what I thought except maybe that they wouldn't hurt me in front of witnesses.

Suddenly I flew forward on the ground and they were over me. They must have seen me turn to the right and cut through between the vines to intercept me, guessing I'd turn back toward the house. Tall One had stuck his foot out between the vines and tripped me.

I rolled over and was on my feet. Flight had failed, so it was fight time. I was back in the jungle and it was Dau Tieng and it was hand-to-hand with Charlie. I'd survived that and I'd survive this. I swung around and was suddenly on the ground again with a terrible pain in my chest. I didn't even see what he did, but Tall One had done something.

Short One leaned over me.

"You okay? Can you talk?"

I wasn't sure. I tried.

"Yeah," wheezed out of me.

"Good. Here's the deal. Take the offer or people you like will get hurt. People like your hippie friends here on the farm. That nice girl and the head guy. Take the deal and everyone stays healthy. Even back in Brooklyn, no one gets hurt. You know I'm not kidding, right?"

"You blew up the Jeep, you fucker."

"It's not good getting attached to material things."

"Cocksucker."

"Besides, you should think positive. It could've happened while somebody was driving it."

I was listening to him but watching Tall One out of the corner of my eye. He was looking down at me, smirking. He came closer.

"An explosion like that," he said, "a body melts like it was made of wax."

He held out his right hand. He was holding a lighter. He flicked it open and held his left hand over the flame.

"The smell of human flesh burning can make you sick. Did you ever get a whiff of that in 'Nam? Maybe call in a napalm strike and watch the gooks go up in flames?"

His hand was burning. I could smell it. I was getting sick. Tall One stopped burning himself, put his knees down on my chest, and stuck his seared palm in my face. I gagged. I thought I might throw up, which was bad since I was on my back. He flicked the lighter on again. Short One grabbed my left arm and pulled my hand toward to flame. I kept my fist closed until my knuckles started to burn. I tried to pull away but it was no use.

"You know we'll do whatever we have to," said Tall One. The flames were licking at my hand. I was close to passing out.

"Don't make us," said Short One. "We're the good guys here, see? We want you on our team."

"Yeah," said Tall One. "Uncle Sam wants you."

He closed the lighter and Short One released my arm.

"Uncle Sam?" I was dizzy from the pain.

"Sure," said Short One. "You have to see the big picture. Roger's a traitor. Get him and you score points for the whole team, not just McWilliams. And you wind up with that big fat pardon."

"Don't you want to be on our team?" said Tall One.

"Sure," I said. The words came out a little easier.

"Good!" said Short One. "Everybody likes a team player. And nobody gets hurt except Roger. So, we got a deal?"

"Sure."

"And we can tell McWilliams to call his country neighbor in Connecticut and get the ball rolling?"

"Sure."

"And you won't do anything stupid," said Tall One, "like try to run away? 'Cause you can't. You understand?"

"Call McWilliams," I said.

- Eight -

I didn't tell Ori or Wildflower about the seersuckers or their threats, or what really happened to Java the Jeep or my hand. I didn't want them to be afraid for no reason. I was sure everything was going to be all right now, at least for them and everyone else but me. I would be going to Cuba. I would find Roger, I'd poison him, I'd come home. I made up my mind it was going to be as easy as Lauren had described it, after all.

Driving to town the next day, I was intercepted by the seersuckers. They had a pickup truck and were stopped by the side of the road. I slowed down, looking to see if help was needed before I recognized them. They had changed into outdoor gear, bright orange hunting vests and camouflage pants. Short One stepped out into the road and waved for me to stop. I could've run him down, but I pulled over. I was on the team now, a team player.

He handed me a thick manila envelope.

"The deal is set. You have to be in St. John, New Brunswick, in a week. That's where you catch the ship to Havana. Here's all the information and a brand new passport. Everything you need for the trip will be waiting for you when you get to St. John. Just get your ass there and go to the address on the papers. Here's some dough."

He took a wad of bills out of his pocket and pulled out five hundred-dollar bills, along with some fifties and twenties, and handed them to me.

"That looks like a lot," I said.

"It's a grand. Should be enough to get you to St. John."

"A grand? You mean a thousand dollars?"

"What'sa matter? Not enough?"

"Uh, no. Fine."

"Do you *habla* any *Español*?"

"*Buenos Días.* That's about it."

Short One turned to Tall One, who was leaning against the truck. "Get him the dictionary."

Tall One opened the passenger door and took a dictionary from the glove compartment and handed it to me.

"Study hard," he said. "There may be a quiz."

"Anything else I need to know?"

"Yeah. Don't miss the boat."

- Nine-

I had my marching orders. It was time to go. I hadn't told Wildflower and Ori about the seersuckers' threats or my change of heart about killing Roger, so when I told them I'd decided to move on, it was just about moving on.

"You know how it is," I said. "I got the highway blues."

I had once mentioned an Army buddy who'd gone up to Montreal and said it was pretty cool. There was a solid music scene, a section of town where the hippies all hung out, and I could probably get work bartending.

It was easy for them to think I was taking myself out of the picture so they could finally be together. That was going to happen whether or not the whole Roger thing had come along.

We had a little going-away party at Pacific Breeze the night before I left, wine and beer and some whiskey, too. We smoked a lot of pot and everyone was pretty stupid by the time we all went off to bed.

It was my last night with Wildflower. We made love like it was something new, like those first nights after she picked me up in the park way back in another lifetime. We talked a lot. I managed to avoid spilling the beans, as much as I wanted to tell her. We had not kept secrets in our short time together. It was a mark of how tight we were right from the start.

I think I might have slept an hour or two. It didn't really matter. I had five days on the Greyhound in front of me, from Vancouver to St. John.

I'd have plenty of time to catch up on my sleep.

I said goodbye to the gang, to the girls I hadn't slept with and the guys I hadn't really gotten to know. Ori gave me a sack of sandwiches, a full wineskin, and a bunch of joints tucked into a used Marlboro box to take on the road. I hugged him for a long time. I don't think I ever loved a guy like I loved that little Eagle Scout.

Wildflower drove me to the bus station.

"Jay," she said before I got on the bus. "Did you ever feel like you had the world by the balls?" Her smile was radiant.

"No, honey, but I'm glad you do."

I kissed her one last time. She shoved a roll of bills into my hand as we parted.

"Oh, no—"

I tried to give it back to her, but she pushed my hand away.

"It's a loan. Until you get settled. You can pay us back."

I felt like an idiot. The envelope from McWilliams had included a thousand dollars Canadian that was now divided up and stuffed in my pockets. The commune needed this money more than I did. But it would easier to take it now and send it back than to argue. I never won an argument with her anyway.

The bus was ready to go. I kissed her again and boarded. We waved at each other until the bus turned a corner and headed out to the highway.

- Ten -

I was supposed to take the train, but I knew that either Ori or Wildflower would drive me to the station and it would have been hard to explain how I could afford the train rather than the bus. Besides, I felt guilty about the whole thing, so I figured taking the bus would be a kind of penance. It was, too. A long bus ride is nothing if not an act of self-flagellation.

It was awful to sit for so long. At least on a train you could get up and stretch your legs. On the other hand, the scenery went by closer and slower than on the train, and the bus stopped more often so you could get out and get a little taste of the changing environment along the way.

I don't know if it helped me to think things out better than on the train, but it made it easier to smoke the dope Ori had given me since I could stroll off behind the gas station or grocery where the bus stopped and take a few tokes before the driver called us to reboard.

Canada was beautiful. It was clear for most of the trip, and I saw the great snow-covered mountains, the great shining plains, the great rivers frozen over with ice or with blocks of ice tumbling on the flood.

It only snowed once the whole trip, but that once was enough. It was late on the first night out, as we climbed up the high passes that crossed the Rockies between British Columbia and Edmonton. We were climbing up to Banff and the snow was coming down fast and thick. I hadn't ever been in a blizzard and was wondering if this qualified.

I had a seat up front, close enough to see that the driver was sweating as he negotiated the turns and switchbacks that took us up and up. There was an old cowboy sitting next to me, and I realized he was watching the back of the driver's head as intently as I was. With a silent acknowledgment of each other's efforts, we focused our concentration together, sending that driver every sinew of will we could manage to transmit.

It took what seemed like the whole night, but at last we saw the lights of Banff shining through the falling snow. The bus pulled into the terminal and the driver announced we had an hour to stretch. He opened the doors and the passengers poured out. He just sat. I went out the front door. The cowboy was behind me, and as I stepped down, I saw him pat the driver on the shoulder as he passed by.

"Thanks, partner. You done fine," he said, then continued on out.

"Let's go get us a drink, son," he said as he joined me on the sidewalk. "There used to be a snug little place up this way around the corner on Railway Street."

"Sounds good to me," I said.

I lit a joint as we walked and offered it to him. He took a healthy toke, held it in, let it out, and took a smaller one before handing it back to me.

"Good shit."

The frozen night air felt like a miracle after the confined tension of the bus. But I was ready to be warm again by the time we reached the bar. It was called the Singing Brakeman, and sure enough, Jimmie Rodgers was yodeling away on the jukebox as we stepped inside.

The place catered to a country-western crowd that looked authentic instead of like a costume party. It was busy, but not so busy that we couldn't get a couple of stools together at the bar. We ordered whiskies and beer chasers and drank the whiskey down fast and about half the beer. I felt the whiskey warm me. My muscles sagged as the tension of the last few hours lifted. I felt good. We ordered a second round.

I looked at the cowboy and guessed that he was having much the same experience. He was about as old as my dad, which is to say in his early fifties, and weathered like him, too. He wore Western boots and a Stetson.

"You come here often?" I said to him.

"I know you're making a joke," he said. "But yes, I used to come over this way a lot, and this would be the place where I liked to drink. Good people and a good jukebox. Name's Lydon, by the way. John Lydon."

He held out his hand. I shook it.

"Jay Cardinale," I said. "So, where you from, John?"

"Got a little place about halfway between Calgary and Red Deer. How 'bout yourself?"

"Brooklyn. Brooklyn, New York."

"No foolin'? I knew a coupla fellas from Brooklyn. Bronc rider, went by the name Flatbush Phil, and a roper called himself Coney Island Cassidy."

"Brooklyn cowboys. Yeah, I knew a few myself."

I did, too. I used to go riding out in Bergen Beach and they kept their horses at the stables out there.

"So, you a rodeo cowboy?" I said.

"Was. Broke my back. Had to give it up."

"Wow. You okay now?"

"Just a little stiff now and again."

The second round came and we downed the shots, ordered another round, and drank some more of our beers. The whiskey began to massage me from the inside out. It didn't matter if I got drunk. I just had to make it back to the bus, eat one of Ori's, sandwiches and go to sleep. On the jukebox Jimmy Rodgers had given way to Bob Wills and His Texas Playboys. I was relaxing, happy to be in this bar, happy to be listening to great music, happy having a respite from the bus and a drink with a man of fine character such as Lydon clearly was.

And yet the awful reason I was there, on that bus, on this journey, was as present in my mind as the moment's joy. Was I really going through with it? Was there really no alternative?

We sat silent listening to the music, watching the happy crowd. After a while Lydon spoke.

"Quite a drive there for a while."

"Yep," I said. "Made me forget everything else I was worried about."

The third whiskies came along with a second round of beers. I sipped from the whiskey and finished my first beer.

"Got a lot on your mind, son?"

"Not a lot. Just one big thing."

"Well, at least you got it narrowed down."

"That's very philosophical."

"Is it?"

"It is."

"Never been accused of that before. Guess there's a first time for everything." He drank some more. "This big thing waiting for you at the end of the line?"

"Cuba."

"Didn't know Greyhound went that far."

"Supposed to kill a man there."

I don't know why I said it. We were just talking.

"Just one?"

"Just one."

"Long way to go to kill a man. Go that far, might as well kill a dozen."

"I did kill a dozen. But that was a different trip, different destination. This time only supposed to kill the one."

"Is that what you do? I mean, by way of a livelihood?"

"Last job I had was soldiering. So, yes, I guess you might say killing people was my bread and butter."

I drank the rest of the third whiskey and swallowed more of the beer. My troubles seemed objective, as if they were not mine but belonged to someone else. Someone I felt sorry for. I thought it would be good to have another whiskey and stick around to see what that someone would do.

"Do you want another drink?" I said. "It's on me. They're all on me."

"Mighty kind of you, Jay. I wouldn't mind one more at all. Might help me sleep through to Calgary."

I waved to the bartender to bring us another round.

"How you get from Calgary to Reindeer?" I said.

"Red Deer."

"Sorry. Red Deer."

"My woman'll pick me up."

"Got a woman."

"Yep."

"Got a ranch?"

"Yep."

"Big?"

"Nope."

"But it's home."

"That it is."

"Don't have no home."

"Do you want one?"

That stopped me. I had to think. But not for long.

"Yeah. But first I want to be free."

"This killing make you free?"

"Supposed to. We'll see, I guess."

"Know the guy you're supposed to kill?"

"I do."

"Do you want to kill him? I mean, would you kill him just 'cause he needs killing?"

"No. He's no good. But I wouldn't kill him if I didn't have to. Wouldn't kill anybody."

"Do you have to? Kill him?"

The cowboy had got to the heart of the matter just as the next round arrived. We both drank our whiskies then went on talking.

"Some people might get hurt if I don't. Good people. Better than him. Better than me."

"Can't have that."

"So you think I should do it?"

"Don't know, son."

"Would you do it?"

"Don't know. Do know I'd feel pretty well fucked one way or the other."

"That's it. I feel fucked."

"Sometimes that's all there is."

"You think?"

"Yup. Sometimes there's nothing but that you're fucked. Screwed. Can't win for tryin'. You know, most of the time in life we do lose."

"Shit."

"Yep. Can't always have a happy ending." He finished his whiskey. "Wish I had some better news for you."

"Truth's the truth."

"Still, if you've got nothing but bad choices, one is usually less bad than the rest."

"But how do you know which it is?"

"You'll know. When you get down to it, you'll know."

He finished his beer.

"We should be getting back to the bus. Can you walk?"

I finished my whiskey and my beer and got off the stool. The booze had multiplied the impact of the dope. I'd have preferred to stay right where I was and take a nap. But the bus was waiting. It would be warm and I could sleep there better than at the bar.

"I can walk."

- Eleven -

We managed to stay on our feet all the way back to the bus. We smelled of booze, but the driver smelled of coffee. That's the way it should be, I thought. Cowboy John Lydon and I switched seats—me by the window, him to the aisle—settled in, and said good night.

When I woke up, it was morning and he was gone. I'd slept through the stop in Calgary. He had left a note with his address saying if I were ever back that way, etc., but had decided not to wake me to say goodbye. That was okay. We'd always have the Singing Brakeman.

My head ached and I didn't have any aspirin. I ate a sandwich and that helped. The day was bright. No one had filled the seat vacated by the cowboy. I stretched out and watched Canada go by. We were down out of the mountains now and traveling through farms and open range. I wondered if the people living out there had lost more than they had won. The cowboy was right. You were bound to lose. The odds favored the house. There were winners, of course. Every once in a while someone beat the house. That kept the rest of us going.

I wondered if the people out there even thought in those terms. And if they did, did they think it was the way life was supposed to be? That God wanted us to keep score?

Or maybe they didn't think about it. Maybe they just got up every day and did the best they could and didn't keep score.

When did I start keeping score? Had I always? I had an idea of myself as happy-go-lucky until I got to Vietnam where everyone was keeping score. Maybe that was just a story I was telling myself now. Maybe I was the kind who always kept score. I tried to remember. I don't know why it became important, except for what the cowboy had said about losing more than winning, and why I was on the bus and going where I was going to do what I was supposed to do. Maybe it was a new kind of hangover.

I tried to remember if I kept score in school. I didn't think so. I was smart, but there were a lot of kids who were smarter. I wasn't going to be valedictorian, not by a long shot. I wasn't going to be captain of the baseball team, either, or Homecoming King, or have the lead in the school play. I wasn't going to be the best at anything, so I didn't really bother trying.

It was one of the things that really pissed my father off about me. He worked so hard and I just floated along. He lectured me on the subject more times than I care to say, usually following up his talk with a chorus of one or both of his favorite songs—"Lucky Old Sun" and "Old Man River"—just to drive home his point. He had to sweat and strain, body all aching and racked with pain, while I had nothing to do but roll around heaven all day.

I didn't think I ever begrudged the kids that did become number one at whatever thing it was. It seemed so long ago. Everything before the war seemed so long ago. Did I keep score about anything?

Girls. It wasn't like I was counting how many girls I slept with. I wasn't a Don Juan with a list. It was more a matter of finding a challenge, a girl who didn't even see me because I wasn't any of those things—valedictorian or future Marlon Brando or All City third baseman. When a girl looked right past me like I wasn't there or looked down on me, she became the one I wanted. That was the game I played, winner take all. I had to work for every girl I got. There was a lot of romancing. And I loved that. I was playing to win, but I was playing for the sake of the game as well. It was perfect.

How could I forget that about myself, except it had been so long since I'd experienced it? The war put a hold on that game, and when they brought me back to the States, I found myself in a world where the game had been, in effect, cancelled. Now the girls came to me. I didn't have to romance anyone. I was that hero deserter they'd heard about. It was their game and I was their score.

There hadn't been any romancing with Sheri, either. But that was different. We found our own special loving friendship right off the bat. But otherwise, romance was gone. Lost. If that was where I kept score, then I had lost there, too.

- Twelve -

I called home to Brooklyn from Medicine Hat. My mother was surprised to hear from me.

"You never call twice in one week."

"I wanted to know if Uncle Frank got Daddy to see a doctor."

"No, but the union did. They told him he could lose his job if he didn't go."

I should have thought of that. The only authority my father had any use for was Local 584.

"So when does he go?"

"Three weeks. It was the first appointment they had open. I'm sure if his name was Rockefeller instead of Cardinale, they would have had an opening that day. But what're you gonna do? That's how the world is."

"Yeah, it sucks. But that's good he's gonna see the doctor. I bet they wind up giving him some vitamins and Geritol and send him right back to work."

"That would be a miracle."

"Well, you never know, Ma. Miracles happen."

"Not to us."

- Thirteen -

When I was seventeen my mother wanted me to join the Navy so I could avoid the draft and not go to Vietnam. It was a good idea and I might have done it if I wasn't seventeen and it wasn't my mother's idea.

So I went to college and dropped out in the middle of my second semester and got drafted.

This time my mother said she would go to the Mafia to get me out. There was a family connection—which I won't go into—and she was ready to use it. But, as it turned out, there was already a waiting list for wise-guy kids trying to stay out of the Army. I was through my physical and drafted long before my turn would have come.

My father thought it wasn't such a bad idea if I got a little discipline, but my mother was disgusted with me for letting myself get drafted. They might as well just come and shoot me and put an end to my miserable life was what she said.

I didn't think it was so miserable. In fact, I thought it was very much worth saving. But my mother had a point. If I thought staying alive was so important, why didn't I do a better job of staying out of the Army? She was right, of course. But back then, I couldn't possibly admit it to myself or anyone else, least of all her.

- Fourteen -

The rest of the trip was quiet. No snowstorms or philosophical cowboys. I filled the time looking into the English-Spanish dictionary Tall One had given me, and read all the papers the seersuckers had delivered to me back on Vancouver Island along with the money and the new passport.

The dictionary had a bunch of handy phrases up front, the basic basics like "hello" and "goodbye," "good morning" and "good night," "thank you" and "you're welcome," and so on. I worked at memorizing these and other biggies, like "where is the toilet?"

When I needed a break from that, I examined the papers in the package. There was a passport in my name with my Army photo. There were documents showing that I had been vaccinated for smallpox and tetanus. Even though the documents were phony, I had, in fact, had my shots in the Army, so I was okay. There was another document, a tourist card permitting entry into Mexico. I figured that was there in case the volunteers couldn't come back from Cuba directly into the States and had to go to Mexico first.

There was also a checklist of stuff we were all supposed to bring, like toothpaste, shampoo, and contraceptives. (I guess they realized we wouldn't be working 'round the clock.) We were encouraged to bring cameras and tape recorders and notebooks. They were hoping for as many different impressions as they could get to use in a book that was supposed to get written when the cane cutting was over.

The list of clothes included a bathing suit (another sign that we would have time off), as well as work boots, work gloves, and sunglasses. Long-sleeved shirts were encouraged, as sugarcane had "prickles." Jeans were discouraged as too heavy. Army pants were recommended as a good replacement. I was ahead of the game there. There was a note attached to the checklist telling me it would all be there waiting for me in St. John. There was an address for me to go to and the name of the person to ask for, Peter Ward.

The last document I looked at was a questionnaire about why I wanted to join the Brigade. It started a spiel about how this *zafra*—the Cuban word for the harvest—was special, bigger than any that had come before, aiming for ten million tons of cane that would save the Cuban economy—which was otherwise in the toilet—and save the revolution, as well. Of course, that's not how it was written, but that's what it was saying.

There was a note attached to this one from the seersuckers saying I needed to have my answers ready, as I would be interviewed before I would be allowed to join the Brigade. This kind of freaked me out as I had thought the whole thing was a done deal. What if they didn't like my answers and left me behind? How was I going to explain to the seersuckers that I didn't do it on purpose? They were clearly not the understanding kind.

The questions were pretty straightforward. Why did I want to go to Cuba and why did I want to be in the Brigade? When and how did I get involved in the movement? What kinds of activities had I been involved in? What did I think people should do to change America?

I thought first of the answers I couldn't give. I wanted to go to Cuba with the Brigade so I could kill someone, get my pardon, go home, and make peace with my dad. I was never involved in the movement, except as a freeloader taking advantage of the free food and free bed at the McWilliams house. My activities had mostly consisted of messing up their sheets. And I didn't give a crap whether or not America changed, as long as I could go home.

So much for being cute. Afraid of being rejected, I started thinking seriously about what I would say. I reached back to the days I'd spent in the McWilliams house and the non-stop talking that had gone. From the depths of suppressed memories, I dredged up Roger's lectures on capitalism, imperialism, racism, and socialism. I had stopped listening to him almost immediately. I thought he was a lot like me, spinning out his yarn, saying whatever needed to be said in order to snare the pretty young things that always seemed to be so present in the house. But his endless yakking filled the house and was hard to avoid.

I didn't have to compete with him, since I got to be the strong, silent, suffering type that needed tender loving care after having been brutalized by my experience in the war. But now I tried to remember the things he'd said. Why would Roger want to go to Cuba? Why would he want to join the Brigade?

"Why go to Cuba? Because reading about Cuba, seeing a documentary film about the revolution, or hearing a lecture about it can't give you the same visceral understanding of what the revolution 'feels' like. Only firsthand experience can do that. Mao taught us that." (Yes, throw some Mao in there. Try to work Che there in, too.)

"And by the same token, I need to express my solidarity with my brothers and sisters in the Third World through my actions, just as Che did by going to Africa and Bolivia. (Got Che in!) Words aren't enough. We have to act, otherwise it's just a lot of hot air." (Roger was the king of hot air, so he would know.)

This was going well. I ran it through my head again, only this time I imagined I was saying it and Roger was the interrogator. Then I did it again, only imagining that it was the seersuckers sitting across from me asking the questions. In my mind, they were extremely impressed by my bullshitting.

What was next? About the movement. Yes. "I was just a dumb teenager. All I thought about was sports and movies and girls. I didn't think about anything important or anything outside myself. But then guys in the neighborhood started getting drafted and going to the war. One of the guys got killed and a couple of others were wounded. Everyone was scared. I went to college but I wasn't much of a student, and when I dropped out, I got drafted. I didn't know anything. I didn't know where to go for help or advice. I didn't think I had any choice but to do what they told me.

"The next thing I knew I was in Vietnam, in the jungle. I was never so scared in my whole life. We were all scared. But the crazy thing was that everything got real clear over there. Even though it was like a nightmare, all the contradictions were right out in the open—killing people to save them, destroying a culture you know nothing about. And that's without saying what it was doing to our own guys, brutalizing them, dehumanizing them.

"A lot of us, more than you know, we stopped hating the Vietnamese. We realized we had more in common with them than our own officers. And yet we had to fight, even though we didn't want to. It was all so insane.

"And then I was wounded and sent home to recuperate. I swore I'd never go back. A buddy at the veterans' hospital tipped me off to a war resisters' counseling center. When I went there, I thought there was no hope for me, but they gave me hope. And I met a whole bunch of people who thought about things in a different way than the people I'd grown up with. Thought of things in political terms. Thought about class issues and race issues and gender issues. I was in a whole new world. And I liked it. It made sense. And then, after a while, when I felt like I could talk to people, I started counseling other guys coming in who had been just like me, demoralized, dehumanized. I only wish I could have done more before I had to leave for Canada. But then, up in Vancouver there were a lot of guys like me. We had a support group and we worked together to ease the way for the new guys who kept joining us."

I didn't know if I would really go that far in making stuff up. I mean, all those things were happening and I knew about them and I did go to one vets' meeting when I first got up to Vancouver. But I never counseled anyone, and if they talked to any of the vets who were up there doing those things, I was screwed. I didn't want to get too creative, but on the other hand, were they really going to check? Would there be time?

So that was me and the movement. But now for the grand prize: What did I think people should do to change America? I could say I didn't know. That was why I was going on this journey, hoping to find answers in a true revolutionary society. Would they think that was too evasive? What would Roger say? "Blow it the fuck up!" The tough talk really impressed the little boys and girls around him. Mostly what he meant was, "I want to fuck you and your sister at the same time," but that might have been a turnoff if he actually said it. As I recalled, none of the older girls, I mean the ones about twenty-three or twenty-four, had much to do with Roger. But the teenyboppers gobbled up his line like it was candy.

I had a feeling that was not going to go over with my interrogator, whoever he might be. After all, the question was about how to change America, not destroy it. I thought for a while and remembered another guy, Evan Something, who had stayed at the house for a couple of nights when he came to New York for some big Marxist convention. His rap, and it was a good one, was "Educate, Agitate, Organize, and Arm." I decided that would be the way to go.

I'd tell whoever it was I had to talk to that Americans were not at a level of consciousness where real change could take place. The ice had been broken by the antiwar and civil rights movements, but it was still just the beginning. The demand for equal rights by minorities and women was raising consciousness more effectively than anything else, and everyone should be working together behind the leadership of these movements. I didn't know what that actually meant, but the more thoughtful people at the house had seemed to agree.

What did I really think? What should people do to change America? I thought about people like my dad deciding they'd had enough and making a revolution. It was a stretch, but I knew enough about the Teamsters and the Auto Workers and some of the other tough unions to think it could maybe happen one day. But there was a part of me that wasn't so far from Roger, a part of me that thought the thing to do was kill all the politicians and all the generals.

- Fifteen -

More dictionary, more joints, more sandwiches, more sleep, more rehearsing my answers, and then we were in St. John. The Greyhound station was in the Port Authority in the old waterfront area. I took a cab to the address I'd been given, which turned out to be just a few minutes away. For some reason I thought I'd be going to an old-fashioned building. I have no idea why. Maybe because it all seemed like something I'd seen in an old movie, so it was hard to imagine it being someplace new and shiny. But that is what it was, a modern building, glass and steel rather than brick and iron, standing tall in the heart of the business district.

That was another thing. I'd pictured a dark side street, with no one around to hear the screams that I was sure would be emerging from the basement dungeon where prisoners were tortured into revealing their secrets. Everyone going in and out as I made my way to the elevator looked like an accountant or a librarian. It must have been my encounters with the seersuckers that had me expecting the worst.

The office was on the fourteenth floor, the highest in the building. The door bore the name and title "Peter Ward, Cuba Import Advisor." I went in without knocking. It seemed the right thing to do. Inside were a couple of large floor plants, a coat rack, a loveseat, and a few comfortable-looking upholstered chairs. Facing the door was a large reception desk. Seated behind the desk reading a magazine was a woman in her early twenties. There was a nameplate on the desk that read "Miss More."

She looked up as I entered. She had long blonde hair and a smile that was at once demure and incendiary. I was not sure she was real. She was more like the kind of fantasy creatures who only exist in *Playboy*.

"Mr. Cardinale?"

"Yes, I am."

"Mr. Ward is expecting you." She stood up, which did nothing to change my mind about her not being real. "May I take your coat and your bag?"

I handed her the bag and she placed it behind her desk. She was back in seconds, just as I finished unbuttoning my coat. She stood behind me and slid it down off my shoulders. She smelled like heaven.

"Go right in." She nodded toward a door in the corner of the reception area. I went to it and looked back at her before I went in. Her smile got bigger and hotter and she nodded for me to go on in. I did.

The office was spare, a desk, a few file cabinets, a few chairs, and a couch that looked like it was meant for napping. Or maybe for "conferences" with Miss More. The wall behind the desk was all glass. Even from the door I could tell it had a terrific view out over the harbor. Peter Ward was seated at the desk, but with his back to me, staring out at the view. He spun around to face me. It was Short One. No seersucker this time: wool worsted. I looked around for Tall One. He wasn't there.

"How come you took the bus?"

"You're Ward?"

"You were supposed to take the train. We don't like mavericks. I thought you were going to be a team player."

"Can I play with your receptionist?"

"Some piece of ass, huh?"

"She's like a centerfold."

"Not *like* a centerfold. She *was* a centerfold. Why did you take the bus?"

I explained about not wanting questions from my friends about where the money came from for the train. He thought about it for a second and seemed satisfied.

"You read the stuff we gave you?"

"How did you know I took the bus?"

"You weren't on the train."

"But how did you know I took the bus? That I didn't fly or rent a car or hitch a ride?"

"We didn't know. When we found out you weren't on the train, we checked the bus."

"Checked the bus?"

"Yeah. Did you read—"

"How did you check it?"

"We had someone waiting at a stop and they saw you, okay? Did you read the questions?"

"Yeah."

"Do you know what you're going to say?"

"Yeah. I've been rehearsing it."

"Let me hear."

He pointed to one of the chairs and I sat. He shifted himself over to the couch. For all his cool, I could tell he was tense about whether or not I was going to pull this off. It occurred to me as I got ready to talk that he had to answer to someone, just as I had to answer to him. And he knew there was the chance that despite whatever strings had been pulled to get me in, there was still the chance of a veto. What would that mean to him? Were his friends and family going to get fucked over if I screwed up?

"Do you want to ask me the questions or should I just do my thing?"

"Why do you want to go to Cuba? Why do you want to be in the Brigade?"

I was going to go back to the reception area and get the questions from my bag, but his words stopped me. He asked the questions as if he had written them himself. For all I knew, he had. After all, everyone knew the movement was riddled with undercover agents.

I went into my spiel, as I had thought it through on the bus. I hadn't expected a chance for a rehearsal, but it came as a welcome surprise. I had imagined him as my interrogator, so in a way it was sort of comfortable delivering my answers to him as he went through the other questions. I played it straight, no smart-aleck stuff. I didn't need to piss him off. When I finished with how to change America, he sat silent for a moment before he spoke.

"Okay. Do it like that and I think you'll get by."

"Gee, I don't know whether to thank you or throw up."

He ignored me and went back to the desk. He took an envelope from a drawer and handed it to me.

"Look this over."

I opened the envelope. There was a brochure from a hotel and a key and some more money.

"That's where you'll stay tonight and tomorrow. All your clothes and stuff are already there. Stay in the room, order room service, don't go out. Day after tomorrow, you check out at five in the morning. Ask for a wake-up call so you don't miss it, and have them order you a cab. Go to Pier 8. Tell the driver you'll want to get out when you're about five blocks away. Tell him you need to walk a while on solid ground before you get on a ship. When you get to the dock, you'll see a bunch of seedy bums hanging around the gate. That's the Brigade leadership. Ask for Avis Watson. She's the one expecting you. Remember, it was Donald Baldwin who recommended you."

"I know all this."

"I hope so."

"Is she the one going to interview me?"

"Maybe. No hard information on that. If we get confirmation on the interviewer, we'll let you know at the hotel."

"And if I get rejected?"

"You won't."

"But if—"

"Don't think about that."

"But—"

"You don't want to know."

He was right. I didn't.

"You have any of that money left?" he said.

"The thousand? I was on a Greyhound bus for five days. How much you think I could have spent?"

"Okay."

"You want it back?"

"Nah. Keep it. McWilliams is loaded, he don't care. Send it to your folks. Now take this, too."

He reached into his desk drawer and took out yet another envelope and passed it to me.

I opened the envelope. It was a stack of Cuban bills.

"Pesos," said Short One. "About five hundred dollars' worth."

"What am I supposed to do with it?"

"What do I care? Buy souvenirs. Have a Cuban sandwich."

I shoved the envelope in my pocket.

"One more thing," said Short One. He handed me a small bottle of pills. The label had my name on it and the name of a doctor I'd never heard of. There was an Rx for a drug I couldn't pronounce and instructions to take one every 24 hours.

"What's this?"

"That's the poison."

Everything surreal and nightmarish about the whole deal suddenly became very concrete.

"There's a lot in here. Do I use all of these?"

"It only takes one to do the job. The prescription's for a painkiller. In case anyone goes through your things, it'll look like something you take to deal with the lingering pain from your war wounds. Now listen, if for any reason somebody wants you to take one, just to prove they're not poison—"

"What?"

"Just listen—"

"Why would someone do that?"

"Because there's a lot of suspicious assholes in the world."

"Oh, jeez—"

"It's a crying shame, but that's how some people are. Anyway, all these pills are just aspirin. Hold out your hands."

I did. He poured the pills into them, then held the bottle up so I could look into it.

"The poison is taped down at the bottom. Three pills. But you just need one."

"What if they empty the bottle and look inside?"

"Then you're screwed."

"What if they want me to take one of them?"

"Then you're dead."

"Oh, jeez. Isn't there, like, an antidote I can maybe carry in a separate bottle? Just in case?"

He laughed. "You been watching too many movies, kid. There's no antidote."

"So I just die? That's it?"

"You could try throwing up."

"Will that work?"

"I don't know. It's all I can think of."

"Jeez—"

He started laughing. "Sorry, kid. Look, you're gonna be fine. No one's gonna make you take a pill. Okay? You're going to slip one to Roger. That's all you need to know. You put this in his cup of coffee, in a glass of water, in his *cerveza* or his Cuba Libre. In about a half hour, it'll look like he's having a heart attack."

"But what if there's no way to slip him a pill? Like if we're never anywhere that we're having a drink? What am I supposed to do then?"

"Then you get a fucking carving knife and stick it in his fucking heart."

- Sixteen -

Two days later, at six in the morning, I approached the gate to Pier 8. It was freezing, bitter cold made worse by a mix of rain and sleet that didn't seem to be falling so much as surrounding me. I was still sleepy. The 5 A.M. wake-up call from desk had done its job, as did the follow-up from Ward, which came two minutes later.

"Are you out of bed?" he said.

"Yes," I lied.

"Fuck you! Get out of bed right now!"

"I'm up."

"Get out of bed! Stand up! Are you standing up? Stand up!"

I got up. "Okay, I'm on my feet. Really."

"Okay. Good luck. And don't get back in bed! You don't want to fuck this up."

He hung up. I thought about getting back into bed, sliding under the covers to warm myself against the soft body of Miss More, whose first name was Candy. But Ward was right. I didn't want to fuck this up.

There was still some champagne in the bottle in the ice bucket, and I drank it down then got in the shower. I thought about Miss More while I washed myself. She had come to my room the first night and came back again the second. The first night, I'd asked if Ward had sent her. She said no.

"You just looked like you needed a friend."

I didn't believe her, but I didn't care. She was a luscious surprise. And she knew things, more tricks even than Wan Woo, who was my Number One girl in Saigon. Maybe Wan knew the same, but she didn't want to scare the farm boys away. Miss More knew I wasn't going anywhere.

Between rounds, I asked her about Ward. She didn't know much. She was modeling. A photographer she was working for had told her about a guy he knew needed a pretty girl to be a receptionist. Good money, no typing, no dictation, just answering the phone and smiling brightly when people came to the office. She said sure. Ward came around the next day, looked her up and down, and hired her on the spot. He had never made a pass at her and was always polite.

His pal Georgie, on the other hand, was always trying to corner her.

"Some guys use a line and keep up the come-on even after you turn them down. They figure a girl can always change her mind and they want to be there when it happens. With Georgie, it was like he was waiting for the chance to pull me into a closet. He actually tried a couple of times, but Mr. Ward stopped him."

She described Georgie to me and, as I guessed, she was talking about Tall One. She didn't believe they were really in the import/export business. Sometimes she was sure the messages she took for them were in code. She wondered seriously if they were spies. She asked me if I was a spy. I told her I was, but she shouldn't tell anyone as it could be a matter of life and death. I told her Mr. Ward knew, of course, but nevertheless, she should never try to discuss it with him. I told her she made me forget all my troubles and woes, and she was so happy that she did it some more. She had the right last name. When I left in the morning I was pretty sure I'd never see her again.

At the gate to the pier, I went up to a couple of long-hairs standing inside a small guard station. They were smoking cigarettes and drinking coffee out of paper cups and trying to stay out of the wetness that came in through the open sides of the station. I asked for Avis Watson.

One of them pointed to a long building not far from the gate. "She's in the potato shed."

The door to the shed was closed against the cold morning air. I knocked. Someone inside yelled, "Come in," and I did. Throughout the shed were sacks of potatoes. I shuddered, remembering my time on KP.

A young black woman sat at a desk next to an electric heater that was doing an inadequate job. She had a short Afro sticking out from under a knit watch cap and high cheekbones, and the beauty in her face was intensified by the look of anger she wore.

"Close the door, dammit! It's freezing."

I pulled the door shut behind me.

"Who are you?"

"Jay Cardinale. I'm supposed to see Avis Watson."

"Oh," she said. "You're Cardinale." She looked me up and down. The anger on her face did not go away. If anything, it increased. I was in big trouble.

"I'm Avis," she said. "Sit down."

There was a folding chair set up on the other side of the desk and I sat in it. It was small and wobbly.

"Look," she said, "I don't pull any punches. As far as I'm concerned, you don't belong here. The idea that somebody with some money pulled strings to get you in when we were turning away a lot of people who were desperately wanting to go is a crime. And you could make me very happy if you said you had changed your mind and decided not to go."

I wanted to make her happy, both by not going and by doing whatever I could to slice away the anger and let her beauty shine through. I would rub her shoulders, rub her back, massage her temples, or massage her feet. I would pet her, lick her, peel grapes for her. I had to catch myself from going further. There would be time for all that later. But first, against both our wishes, I had to persuade her to let me join the Brigade.

Everything I had practiced saying on the Greyhound and had rehearsed with Short One flew out the window. It was all too pat and she'd piss on it. I had to come up with something better, something truer, or at least, something that sounded truer. An officer back in the war had once told me I had a gift for improvising, for adjusting quickly when reality did not match the battle plan. That was what kept me alive in the jungle. It was the gift I needed to keep on giving, and I needed to do it right now.

"Look," I said. "I don't blame you. I'm sure there's a lot of people who should be going but aren't. But that doesn't mean I don't deserve to go."

"And what makes you so deserving?"

I'm not, I thought, and then realized that was where to start.

"It's not me. I'm not doing this for me. It's the guys in country, my brothers out there in the jungle. Word got back that I was going to be in the Brigade and they started to cheer. Don't you know how much they hate the war? They need to know that it's possible to escape. To get out from under. If I could do it, not just make it to Canada and hide out, but go to Cuba and really stick it to Uncle Sam, then maybe they can, too. Maybe another guy deserts, and then another and another and another. Maybe word gets around. Maybe a squad refuses to fight, then a whole platoon stops fighting. Maybe it spreads to a company or a battalion."

She tried to interrupt. "Do you really think—"

"I don't think, I know. You weren't there. What did you do? Read a magazine article? I was there and my brothers are still there, and I tell you, there's a shitload of soldiers ready to quit. They need to be inspired. They need to believe."

I was a little worried about piling it on too thick. It was such bullshit. But it was all or nothing at this point.

I said, "You know who I am, right?"

"I know—"

"Well, so do thousands of guys back in the 'Nam. Their eyes are on me. What I do means something to them. Maybe means a lot. And maybe you're a big shot here, putting this trip together. Maybe you hope you can build some kind of revolutionary bond. Well, sister, nothing builds a bond like war. I hope your little adventure here lets you feel even a tenth of what I feel with my brothers in the jungle. So fuck you and fuck your Brigade and all the desperate, deserving little rich kids who want to go play peasant for a couple of months so they can have something to look back on when they get home and go off to work in daddy's business. I'm sure that's much more important than anything I'd get out of it."

I went to get up and realized I was already on my feet. I picked up my bag and slung it over my shoulder and prayed that she would stop me before I got to the door, which was only a couple of steps away.

No luck. I opened the door and the cold air blasted in.

"Shut the door," she said. I hoped she meant from the inside because I turned to her without leaving the shack.

"Why do they stay and fight now?" she said.

"Because they're scared. And because they're trained to. And because, in the end, when the shooting starts, you can't let your brothers down. They're all you've got. They are your whole world. That's why whole squads have to decide together, not one soldier at a time."

The door opened. One of the long-hairs from the gate stuck his head in and said, "The buses are here," then left, closing the door behind him.

Avis stood up. She looked at me for a few seconds. I didn't think she'd bought it, but she was trying to figure out why I was trying so hard. Maybe the law was coming down on me and I needed to get out of Canada, or maybe I thought it would be easier to get to Europe or even back into the States somehow from Cuba. It didn't especially have to make sense. People convinced themselves of a lot of really dumb ideas back then, as they still do today. And if your conviction was strong enough, it could carry others along with you.

I was still by the door with my bag over my shoulder. "All right," she said. "I'll fix you up with a Brigade ID card when we're on the ship. Let's go meet the rest of the Brigade."

- Seventeen -

There were ten buses parked in a line on the pier, parallel to the ship. For the first time, I saw the name of the ship, *Luis Arcos Bergnes*. I wondered if Luis was a famous revolutionary or the guy who financed the shipbuilding. Maybe he was both. I put it away to ask about him later.

"These are people coming up from the east coast and Midwest," said Avis as we walked toward the buses. "There's a west coast group flying over from Mexico, but they don't have to leave yet."

"Does everyone know each other already?"

"Some people knew each other before. Otherwise, most people met at the orientation sessions or on the buses. There'll be time to get to know one another on the trip down."

Standing on the pier, I realized that from New Brunswick down to Cuba by freighter was not an overnight journey. In my mind, I'd been imagining that I'd get to New Brunswick and the next day I'd be in Cuba, and by the end of the week Roger would be dead and I would be able to breathe again. What other fantasy worlds had I been living in?

The buses were emptied out, and what looked to be about five hundred people were standing alongside them, talking, laughing, some smoking cigarettes, some stretching. I expected them all to be about twenty, but there were several older faces in the crowd, including a couple of old-timers who looked to be the same generation as my dad. I'd met some old Wobblies and communists when I was in San Francisco, guys even older than these, and I knew there were revolutionaries long before there was an SDS or any of the radicals of my time, but it was still a shock to see these geezers in among the shiny young believers heading to Cuba to improve their revolutionary skills.

I'd gotten a little information from the papers the seersuckers had given me, and I knew the aim was to balance all the different elements of race and gender. It was hard to tell for sure, but the crowd seemed more white than brown and black, and about fifty-fifty male and female. Maybe it was all mathematically correct and I just wasn't seeing it yet.

Avis moved forward to the crowd and called them to gather around her as best they could. The long-hairs from the gate helped wrangle them to her.

"If we haven't met, I'm Avis Watson. I'm one of the organizers of the Second Brigade. As you can see, our ship, the *Luis Arcos Bergnes*, is here. But we can't go aboard yet. The first Brigade is still on board and the Customs people have to do their thing before they can come off and we can go on. I'm really sorry about the hang-up, but the Canadian government has been very cooperative with the Brigade and it's only right that we be a little patient. Does anyone have a problem with that? Speak up."

A young guy in the front of the crowd did. "So we have to stand here freezing our butts off while they go through the fine print?"

"No," said Avis. "You are going to get back on the buses and take your seats. We'll keep the heat on, and as soon as we can, we will all go on board."

"Do we have to stay here?" said a young white woman. "Can't we go into the city and come back when they're ready for us?"

"That would be great," said Avis. "Except we don't know when they'll be ready for us and we really can't have five hundred people spread out with no way to be in contact. The buses are not a great solution, but it's the only one I can think of."

Someone toward the back shouted, "Well, ain't there someplace we can all go together and get something to eat?"

"We looked into it. No place big enough or close enough. You're just going to have to tough it out on the buses."

There was a lot of moaning and griping. Tough revolutionaries, I thought. Avis thought the same. She put her fingers in her mouth and a loud, shrill whistle came out of her. I imagined there were cabbies in New York stopping short and looking around to see who had hailed them. The crowd quieted.

"Did you come all this way just to complain? What the hell are you gonna do when it starts raining while you're cutting cane? Let's show a little revolutionary discipline and get back on the buses—and maybe try a little self-criticism. I'll let you know when we're ready to board. Group leaders, get your teams back on your buses now. I mean NOW!"

I enjoyed watching her deal with the crowd. Everyone who needed to shoot their mouths off got to have their say and then she told them what to do. It was like the Army. Soldiers gripe constantly, but when the orders come, you jump to it.

As far as I could tell from my limited exposure to the revolution, movement leaders tended to fall into three groups. There were the bullshitters like Roger, who would eventually go on to careers in public relations or commodity trading; true believers, like Eddie, who, however sincere they were as either apostles of nonviolence or storm-the-barricades types, were looking for personal salvation more than anything else; and then there were the long-haulers, the ones who would go on to be union organizers or community activists, or lawyers who only represented the downtrodden and made a tenth or even a hundredth of what they could get in the business world.

There was something about Avis, an evenness, that made me think she was clearly a long-hauler. I could see her spending her whole life fighting the good fight, fighting for pennies, fighting for each little scrap of justice that could be torn out of the system. She had no time for a petty distraction such as I would be. Which made me want her oh, so bad. Anyway, chasing her would be something to do until I had to deal with killing Roger.

"Where do you want me?" I said as she went forward to help the group leaders herd the troops back on their buses.

"Let me see if there's an empty seat somewhere," she said.

Before she could do that, someone called my name. Even though it was a man's voice and he was really calling my name, I thought that I would see Sheri when I turned around. Instead I saw Walter Solomon hurrying toward us.

"Jay! What the fuck, man! What the fuck!" he said, throwing his long arms around me in a huge embrace. I hugged him back. His embrace brought an unexpected feeling of relief. I'd been dreading having to go through a meet and greet with the other Brigade members. Everyone here, even the few gripers who had spoken up, was an enthusiast. In the closed world we would inhabit, I would be challenged at every moment to keep up the pretense of my own enthusiasm. Walter knew me as a symbol of resistance, and his presence would give me someone to play off of in building my revolutionary identity with this crowd.

Tall, thin, and balding at 24, Walter had been one of the regulars at the McWilliams house when I was there. He and Eddie had been best friends. They'd been classmates at Stuyvesant, one of the special high schools the city has for very smart kids, getting their start in political activism there before going on to Columbia together. Walter was a lot like Eddie. He was sincere, dedicated, sexually uncertain, and, until Roger began working his evil magic, all for nonviolence. When I left, Eddie was already turning toward Roger's "at all costs" point of view. Walter was, as I recall, still reluctant to break from the path of Gandhi and Dr. King. Maybe Roger turned him and maybe he didn't. I figured I would find out soon enough.

"I should have guessed you'd be here!" I said, shaking him by the arms. "Wow! This is great!" I turned to Avis. "Is it okay if I find a place in Walter's bus while we're waiting to board? I mean, if there's room there?"

"You're coming to Cuba?" said Walter. "Holy shit! I thought you were just here, like, to see us off or something."

"Well, you know, I couldn't come down to Boston to get on the bus without getting busted. So I had to meet you here."

"Oh, shit. Of course! This is fantastic." He turned to Avis. "Can Jay come on my bus? We've got some empty seats."

She looked at me. "I guess I'll know where to find you."

- Eighteen -

Walter being there was a piece of luck, but like a lot of luck I've had in my life, it came with a price, which in this case was Walter being there. For one thing, it meant there would be someone around who knew I knew Roger. If I was actually able to get in touch with Roger, and actually able to go through with the deal and kill him, it would probably be better if no one was around to point out my previous relationship with him.

For another thing, there was a chance that Walter was in love with me. This may sound completely crazy, but, as I already mentioned, when we knew each other in New York, he was sexually uncertain. Whenever we spent time together, in a small group or just the two of us, having one of those convulsively serious conversations about the war and politics that inevitably broadened to include the Meaning of It All, I could feel the heat of his attention and recognized it as the same vibe I sent out when I was after a woman. (Until then, I'd never understood how annoying I could be.) After a while, I noticed there were fewer group conversations and more one-on-ones, especially late at night in those rare moments of quiet in the house after most of the crowd had passed out or gone on their way.

I began to avoid him or always had an excuse ready as to why I was on my way somewhere else. After a little while, he apparently gave up. Walter was, to repeat one more time, uncertain, so it may have been that my turning away made him decide to be straight. Or he may have found another object for his affections. I didn't know and was too relieved to be curious. And it was not much longer before I was gone from the house to start on my way to San Francisco.

I didn't care whether Walter was gay, if that was what he did choose. Under different circumstances, I might have even said what the hell and gone to bed with him. He was a handsome young man, despite his emerging bald spot, smart and sensitive and very funny, too. I had a great time in his company. The whole gay thing was changing then, too. There had just been the Stonewall riot in the Village and there was a lot of gay macho pride strutting around. On top of that were all the androgynous images coming out of the music world, starting but not ending with Jagger and the Stones. Walter was far from being the only one who was uncertain. But I had too much else going on to help Walter work through his problems. And whatever sexual uncertainty problems I might have had were way down on the list of things I needed to deal with.

It was warm inside the bus. Walter had been sitting next to one of the Brigade members who had gotten on in Boston and who he hadn't known before the trip. Walter introduced me as an old comrade from New York who had been hiding out in Canada, and asked if his new friend would take a different seat so that he and I could catch up. I thought about us being "old comrades," as if we had stormed the Winter Palace together. It was the kind of thing Walter could say and I wouldn't be able to tell if he was caught up in the self-romanticizing of the movement or consciously exaggerating. Most of the time when we had talked, he was serious and sincere, but every once in a while it hit me that what he was saying was a parody of the clichés that passed for received wisdom among the young and revolutionary. I remember once listening to him lecture a newcomer to the house about how we had to learn to use our night soil as Chinese peasants did for fertilizer, and noticing Eddie across the room burying his face in a pillow trying to hide his laughter.

We settled into our seats. All around us, the conversation was about how long we were going to have to wait before we boarded the ship. No one had a clue, because it was not anything that even the Customs people on the ship could have known. That didn't stop the construction of elaborate theories based on the number of people on the ship, the time it took to interview each one, the number of inspectors, and the time they had started. Was it a typical Customs inspection or would it take longer because the ship was filled with dangerous revolutionaries?

"Do you have any idea?" said Walter.

"No," I said. "It's probably better not to think about it. So, what have you been doing? What is it? Five months since I saw you?"

"Forget what I've been doing. That's dull! What have you been doing? Where have you been?"

I told him about my trip across country to San Francisco, the places I'd stayed and people I'd met, about San Francisco, going to Vancouver, and the commune. While I talked, I figured out a story about how I came to be in the Brigade. I kept it simple. I'd met some people who told me about the Brigade. I decided it was what I needed to do, and they put me in touch with someone who put me in touch with someone else who had enough pull to get me in at the last minute. I told him I hadn't been sure that Avis was going to approve me, but she had and here I was.

"You're lucky," he said. "She can be a real bitch."

"Have you known her long?"

"Long enough. She's one of the organizers of the Brigade. She interviewed me and I just wanted to reach across the desk and strangle her."

"How come?"

"Oh, she was just mean." He hesitated before he continued. "She's SWP."

"SWP?" I'd heard it before but couldn't remember what it stood for.

"Socialist Workers Party. The working class must lead the revolution."

"Is that your beef with her?"

"No, that's okay. It's just that, being so fixated on her macho workers, she…well, let's just say she didn't think I was strong enough to do the work. Or maybe tough enough. I don't know. She just didn't like me."

He was dancing around the gay thing.

"But here you are," I said. "So you must have impressed her."

"I did push-ups."

"Really? Are you kidding me?"

"I told you I wanted to strangle her. But I didn't think it would help me get in, so I just took all my rage, got down on the floor, and started doing push-ups. I probably got to thirty when she told me to stop. Thank God. I might have had a heart attack if I had to do any more."

"Thirty is a lot."

"I started working out as soon as I heard about the Brigade. If I got in, I didn't want to be a limp-wristed fairy when I got to the sugar fields. Pretty smart, huh?"

"No flies on you."

"And I wanted to look good for Roger."

I gripped the arm of my seat so tight I nearly tore it off. Visions of sugarplums danced in my head. Act natural, I said to myself, act natural, act natural, act natural.

"Roger?"

"Roger Chumley. From the McWilliams house. You must remember Roger."

"Roger. Of course. That's who I thought you meant."

Could he hear my heart pounding in my chest? I was thankful for all the layers of clothes I had on.

"He's in Cuba. I forgot," I said. "I guess I was so caught up in my own shit lately, I just wasn't thinking much about anyone else. So, you're going to see him?"

Act natural, act natural, act natural, act natural.

"Yes," said Walter. "We've been writing."

"Were you close to him? I don't remember."

"We got to know each other more about the time you left. You remember what was happening."

"I remember things were getting serious down in the basement."

We were talking in code now about the explosives that Roger had started bringing to the house.

"Exactly. I know you left, but you had a lot of influence on what happened."

"I did?"

"You were so messed up by your experience in the war. And then, the fact that they were after you, that you had to take off. It made everything so much more immediate. It made taking action so much more necessary."

This was depressing me no end. If I'd stayed, I might have helped stop these kids from going off the deep end. Instead, by leaving, I gave Roger ammunition that helped him to turn them.

"It's not what I wanted."

"You never said that. We thought you did."

It was true. I had never spoken against the bombs except to tell Eddie that I thought it was crazy. But I never really tried to stop Roger. I just got my ass out of there. Maybe I did want it. Maybe I wanted them to start blowing things up as long as I wasn't anywhere around it. Or maybe I didn't want any of them, especially the girls, to think I was less than a fire-breathing revolutionary, just in case I ever got to see any of them again. Or maybe I just didn't care one way or another.

"Do you have any idea what actually happened?" I said. "I only read what the newspapers said, and there wasn't a lot of detail except for the little bit Linda Rosenbaum told the cops when they caught up to her."

He didn't say anything. I waited. The silence started to stretch.

"Did you talk to Linda?"

His face shrank into itself. He was disappearing.

"Were you there?"

"Do you have any cigarettes?" he said.

"Yeah."

"Let's go outside and have a smoke." He was up quickly and heading toward the front of the bus. I followed him out. He walked toward the edge of the pier. I joined him there, shaking a cigarette out of the pack and lighting it for him and one for myself. His hands were shaking. He took a couple of drags before he spoke.

"We were in the basement working on the bomb. Me, Roger, Eddie, and Michelle Friedman. Roger sent me to get an alarm clock to use as a timer. It was crazy. It was exciting. I was a real revolutionary. I brought the alarm back and Roger hooked it up to the explosives. We had a bomb. A real bomb. But then he said it was the wrong kind. It wouldn't work. He didn't say why. I asked, but he said he would explain another time. He said he would have to get the right kind himself. I felt he was upset with me, disappointed. I felt terrible. I went after him. When I got outside I didn't see him. He must have been hurrying to the store, the one on Seventh Avenue that was like a five and dime, where I got the alarm I brought back. I needed to tell him that was the only kind they had there and he'd have to go somewhere else. And I wanted to apologize. I wanted him not to be mad at me. I had just reached the corner when …"

He stopped talking and took another drag on his cigarette. I waited.

"The explosion knocked me down. I wasn't unconscious, but I was in a daze. Then I saw Linda come running out of the house. She was a mess, covered in blood and her clothes all torn. I got up and ran to her. She was hysterical. We got to the corner. I guess I knew enough to get as far away as we could as fast as we could. There was a taxi and I got her into it before the driver could say no. I wanted to take her to the emergency room at St. Vincent's, but she wouldn't go. We went to my apartment. She took a shower, we cleaned up her cuts, I gave her some clothes, and we drank brandy and watched the news on TV. She stayed at my place for a couple of days then went to her parents."

"She told her parents what happened. They called the cops," I said.

"They felt bad because the cops weren't sure who the girl was that they found. The Rosenbaums wanted Michelle's parents to know."

"But Linda never told anyone you were there."

"She wanted to pay me back for helping her."

He went silent again. His cigarette burnt itself out.

"I'm sorry," I said.

"I don't know what could have happened. Roger told us not to touch anything while he was gone. Everyone backed away from the bomb. When I left, Eddie and Michelle were talking about what we should blow up."

I wanted to talk more about Roger, but I stopped myself from asking. There would be plenty of time on the ship to get back to that.

"I'm cold," he said, and started back to the bus.

- Nineteen -

Walter closed his eyes as soon as we returned to our seats, but I don't think he fell right to sleep. He mostly needed to retreat from where he had been in our talk outside. I stayed with it. I remembered the news stories and Linda Rosenbaum, who was a sweet, smart girl who liked to flirt with me, telling the police that she had been upstairs in Eddie's room when the house exploded. She had been asleep and had just gotten out of bed moments before. She told them she was pretty sure that the only people there when the bomb exploded were Eddie and Michelle because everyone else who had been in the house the night before had gone home. She also said she had pulled up the shade just before the explosion to see what the weather was like and happened to see Roger leaving the house and walking down the street.

After what Walter had told me, it was clear that Linda had not known who was in the house and had not seen Roger leave. She had gotten all that from Walter. It had struck me as odd when I'd first read the story that she had fingered Roger. I remember speculating that he must have fucked her over somehow and she was getting even. It seemed even more likely now that I knew she had protected Walter.

It didn't matter much anymore. Roger was a fugitive and Eddie and Michelle were dead. Michelle Friedman. She had started coming to the house right about the time I was getting ready to leave. A nice girl. I talked to her once or twice. I remember the first time, because she had me mixed up with Roger, started talking to me like I was him, and was very embarrassed by her mistake. She said it was because we kind of looked alike. I wondered if she had gotten caught up in the bomb-making to get in with the "in crowd" as fast as possible. Like a high school movie where the new kid has to do something crazy in order to be accepted.

    They all wanted to be revolutionaries and to be accepted by the other revolutionaries. They were all good kids, caring, wanting to make a better world. But they were still kids. I looked down the aisle of the bus. It was the same deal. Kids, good kids, driven crazy by the stupid war. It was weird. I wasn't any older than they were, but they seemed like kids to me. I wondered how many of them were ready to make bombs. I thought about a rally I'd gone to in the park in San Francisco where kids were singing "Revolution has come, Time to pick up the gun." I'd picked up the gun. Well, really, I guess I'd had it handed to me. All I wanted to do was put it down. I thought about how nice it was to cuddle up under the covers with Wildflower. I thought about what it would be like to cuddle up with Avis Watson. I fell asleep.

- Twenty -

It was hours before we got on the ship. Everyone was awake and cranky when we finally saw the First Brigade start down the gangway. The bus doors were opened and people hustled out to greet the heroes back from the real revolution. Friends found friends. The mood turned jubilant.

I didn't know anyone getting off the ship. I stood back and watched them. They looked tired but joyful, glad to be home, but also glad they had done what they had done. What had they learned? I had a sudden urge to be one of them, to test myself and win and have that look as if I knew something worth knowing.

I thought I did have that once, coming to Saigon with my buddies for a break after some hard fighting in country. It had been our first time in the jungle, our first time in combat, our first time killing. By some miracle, we all came out of the first fighting alive and in one piece. Crazy luck. But we didn't know that. What we knew was that nothing would ever be the same.

Except for that look of knowing something, the people coming home were like the people getting ready to go. They were mostly kids, white and black and brown, boys and girls, and some grown-up men and women, too. I saw one Asian guy, but I wasn't sure if he was with the old Brigade or the new one now that the groups were together, everyone wrapped in winter gear.

Walter had plunged into the crowd, waving down a guy who had just stepped off the gangway, then running up to him and embracing him as he had embraced me a few hours earlier. Walter spotted me as they walked back toward the buses, which were going to take the arrivals back into the U.S. He called me over.

"Jay, this is Alan Stone. We went to school together."

We shook hands. His hand was hard from two months of cutting cane. He had a firm, manly grip, too. Stone was short and compact. He had good color in his face and a big smile. He looked like he was on a great acid trip.

"Jay was a friend of Eddie's," Walter said.

"Oh," said Stone, not sure how close a friend I might have been.

"So, how was it?" I said.

"Great, man. Eye-opening. You're gonna love it. It's like nothing you ever experienced in your life."

"Great," I said.

The mixed Brigades drifted into the potato shed to get out of the weather. It was a weird party, everyone in winter clothes, everyone's words visible as mist coming out of their mouths, and not a drink to be had. But no one, except maybe me, needed a drink. They were high on their own enthusiasm.

Stone rattled on at us. What it was like in the fields, in the camp, the time off that they had to travel around Cuba and meet the people, the revolutionary fervor everywhere. At first I wasn't listening, looking around instead to see if I could catch a glimpse of Avis. But slowly I started taking in his words. It was dawning on me that I was going to be part of this. I had only been thinking of my own mission, but now I saw that however I was going to get to Roger, most of my time was going to be spent cutting cane. I thought back to when I had been drafted. In boot camp, I had made up my mind that life in the Army would be a lot easier if, instead of pretending I wasn't really there, I became the best soldier I could be. As it turned out, doing that had saved my life when the real soldiering began.

It hit me that I would have to do the same thing in Cuba—be the best cane cutter I could be. I began to pay attention as Stone explained what he had learned about cutting cane, the best way to hold a machete, the best place to strike the cane, the right way to move down a row, the right way to stack the stalks. I didn't know if it would save my life in Cuba, but it couldn't hurt.

Before Alan could get very deep into his lesson, Avis did her whistle thing again and the shed quieted down.

"Time to board," was all she said.

PART II
The *Luis Arcos Bergnes*

- Twenty-One -

The interior of the *Luis Arcos Bergnes* was warm and dry. The ship had been a cattle boat but was converted by the Cubans into a floating barracks, with a double layer of bunks in what had been the hold. The men and women had separate areas. I'd thought I'd been in close quarters when I was in basic training, but that was spacious compared to this scene. There was hardly any room to stow our gear, and most people would up sleeping with their bags and suitcases.

We finally got to eat some hot food, the women first and then the men. I don't remember much more about that first night except saying good night to Walter. I probably passed out.

The seas were rough in the North Atlantic, and a lot of people were seasick through the first part of the trip. I was one of them. Being seasick on this trip wasn't such a bad deal. From the time we got on board it seemed like an endless meeting was taking place with everyone trying to shout down everyone else. Whatever the meetings were supposed to be about, they always wound up focusing on a few themes: white guilt, Third World leadership, women's liberation, and evolution versus revolution, that is, whether to wait for the workers or take matters into our own hands.

Everyone was extremely serious about the whole thing, as if they had to come to some decision because tomorrow we were going out to storm the Bastille or the Winter Palace, and the day after that we would be in charge so we had better have our act together. I really didn't know much about the revolutionary movement before I started hanging out in Eddie's house. But there were books about it all over the place and I ate them up. To me they were adventure stories, war stories. Even our own revolution.

I'd sit in a big armchair in the McWilliams's library room smoking a joint and reading Lenin and Marx and Mao. There was some Stalin, too, and Ho Chi Minh and that guy from Albania. And while I was reading, all around me the kids were having their endless arguments about whether we should be focused on educating the working class or moving ahead as a revolutionary cadre to act immediately, and whether whites could only follow the lead of blacks in making a revolution in America, and whether women should be in the forefront.

Did Lenin and Trotsky sound as pompous to the casual listener when they were having their arguments while living like paupers in exile? Did the guards watching over the reading room in the British Library know that the scruffy mountain of unkempt hair who came in every day was KARL FUCKING MARX, who actually was going to change the world? What about the waiters at the posh hotel in London where Ho washed dishes? Did they have any idea that the skinny gook was going to be the father of his country and stop U.S. imperialism dead in its tracks?

Maybe some kid on the *Luis Arcos Bergnes* was going to be president someday. It didn't seem possible, but most people listening to Lenin no doubt thought he was just another delusional windbag.

Although I was so sick I mostly wanted to die and be buried at sea, I was glad not to be in the meetings. I knew I would have gotten caught up in the heat of the moment and started spouting a lot of nonsense that I didn't understand. Not that there were a lot of meetings I could have been in. The blacks had their own meetings and the women had their meetings, and the white men had trouble figuring out where they belonged. What was our common identity except we were white and men and were at fault for everything that was wrong?

Walter wavered between being upset that he wasn't in any group and being glad that he wasn't.

"Sometimes I want to shout 'Enough already!' but then I think of something I want to say and I have no one to say it to," he told me.

"But you're a white man," I said. "What could you possibly have to say?"

"Very funny. But, come on, don't you feel the same way?"

"Sure. But you can't fight history. And history says it's their time. If we're really supposed to follow, then shut up and follow."

"But when I think they're wrong—"

"It doesn't matter. You have to step aside and let people find their way. You know I'm right."

"Yeah, but that doesn't make me like it any better."

Another benefit of being at the rail was getting to spend time with Avis, who was also in the seasick club. The first morning out, I met her clinging to the rail as the ship tossed and the wind cut through us as if we were naked.

"I hate this," she said.

"Kind of undermines your image as an authority figure."

"Fuck you."

"Think of it as your martyrdom for the cause."

"You suck."

"This is what your statue will look like after the revolution, bent over the rail giving it all up so that others may have smooth sailing."

"I hope you fall overboard."

"I've always gotten seasick. I didn't even think about it when I decided to come. I guess that's how dedicated I am."

"This is my first time on a ship. I'm going to walk home."

"I used to go out fishing all the time when I was a kid and almost always got seasick. It really pissed me off because no one else in my family did. We all went out on the fishing boats from Sheepshead Bay, my father and grandfather and uncles and cousins, and of the whole gang of us, I was the only one who ever hit the rail. It was a family joke. *I* was the family joke."

"Did it ever stop?"

"Yeah, when I stopped going."

"Too bad."

"Nah. It wasn't one of my favorite things to do anyway. I like being warm and dry and going out for blues and flounder was cold and wet. The only part I liked was when the captain would take pity on me and let me hang out on the bridge. Taught me the controls and even let me steer. Took my mind off being sick."

A really big wave lifted the side of the ship and for a moment we were thrown together. Avis pulled away as soon as she had her balance back.

"The captain says it'll stop when we get closer to Florida," she said.

"When is that?"

"Three or four days."

"We'll be dead by then."

"I hope so."

We both threw up and then went back inside.

"Hey," I said, "thanks for letting me come."

"Don't fuck up."

She walked away. I was happy. The ice was broken.

- Twenty-Two -

Over the next couple of days, it was rough seas and several visits to the rail for both of us. The circumstances were not very romantic and the conversation stayed short and guarded. I looked forward to better weather and a chance for something beyond black humor. She did surprise me, though, during one of our last encounters before we hit smooth sailing.

"Why did you really come?" she said.

I almost blurted out the truth, but my churning stomach gave me a moment to collect my thoughts.

"I needed a vacation," I said.

"You think this is going to be a vacation?"

"Look, I'm a college dropout with no skills. In Canada I was trimming grapevines. I figured this wouldn't be so different, it was for a good cause, and it was south. I could work on my tan."

"Not a priority for me. You think you're going to figure out some way to get back into the States when this is over. Right?"

"Hadn't thought about it. But if you have any ideas how that could happen, let me know."

"Maybe you think you can stay in Cuba?"

"Hadn't thought about that either. But maybe I'll like it, and yeah, why not?"

"Or maybe you're thinking you can get to Europe from Cuba."

"You let me know how that one works and I'll consider it."

"Just don't—"

"I know. Don't fuck up."

She went inside. I had her eating out of my hand. I threw up again and went in myself. Almost telling her about Roger made me think I needed to get back on track. When we were waiting to board, I had imagined that Walter would tell me everything I wanted to know, and sooner rather than later. But he hadn't mentioned Roger since we'd left Canada. I was thinking I'd have to prompt him somehow, but without making him suspicious. I thought about it for a while but nothing came to me. Then the Cubans did it for me.

Maybe from their experience with the first Brigade, the Cubans had learned they had to keep us entertained or we would tear each other's heads off long before we reached Havana harbor. So they showed movies. It worked. There was a how-to film demonstrating proper cane-cutting techniques, but mostly there were American movies that were just for fun. One of them was the Chaplin movie *Modern Times*. Everyone was appreciating Chaplin the clown, forgetting for a while Chaplin the Communist. I was sitting with Walter, both of us laughing along with everyone else.

"I can't wait to tell Roger they showed this," he said. "It's one of his favorites."

I forgot about Chaplin.

"You're going to see Roger?"

"As soon as we get a day off. He's in Havana."

"Great. Say 'hi' for me." What I really meant was invite me to come along.

"Why don't you come along?"

Act natural, act natural, act natural.

"Well, if I wouldn't be in the way …"

I think Walter suddenly regretted having asked me. But it was too late.

"No, of course not."

"I can just say hello then head out to the beach. Leave you two to catch up."

That made him feel better and sealed the deal.

"Okay. Whatever."

Act natural. Whatever. Yes. Act natural. I was going to see Roger. I had something for him.

- Twenty-Three -

I almost made it to Havana without having to talk politics. But given the circumstances, our close quarters, and the fact that other than cane-cutting techniques hardly anything else was discussed, it was too much to expect. We were off the coast of Florida in waters that were at last calm, and it seemed like everyone was on deck to get some sun. One of the ship's officers lent us his binoculars, and they got passed around as we tried to make out as much detail as possible of Miami Beach.

While I was taking my turn, someone tapped me on the shoulder. I recognized him as one of the Weathermen. There was a group of them in the Brigade, strutting around with a "we're the only real revolutionaries here" attitude. They reminded me of some of the Marines I'd met in Vietnam who were always looking down on us lousy Army mutts. The Weathermen had made a lot of noise in Chicago a few months earlier with their "Days of Rage" protest against the Chicago Seven conspiracy trial. But from all accounts, noise was about all they made. For about half an hour they managed to break a bunch of car windows before the cops shut them down. All in all, their days of rage were on a par with a Saturday night beer riot at a midsize college after the home team wins the homecoming game.

I handed him the binoculars.

"Help yourself."

"That's okay," he said. "I've seen Miami."

I handed the glasses to the next person over and turned back to look at the shoreline. The Weatherman stepped up next to me. He was my height with long hair wrapped tight by a red bandanna. He was a handsome kid and had that same quality as the McWilliamses, that look of money. Only he was so clearly ashamed of it, his mouth twisted as if that would show he was disassociating himself from himself.

"You're Jay Cardinale, right? The deserter?"

He made it sound like it was the title of a TV show. I wondered what my theme music would sound like. I was thinking like the music for *The Rebel*. "Johnny Yuma was a rebel, he roamed through the west…." I may have been humming out loud. He was waiting for me to say something.

I thought about the seersuckers. With them I was struck silent with fear because I knew how much they could hurt me. This time I was silent because I knew how much I could hurt *him*, and I didn't want to go there. But he stayed there, waiting.

"Uh, yeah. How you doing?"

"Great, man. It's great to meet you. They call me Geronimo."

"That's your name?"

"That's what they call me."

"Oh. Wow. Cool."

"Yeah."

He was making it hard for me not to want to throw him overboard.

"Who's they? That calls you that?"

"You know I'm a Weatherman, right?"

"Yeah, I seen you with them."

"We know about you. About your experience."

"My experience?"

"The war. Being in combat. You know. We thought you might belong with us."

He was talking loud enough for the people around us to hear, making a show of recruiting me to the action faction. It was like hearing Lauren McWilliams all over again. I had blood on my hands. I was in demand.

"Wow. I'm honored."

"We're just getting together for a meeting."

"Aw, gee, that's great. But I think I'll take a pass."

"Huh?"

"If I joined I'd probably just desert again. It's just the way I am."

"But—"

"No, really."

"Look, man, we're the vanguard. All these pussies are gonna talk themselves to death. We're gonna kick ass. You should be with us."

"But that's just it. I'm a pussy. I'm going to wait for the working class to come to its senses, even if it takes the next hundred years, then I'm going to roll down the street in my wheelchair leading the victory parade."

"I thought you were an action guy."

"No, I'm a working-class guy from Brooklyn, a Teamster baby. Solidarity forever."

Some of the people who couldn't help but listen to us started snickering. He shot them an angry look and they walked away, but were laughing out loud as they left. He turned back to me.

"Well, fuck you, then."

He went to his meeting without me. "Geronimo." Jesus H. Christ.

- Twenty-Four -

Walter was on the deck on the other side of the ship. A space had been cleared so we could exercise. The Brigade had been broken down into smaller brigade units that would cut cane together, and each brigade took its turn in the exercise space.

Walter had been elected leader of our small brigade, Brigade 27 (he had campaigned for it, politely and earnestly), and had taken charge of organizing our exercise routine. I figured his success with the push-ups had gone to his head. He would lead some of the exercises and I would lead some, doing basic boot-camp stuff, and then, in the spirit of democracy, anyone else in the group could take a turn as leader.

"People are talking," he said as I joined him.

"Huh?"

"Your tête-à-tête with Geronimo."

"It just happened. How do you know about it?"

"Small ship."

"Smaller than I thought."

The rest of our group had arrived and we got to work. I wanted to know more about what Walter had heard, but I also wanted to drop it completely. Given my reason for being on the ship, I was inclined toward anonymity. I did not want people thinking about me, much less talking about me. Geronimo (what the hell was his real name?) had caught me off guard. Otherwise, instead of mouthing off, I would have simply declined his offer to become a Weatherman as politely as possible.

As our group was ending its exercise set, I made up my mind not to ask Walter what he had heard. If I asked him, he would ask me, and words would lead to more words and then still more words. End it now, I thought. It felt right. But before I could deny Walter the chance to pick up the thread, one of the other people in our group—the youngest, a nineteen-year-old from Virginia named Jerry, who I was sure had a crush on Walter—came over to me and said, "Thanks for sticking it to Geronimo. He's such an asshole." I sighed. He looked at me with wondering eyes and then we both turned, aware that someone was approaching.

It was Geronimo. Behind him the other Weathermen were assembling to take over the exercise space to run through their karate routines, shouting "Smash imperialism!" and "Bring the war home!" as they punched and kicked the air. I'd forgotten that their turn came right after ours. Geronimo had blood in his eye. The other Weathermen watched, some openly, some pretending to stretch in preparation for their drill.

"Hey, motherfucker," he said as he closed in on me. Too close. He started into his karate stance but he should have been a step or two farther away. Before he could get in position, I hit him as hard as I could with a straight right, putting all my weight behind it. His head snapped back and blood poured from his nose. His knees buckled and down he went on his ass. He sat there on the deck, shaking the stars from his brain. Geronimo was now Sitting Bull.

A couple of the other Weathermen started toward me. Everyone in my exercise group was frozen where they stood. An image of the last time I'd been in a fight like this, in the yard outside Edward B. Shallow Junior High School, flashed through my mind. The two Weathermen went into their stances smartly, beyond my reach. I guessed that both would use their feet before their hands. They could stay farther away if they did that.

I kept my hands low. The smaller of the two came at me first, shouting and kicking. It was only when I heard the voice that I became aware it was a woman. She caught me on the left thigh, but I was twisting away from the kick, and though it hurt, it was not a terrible blow and it didn't keep me from grabbing her ankle, yanking it up and back. She lost her balance and went down on top of Geronimo.

Her partner went into his kick and hit my hip. This time I was off-balance and it sent me staggering sideways but not down. I turned to face the kicker, who clearly wasn't sure what to do next. That had been his one big move. He looked down at his two decked companions and then back at the rest of his group. They started moving toward us. Oops, I thought, this is not looking good. To my surprise, Walter and his Virginia friend came up beside me.

Before anything else could happen, there was a whistle, Avis's whistle. She and a bunch of the Cubans were rushing toward the exercise space.

"Stop it!" she said. "Right now."

Everyone stayed where they were except the woman on top of Geronimo. She scrambled to her feet. Avis stood between her and me. I noticed the Cubans were smiling. It occurred to me the woman's name was Beverly, though I don't know why it came to me then.

"God damn it!" said Avis. "Are you crazy?"

"Screw you," said Beverly. "We're not taking any crap from him or anyone else."

Beverly looked like she was ready for round two. If she took a swing at Avis, I was going to punch her in the face. But I didn't need to worry.

"You'll take it from me," said Avis. She put her face an inch away from Beverly's. "Get below." She pointed to the still dazed Geronimo. "And take him with you."

God, I was falling head over heels for her.

Beverly wasn't finished arguing.

"We have a right to be here."

Avis glared at her. I didn't think she could get any closer to Beverly, but she moved forward. She spoke quietly so that only those of us closest to them could hear.

"You're embarrassing the whole Brigade," said Avis. "Get below and cool off or I swear to God, I'll have the Cubans toss you overboard."

The Cubans leaned forward, as if ready to grab Beverly whether Avis said to or not. These were intense guys, and though I'd seen them very happy and relaxed when they were making music, it was clear they didn't go in for nonsense when it came to being revolutionaries.

That did it for Beverly. She turned and headed for the door that led down to the dorms. The Weatherman who had kicked me helped Geronimo to his feet and they and the rest of the Weathermen followed after her. Geronimo never looked at me as he got to his feet or as he left. But Avis looked at me. She was fuming.

"You come with me," she said.

She took a different door than the Weathermen had used. I followed her down the stairs to a space that had been cleared out so the Brigade leaders could have an office. No one was there. She closed the door behind us.

"Sit."

I did. She stayed on her feet staring down at me. I figured she was trying to be intimidating, and she was, but all I could think about was how hot she was.

"Why are you here?"

"I told you. I wanted out of Canada."

"Are you FBI?"

"Are you crazy?"

"That's not an answer. Do you work for the FBI?"

"I work for me."

"And the FBI."

"No."

"You're a provocateur."

"Me?"

I caught myself about to say, "I didn't start it. It was Geronimo." But it sounded so stupid, I had to hold back.

"You're making trouble," she said.

"Okay. I guess I did kind of provoke him. But he's such a prick."

"No kidding," she said.

We laughed. Just a little, but enough so that I didn't have to worry that she was still thinking I was FBI.

"Really," I said. "I didn't go out of my way to do it. He did come asking for it."

"I don't care. I can't have fighting. That shit's supposed to be left behind. We're all here for one reason, to help the Cubans."

"Right."

"Don't fuck with me, Jay. You can get your ass thrown overboard, too, you know."

"Look, I told you I'm here for me. You all are going to go home when this thing is over. I don't know where I'm going to go. Back to Canada? Stay here? I don't know. But I know that nothing good is going to happen for me unless I do a good job. So I'm down for cutting cane. I'm gonna be a cane-cutting machine. I want to win the gold medal. I'm gonna do you proud. Okay?"

A lot of people would have been satisfied but Avis was sharp. She couldn't help but mistrust me.

"Stay away from Geronimo. Stay away from Beverly. Stay away from all of them."

"Fine with me."

My admiration continued to grow. I had a feeling that she was noticing it for the first time. I couldn't tell yet if she liked it or not. The scowl on her face could mean so many things. I wished we were someplace else, somewhere that I could invite her to go have a drink and talk things over. Maybe once we were in Cuba, when we got our day off, I could give it a shot. Maybe she could come with me when I killed Roger, and then we could go have a beer. For the moment, all I could do was look contrite and smile at her. Her scowl lessened and she looked like she might be on the brink of a smile.

There was cheering from up on the deck.

"Is that for us?" I said.

- Twenty-Five -

We went up on the deck. People were jumping around, hugging, cheering. The trial of the Chicago Seven was over with a verdict of not guilty of conspiracy. Walter hurried toward us, a huge smile on his face.

"It's incredible!"

"Unfuckingbelievable!" said Avis. She and Walter hugged.

"Wow," I said.

"Yeah," said Walter. "Wow!"

He hugged me.

"Wow," I said again. I thought it might get me a hug from Avis, but she had already turned to some of the other Brigade members that had followed Walter over to us. I grinned broadly and shook my head approvingly as the celebration swirled around me, but the truth was I didn't feel the same excitement as the others.

The Chicago Seven trial had started about the time I'd gone up to Canada. A bunch of antiwar activists had been charged with having gone to Chicago in 1968 when the Democrats were holding their convention and starting the riots that had pretty much ruined the party. There were eight defendants when the trial started, but Bobby Seale, the leader of the Black Panthers, had been separated from the other defendants when he got into a major league fight with the judge who had him gagged and shackled. That was about as depressing a moment for the country as I could ever remember. I was glad to be in Canada.

The commune members were all for the defendants, of course, but I don't think anyone was following the trial on a day-to-day basis. We didn't have TV and we didn't get a newspaper every day, and the radio news was not all that expansive and tended to give more time to local events, with the major global news wrapped up in less than a minute. The trial only became something I was familiar with in any detail after I got on the ship, as there it was a major topic of conversation.

Of course, all the Brigade members were outraged at the injustice of the trial. The judge was a reactionary idiot, the government was trying to crush all dissent, the defendants were all angels. As far as I could tell, it was all true except for the defendants being angels. I knew they hadn't conspired to incite a riot, as the Chicago police and the Democrats had pretty much done that for them by being a collection of cowards and liars. But while they were on the side of the angels, a few of the defendants, certainly the ringleaders, Abbie Hoffman and Jerry Rubin, were clever devils. I dug them. Hoffman was like a guy you'd hang out with on the corner, a smartass loudmouth with a wicked opinion about everything, but always funny, even when he was serious. Rubin didn't have the same flair, but I read somewhere that his father drove a delivery truck and was a union man like my dad and so I felt a kinship with him.

The other defendants were all sincere antiwar activists, a bunch of good guys who scared the government because they really stood for something. I didn't need to know anything else except they had been trying to help me and all the other guys back in Vietnam who should never have been sent there.

I had to admit that I felt a little guilty about them being on trial. If I hadn't been so stupid as to go along with being drafted, so afraid to resist—me and thousands of others—they could have done something else with their lives besides trying to end the war.

And then there was Bobby Seale, the Black Panther leader. I'd met him in San Francisco before I went up to Canada and before he went off to Chicago for the trial. One of Sheri's housemates—I only knew him as Big John—belonged to a radical film group called Newsreel that made documentaries about the war and all the other political stuff that was happening in San Francisco. Their specialty was making movies about the Panthers, and I went along with Big John on a couple of shoots and that's where I met Bobby. Everyone referred to him as Bobby, just as his partner in founding the Panthers, Huey Newton, was simply Huey. There was no other Bobby or Huey. If there was, they had to have nicknames or else be called by their last names.

We were in a kitchen in a small house somewhere in Oakland, waiting for Big John, who was supposed to know how to use the camera, to figure out why it wasn't working. While we waited, Bobby, who had the most soulfully weary eyes I'd ever seen in a man's face, told jokes. They weren't race jokes, but the kind of thing you'd hear on Johnny Carson's show, the kind of jokes a Borscht Belt comedian would tell. Somebody told me later that one of Bobby's secret ambitions was to be a stand-up comic.

The following day Bobby was arrested and shipped to Chicago for the trial.

- Twenty-Six -

The celebrating died down and the mood turned to one of anticipation. The next day we would be entering Havana Harbor. I don't think anyone slept that night. I know I didn't. The Cubans on board were the most excited of all. They were going home.

Lying in my bunk, I thought about the other Brigade members. From the conversations I had heard, I knew they were worried about how they would do. For all the exercise and all the revolutionary bravado, they were scared. Would the softness of their student lives undermine their political ambitions? Would they have the stamina to face up to long days of working in the cane fields?

We had a lot of tough guys in boot camp, but except for the ones who had been on varsity teams, we all thought we were going to die from exhaustion. Would the Cubans push these kids the way the Army had pushed us? Did they really need all that cane cut for the sake of their survival, or was it all a publicity stunt where it didn't matter whether we cut cane or not, just that we were there? When the trip had started, I'd figured it was for the publicity and that the kids were worrying for nothing. But as we got closer, it hit me that this was for real. Maybe Avis's seriousness was rubbing off on me, or maybe it was something about the Cubans, their hard edge even when they were playing music or just hanging out. Whatever it was, I figured, as I had learned in the Army, be prepared for the worst.

I didn't worry about holding up my end when it came to the cutting.

PART II *The Luis Arcos Bergnes* 99

Once we got past the rough weather, I'd been up on deck at night running through my own drill in addition to the exercise we did as a group, and I felt ready to go into the cane fields. My worries were about Roger. I'd caught a huge break with the Walter connection. It eliminated having to track Roger down and figuring out a way to get to be with him, neither of which I had any clue how to do. The seersuckers had been awfully loose about that kind of detail, especially given how well they'd taken care of things like paperwork and poison pills.

I hadn't thought much about them since the trip started, but as I looked ahead to Roger, I wondered at how it had all come together—Mr. and Mrs. McWilliams, the seersuckers, knowing about my dad, the pardon. I guess I had figured it was all due to McWilliams's government connections. The seersuckers either worked for some spook agency and had been assigned to help McWilliams, or else they were former spooks who'd been hired for the job and used their connections to get the dirt on me. In either case, it was an awful lot of effort to get even with Roger for poor dead Eddie.

However it had come about, it was all on me to get it done. While the other Brigade members were staring into the dark of the ship's hold picturing themselves cutting cane, I was envisioning myself in Roger's apartment waiting for the moment when he and Walter would both have their backs turned and I could slip a pill into Roger's drink. That was assuming we had drinks. What if he was a cheap bastard and didn't bother? If I asked for a glass of water or something, there was no guarantee that Roger would have a drink, too. Would I have to suggest that we go somewhere for a beer and try it then? How was I going to get them both to look the other way at the same time if we were sitting in a bar? It was beginning to sink in how ridiculous the whole idea was.

What if I tossed the idea of the pill and got myself a knife and just cut Roger's throat? I couldn't do that with Walter around. I'd have to go back to Roger's place once I knew where it was, sneak away from the cane field, go to Havana or wherever he was, kill him, and get back before anyone noticed I was gone. Maybe I could say I was sick, stay in my bunk, and sneak away after everyone left for the fields. But how was I going to get back and forth? How far away from Havana—or wherever Roger was living—were we going to be? Could I blend in among the Cubans so that no one would be able to describe the gringo going in and out of Roger's place?

And what if Roger wasn't alone? What if he had picked up a little señorita to play house with? Or if he didn't have a place to himself but instead shared living quarters with other exiles or with some Cubans?

What if he had a gun?

What if, what if, what if. I was making myself crazy. I thought about Lauren McWilliams and her garden-party idea that a killer was a killer was a killer. It was all too stupid to be real. Surely the seersuckers must have known I wasn't going to be able to do this. Of course they had, but they didn't really care. They did what they had been asked to do, help out an important friend of the president. If I failed, it wasn't on them. It would, at worst, be back to the drawing board to figure out another scheme.

What about their threats? If I tried and failed and didn't wind up dead myself or in a Cuban prison, were they really going to kill my family and friends? That wasn't too stupid to be real. It was too insane.

Back to the drawing board. How was I going to pull this off? Think positive. Think like Lauren McWilliams. Think like a rich person who always got what she wanted. I had to get Roger to drink. I had to have a moment alone to poison his drink. That was all there was to it, really. Use Walter to get to Roger. Once with Roger, play it cool to somehow get drinks into the picture. Once we had drinks, find a way to be alone.

Going to a bar was best. Get a table and volunteer to get the drinks at the bar. Slip the Mickey in before bringing the glasses to the table. Piece of cake. That's the Lauren attitude. That's the "can-do!" spirit that colonels are always touting to the troops. All you had to do was repress the part of your brain that kept shouting, "Bullshit!"

So I had a plan.

Sort of.

PART III
Campamento Brigada Venceremos

- Twenty-Seven -

It took a few hours from the time we saw land until we landed. All the while, there was a great celebration on board. Music, dancing, singing. The joy of the Cubans at seeing their home so close and the Brigade's excitement at having made it so far wound together in a way that had been missing through the voyage up to that moment. It was the first time since we'd left Canada that I thought there might be some real opportunity to connect with what Cuba was all about—a revolution, a new way of living, of being—and not just another empty gesture that gave a lot of spoiled kids another chance to play at being rebels.

I joined Walter and the rest of our little brigade in the singing and dancing. In part, I was trying to distract myself from the thoughts still running through my mind about Roger and what I was going to do. I also wanted to hide myself in the crowd instead of standing off to one side noticeably lost in my gloom and doom to anyone who cared to observe me, meaning, of course, Avis. I wanted her to think that while I might have different motives than most of the kids for being there, they were reasonable. I had to end her thinking that I was up to no good.

Once I joined in, it was easy to get lost in the energy and noise. I stopped thinking about myself. I cheered with Walter and all the others as the sun came up over the Cuban horizon and the fog lifted so that we could see the shoreline clearly. I shouted, "Venceremos!" as we sailed past Moro Castle and into the harbor proper. And I had tears in my eyes when I saw the huge crowd waiting to greet us. I thought about what it had been like arriving home in New York and how completely invisible and ignored I felt. I wished that I was Walter, that all I had come there to do was cut cane and fulfill my revolutionary destiny.

- Twenty-Eight -

We left the *Luis Arcos Bergnes* and walked through a cheering crowd straight onto buses lined up and waiting to take us out to the camp in the cane fields that would be our home for the next six weeks. The ride took a couple of hours. There was little conversation as we all stared out the windows at the countryside. It was low hills and green grass. There were few cars or any other vehicles on the road. Sometimes we'd pass a house or a cluster of houses. Our buses had the Venceremos Brigade "BV" insignia on them, and everyone we passed cheered when they saw it.

After an hour, the landscape changed. We were in the cane fields. The cane lined the road, tall, as tall as the buses, and thin. At least the individual stalks were thin, but the fields themselves were thick, dense with the stalks. I could see the expressions on the faces of my teammates changing. The smiles at seeing Cuba, the rolling fields, the round, soft hills in the distance, and the sharp mountains at the horizon, were replaced by tightened lips on some faces and open-mouthed awe on others. Whatever thoughts any of us had of a revolutionary idyll were vanishing with each passing minute as the cane went on and on and on all the way to the camp.

Avis's voice cut through the dread-filled silence. I was in the back and hadn't noticed she was on our bus, sitting up front next to the driver.

"Yes, ladies and gentlemen, boys and girls, there it is." She was laughing. People turned to her, bewildered. "That's our enemy for the next two months. Look at it, waiting for us, waiting to do battle. Yes, I know, it looks like sugarcane. But it's not. Not really. Do you know what it is?"

No one said a word.

"No one? Then I'll tell you. It's oppression. It's hunger. It's poverty. It's ignorance. And every time you swing your machete, every time you cut one of those motherfuckers down, you are striking a blow for freedom. You are striking a blow for dignity. You are striking a blow for the people. You want to be revolutionaries? Then cut, chop, slice those bastards down! What are you gonna do?"

"Cut cane!" shouted Walter.

Avis shouted louder. "What are you gonna do?"

More voices joined in. "Cut cane!"

"Say it again!"

Everyone on the bus, including me, shouted, "Cut cane!"

God, I was crazy about her.

- Twenty-Nine -

The buses rolled into the camp past a sign that read Campamento Brigada Venceremos. We were directed to our tents and stowed our gear, then headed out to a meeting hall where Javier, the Cuban director of the camp, gave us another pep talk. He talked a lot about Vietnam, about the spirit of the Vietnamese and how they were defeating America. Ain't that the truth, I thought. Between him and Avis, the fear of failure had shrunk to something manageable.

There were a couple of other speakers, camp leaders who pretty much told us the same thing. It didn't matter. Each speech pumped us up even more. We were there for the revolution! We were there to smash imperialism! I looked over at where the Weathermen were sitting. They were in heaven. Geronimo must have felt my eyes on him because he turned and looked at me. Without thinking, I held up my fist, giving him the power salute. He stared for a moment then nodded his head and saluted me back. Then we both turned back to the speaker. Jeez, I thought, what the hell did I just do?

The news that lifted everyone's spirits the most was that we didn't have to go right to work the next day. Instead we were going to get in a day of practice. That was good. So many of the group were students, or had just been students, and they were reassured by the idea of having a lesson. It was familiar.

After a socko finish that had us all on our feet stomping and cheering, Walter and I went out to explore the camp. There were separate tents for the men and the women. There was a dining hall and a first aid tent. There was, to our surprise, a movie theater, an outdoor one to be sure, but still a surprise. Also surprising were the barber tent and the volleyball courts.

There were a couple of guard stations, too. I was not happy to see them. Aside from my concern that I might have to sneak out at some point to get to Roger, I wondered if they were to keep us in or someone else out.

And all around us were the cane fields.

"This reminds me of summer camp," said Walter. "Except for the cane."

"Reminds me of Vietnam," I said. "Except we cut the jungle back much farther from the perimeter."

"Well, maybe that's what we'll do first. Cut the cane right around the camp."

I wondered if other people were having the same experience, looking at the cane surrounding the camp, daring us to keep up the good spirits we had coming out of the meeting.

- Thirty -

No one cut their foot off.

In the years since, I've met several people who, when they hear I was in the Brigade, told me about this guy or this girl that sliced off one extremity or another while cutting cane. I tell them it isn't so, that it's just an old reactionary wives' tale, but it does no good. The story is too comforting for those who didn't go.

Of course, every once in a while I encounter a *Brigadista*, and when the talk gets around to cutting cane, what we remember about what really happened is bad enough.

No one cut their foot off, but some came close. There were assorted nicks and cuts, bangs and bruises. Our instructors were patient with us as they took us through our day of practice. They'd been through this before with the first Brigade and maybe they were even thinking back to when they themselves had first been taught to cut. Even so, we, the instructees, were frustrated as hell those first few days.

I had high hopes for myself, but they didn't pan out. I couldn't get the angle right, and wound up hacking away over and over to get the stalk to fall, just like almost everyone else. I was pissed off. I was used to doing physical things well, and couldn't stand not being able to get the hang of it. What made it even worse was that I noticed Geronimo swooping down and taking a stalk down with a single stroke. He grinned confidently and the other Weathermen gave him a big cheer.

With my next practice turn, I went at the stalk in a fit of anger and got my machete stuck. The instructor had to wrestle it out. Some people laughed. Geronimo looked smug. I could hardly wait for my next chance. I'd show him. Before I got to go again, Walter's little friend from Virginia, Jerry, had his second turn. The first time through, he had, like most of us, gone at the stalk with all his might and managed to shred it without ever actually cutting it down. This time he seemed focused, and his swing, while forceful, was focused and smooth and the cane split just as it had for the instructors. He was saluted with a round of cheers.

My time came again. I took a deep breath and let the anger go and watched the spot on the stalk where I wanted the machete to land as I swung it forward and down to meet the stalk, much the way my father had taught me to keep my eye on the ball when taking batting practice way back when he thought I had the goods to be a major-leaguer some day. (Another disappointment.) The cane split away, falling peacefully to the ground. I snuck a glance at Geronimo as I stepped back to our group. He acknowledged me with a nod. The game was on.

- Thirty-One -

I couldn't maintain. The first day of actually being out in the field, I probably got it right with about one out of every three stalks I hit. Of course, if it had been baseball, hitting .333 would have made me an all-star. But in baseball, there's about thirty seconds between each pitch. In the cane field, you cut down a stalk and immediately moved on to the next. Because the goal of this *zafra* was so much larger than any other *zafra* before it, we would have to work fast.

The key was to get a rhythm going, and I could for short spurts. But then I'd lose my concentration and wind up hacking away like the machete was a sledgehammer. Still, I knew I could do it right and that with each day I would get better.

The rest of Brigade 27 was not as sure about themselves. While I was batting .333, Walter and the others were barely hitting .200. Even Jerry, who had done so well in practice, lost his stroke when it came to having to do it right over and over again. All through our sector of the field, and from the sectors all around us as well, I could hear the shouted curses and cries of disgust and disappointment.

On top of the frustration was the fatigue. We were up at dawn with a shout from the Cuban instructor of "*De Pie!* On your feet!" Then a light breakfast, sharpening machetes, and marching out to the fields. Most of this could be done without actually being awake. I noticed I wasn't the only one saving my consciousness for when it was time to swing our machetes.

And on top of the frustration and fatigue was the pain. Aching backs, burning shoulders, forearms that felt like lead, legs that felt like they were crumbling into pieces.

And then there was the heat. It would still be cool at that hour, but as the sun rose, the heat became oppressive, especially since we were working hard and fast, or trying to, anyway, and for the most part we had to keep a layer of clothes on to keep flying cane splinters from slicing into our arms and legs. Inside my clothes, the sweat stung my skin, already irritated from the humidity.

And with the heat and humidity came a stink. Some of it was from us and some of it was from the field and some came from the jungle around us. A sweet-sour smell of rot that was there even in the morning before the heat came on and made me long for the fresh breezes I'd known back on the commune.

I wanted to quit. But looking around at the rest of my Brigade, I felt like I had to be the positive one. "It's going to come," I told the group when we took our break for the ritual afternoon snack the Cubans called the *merienda*.

"I can't open my hand," said Walter.

"I can't straighten my back," said Jerry.

"It's always like that at the start," I said. "It's like the first day of football practice. Everything hurts all over and you just want to get in a hot bath and never go back. But it gets better."

No one was buying it.

"I just want to die," said Walter.

"It's not about you," I said. "It's for the revolution."

I couldn't believe I'd said that. When the camp leaders had been rallying us the day before, I'd cheered along with the others when they said things like that, while thinking it was the same bullshit as shoveled out by every assistant coach for every team I'd ever played on from peewee on up. I didn't believe in rah-rah back on the playing fields of Brooklyn, and I didn't believe in it any more in the cane fields of Cuba. But believe in it or not, I was the one saying it. And then Avis, appearing out of nowhere and kneeling down beside me, was saying it, too.

"That's right," she said. "We came here to make a revolution, and cutting the cane is making revolution. I know it's not easy. If it was, people'd be making revolutions every day. It's hard making revolution. Hard work.

But I know you all can do it."

Her tone surprised me. It was warm and nurturing. Previously, on the ship and back in Canada, she had been exhorting or chastising. This time she was mothering us. It was weird. Avis was the same age as the rest of us, give or take a couple of years, yet she spoke with the wisdom of the ages. Maybe I was wrong. Maybe she was older and just looked younger. As she knelt beside me, I looked at her more closely than I ever had before. No, I was right. She was our age.

I didn't know if it was a gift she'd been born with, some innate ability when dealing with people to pick the attitude that the occasion called for, or if it was something she had studied in some young socialists' training camp, a course in how to be a great leader. Either way, she had what it takes. It just confirmed for me my earlier judgment that she was one of those who was in it for the long haul.

She spoke a little more and then the *merienda* ended and it was time to go back to the cane. The whole team picked themselves up off the ground where we had collapsed, lifted our machetes, shrugged off our weariness, and headed back to the cane.

"Hey," said Avis.

We all turned to look back at her.

"Venceremos!" she said, smiling at us and raising a fist salute.

Together we all saluted her back, saying in chorus, "Venceremos!" She grinned at us, then turned and walked away.

Watching her, I realized my feelings about her had changed. At first I'd thought pursuing her would be something to do to distract myself from thinking about Roger all the time. Now I thought getting her to pay attention to me, to take me seriously, to become interested in me, was something that might be beyond all the old tricks I'd used back in high school and college. I couldn't just pretend to be someone special to win Avis, I would really have to *be* special because she was. It wasn't a game anymore. I had fallen in love.

- Thirty-Two -

Slowly, it all came together. I began to develop the consistency I was looking for, although occasionally I would lose it altogether and wind up punishing the stalks like I was using a potato masher instead of a machete.

Of course, I couldn't cut as much as the Cubans. None of us could. There were Cubans attached to each of the small brigades to continue our instruction, answer questions, encourage us, and generally try to keep the work moving forward. I figured this was something they had worked out in dealing with the first Brigade, but later I realized it was probably something they had had to do when they started using the masses of volunteers recruited from the cities to help with the harvest. Cubans who had never cut cane had no more aptitude for it at first than any of us did.

Our Cuban was Juan, a lean, handsome young man of about twenty. He came from Aguacate, the town closest to our camp. Juan was a student when he wasn't cutting cane. He was planning to become a doctor like his great hero Che. He had been nine when the revolution succeeded in driving Batista out. His father was one of the small band that had been with Fidel and Che in the Sierra Maestra.

Juan was what the Cubans called a "New Man," the embodiment of the revolution. He had socialist values and a deep sense of justice and solidarity with the international working class. When he wasn't cutting cane, he helped out around the camp as a handyman and custodian. And whenever he could, he rode home to see his family on an old bicycle which he'd resurrected from a trash pile and turned into an admirable piece of equipment. He was gentle and thoughtful and always calm, and without trying to show anyone up, he made clear the difference between the Americans who talked the talk and the Cubans who walked the walk. It was truly embarrassing.

Juan's family was educated and middle class, and cutting cane was not part of his childhood experience. But, being a New Man with a proper socialist attitude, he had learned quickly and become a model for everyone else. So as he and the other Cubans had learned, we did, too. Most everyone in Brigade 27, and in the other brigades as well, began to get in the swing of things, as it were. Production improved. But with success came a new problem.

A lot of it was my fault, mine and Geronimo's. In the days following the practice session, we continued trying to top each other. I don't know if you could call it a friendly competition. And I wouldn't say that it had been replaced by respect. But the kind of schoolyard crap that we had started out with was gone. It was more like we had come to accept the fact that neither one of us was going anyplace until the Brigade's work was done.

So we eyed each other's output, how many *arrobas*—the 25-pound units used for measuring the cut cane—the other had cut that day. If he did more than me, I would try to outperform him the next day and vice versa. I said before I wasn't much into keeping score, but I did like to compete. Maybe I wanted to beat Geronimo like I had never really cared about beating anyone else, and maybe I just needed him as an excuse, something to push myself into the work, which was otherwise an enormous fucking pain.

I didn't know what it meant to Geronimo and didn't much care. To the extent that I thought about it, I figured we were doing a good thing. The competition made us produce more, and it looked like a lot of the other *Brigadistas* were getting into the game. But that turned out to be the problem.

Even though we were producing more, the level of frustration was increasing. People were yelling at each other in the fields. Shouting matches broke out between brigades and within them. The number of meetings kept increasing, which was hard to believe given that every nonworking, nonsleeping minute was already filled with meetings—or so it seemed to me. The biggest problem was between the men and the women, as the men took over the cutting and the women were pushed into collecting and piling the stalks. The women protested, and there were more meetings to argue about who should do what.

I usually managed to avoid all meetings except the ones held by my immediate brigade. Those were hard enough to take. But Avis stopped me as I was heading back to my tent at the end of the day. Having her come to me made me blush. I had to force myself to concentrate on what she was saying as she told me I had to come to a meeting of the Brigade leaders right after dinner in the meeting hall.

"Me? Did I do something wrong? I mean, I've been working my ass off."

"I know."

"So what's the problem?"

"Just come to the meeting."

From the way she looked at me, I could tell she noticed my blush. I had to say something dumb to distract her.

"Will you be serving dessert?" I said.

"Yeah, your head on a plate covered with chocolate jimmies."

"Jimmies? We call them sprinkles in New York. Are you from the Midwest?"

"Never mind where I'm from, just get your butt to the meeting."

She walked away before I could ask another question. I noticed Juan over by the machete rack and realized he had been watching us. When he saw me look at him, he turned away, pretending to clean his machete (which was already clean). I had only caught his eye for a second, but it was enough. I had been talking to Avis, one-to-one. Never mind what we might have been saying. He was jealous. Any exchange with her had to be words of love.

- Thirty-Three -

I went on to the tent. Walter was there. As usual, he knew what was up.
"Competition," he said.
"What?"
"You and Geronimo. You're competing."
"That's bad?"
"Uh-huh. Very capitalist. Sets a bad example. Think cooperation."
"Oh, man …"
"Don't worry. You'll get reamed and it'll be over and you'll be a better man for it."

As usual, Walter was right. I did get reamed. Besides Avis, there was the camp director, the small brigade leaders, including Walter, and the Cuban instructors. Geronimo was there, too, and a few of the other Brigadistas who I recognized as being among the best cutters and also, like me and Geronimo, the most openly competitive.

"First, let me compliment you on your achievements in becoming so productive so quickly," said the director. "But I need also to reprimand you on the way you have been behaving. I am referring to the personal competition that has developed among you. In personalizing your achievement, you cease to be revolutionaries."

Since I didn't think of myself as a revolutionary, I wasn't too upset by this. But I snuck a peek at Geronimo. He looked like he was going to burst into tears. So did most of the others who had been brought in for the criticism.

"You think by cutting more cane than the others in the Brigade you are achieving more for the revolution. But with every stalk you cut for personal achievement, you are undermining the revolution. You are perpetuating the old ways of thinking, the old ways of relating to your brothers and sisters, the old ways of doing business. Cutting more cane to make yourself the champion is not revolutionary. Cutting more cane so that there will be more schools, more health care, more food for the people, that is revolutionary. That is the way of the new socialist man and woman, the New Man that Marx was describing. The New Man Che was exhorting us to become."

He had said the secret word. "Che." I thought a duck was going to come down and give him a hundred dollars. But that was a different Marx.

The director pointed to the Cuban instructors, including Juan. "Why do Roberto or Julio or Juan cut faster than you? Because they have more experience? Yes, that is true. But they were not born *macheteros*. Julio worked in a shoe factory and Roberto sold ice cream. Juan is a student. Juan, when did you first cut cane?"

"Two months," said Juan. He was staring at me.

"Julio, when was the first time you cut the cane?"

"The same. Two months," said Julio.

"Roberto," said the director. "When was the first time you cut the cane?"

"Six weeks," said Roberto.

"You see," said the director, "it is not about experience. It is about purpose. Julio and Roberto and Juan know why they are cutting the cane. They are revolutionaries. And more than that …" He paused dramatically. "They are New Men, they are communists."

This was shocking. I knew Juan was relatively new to cutting, but I thought for sure that Julio and Roberto had been cutting cane all their lives. It seemed like second nature to them. I wondered if they were kidding us, if this was some kind of sideshow scam they ran on the dumb Yankee rubes. Were they really trying to sell us communism like it was some kind of snake oil?

If they were, it was working. There was an awed murmur of approval among the Brigadistas. How could we have been so shortsighted, so selfish? We—and by this I mean the other bad boys in the room—wanted so desperately to be revolutionaries, and yet we were just stinking individualists, stuck in our worst capitalist selves. A vision of Lee Marvin in *The Wild One* flashed into my mind, when the cops are dragging him off to jail and he cries out, "Oh, the shame of it all, the shame of it all."

As we left the meeting hall, Geronimo came up next to me.

"That was some heavy shit," he said seriously.

"Yeah," I said. "Heavy shit."

As we went through the door, I noticed Juan again, still giving me the evil eye. The New Man had some old shit going on for him.

- Thirty-Four -

Despite the slap on the wrist, it still took a while for the lesson to sink in. Individualism dies hard. It was like that in the Army, too. A lot of us, and this time I include myself, were out for ourselves at first. I basically wanted to avoid a hard time, so I worked hard to be a good soldier figuring, as I've mentioned before, that it would make more sense than pretending I wasn't really there. Others started right out with a goal of getting promoted, looking for more pay to send home or for the chance to tell somebody else what to do instead of just having to take orders all the time. A couple of guys, who had played soldier too much as kids, set their sights on becoming heroes, outdistancing the rest of us.

Our sergeants tried to steer us into thinking and acting as a unit, but they knew that, in the end, it was only in combat that all the training aimed toward making us work together would take hold. That was the problem we faced in Cuba. No one was shooting at us. The Cubans, with the Bay of Pigs, the missile crisis still fresh in their minds, not to mention the ongoing U.S. embargo, did feel like someone was shooting at them. No guns needed to go off for them to feel they were in a war.

So we poor unthreatened Yankees did our best to get into that state of belligerence that breeds brotherhood. It was a matter of concentration for some and a matter of letting go for others. I was in the latter category. I stopped trying to beat Geronimo and everyone else and just get a good rhythm going. Mostly, I sang to myself.

My number one song was "Sugar, Sugar." It didn't take long for it to become my song for Avis. I'd be singing in my head, "You are my candy girl," the thwacking of my machete setting a beat, as I pictured the two of us dancing, doing all kinds of elaborate Lindy moves, none of which I could actually do in real life. I cut cane and wondered if Avis was a good dancer. She was so serious, I wondered if she ever kicked back. "I just can't believe the loveliness of loving you, I just can't believe it's true," I would sing and imagine us going out for pizza.

My production soared. The cane seemed to cut itself as I went down my row. I didn't even think about it, didn't look to see what Geronimo or anyone else was doing, just sang and cut and cut and sang.

Sometimes I thought about Wildflower. It had only been about three weeks since we had said goodbye at the bus station in Vancouver. It felt more like three years. Was she out working in the fields of Pacific Breeze? Were she and Ori working side by side? Did they sing to each other as they worked together?

Did they have to struggle with individualism? Here we were, working for the whole of the Cuban people, our efforts directed outward, while the commune was an escape from the rest of American society, isolated on purpose and working for itself, for its members. I didn't know what it meant in any larger sense, only that it was completely different. Maybe the commune was supposed to be a model and someday the rest of America would wake up and say, oh, yeah, that's what we should be doing. Maybe that was how the commune served the nation. And maybe it just was what it was, a place to get away from all the crap.

> Avis came by one afternoon as we were heading back to the field.
> "Quite a change," she said.
> "All thanks to you."
> "Really?"
> "Don't you know? You're my inspiration."
> "You're such an asshole."
> "That I am."
> "Well, whatever is really inspiring you, keep it up."
> She walked away shaking her head. My heart pounded in my chest. "You are my candy girl," I sang to myself, "and you got me wanting you."

- Thirty-Five -

My mood was so good, it seemed like everyone else in our brigade was picking up on it. Our collective production increased, and instead of collapsing during our breaks, we would tell jokes or sing folk songs, then jump up ready to go back to work when the breaks were over.

Despite the good feeling, I was anxious. It was three weeks since I had called home and it was time to call again and see what the doctor had to say. At the information post just to the side of the barracks was a phone that we could use to call New York, Boston, and a couple of other places. I couldn't figure out why it was limited, but there were a lot of things I couldn't figure out, and I was happy to accept that my needs would be met.

It was evening when I called. My mother answered. There were a couple of people seated on a bench nearby and I promised myself I would control myself no matter what.

"Hi, Ma."

"Jay?"

I marveled at the fact that after twenty years of hearing my voice, she still wasn't sure it was me.

"Yes, Ma, it's me."

"Jay, where are you? Still in Canada?"

"Yeah," I lied. I don't know why. It just seemed easier. "How is Daddy? What'd the doctor say?"

"He said 'Here's my bill,' is what he said."

"Ma, what did he say?"

"Nothing. He took a lot of tests and said call back next Monday."

"That's it?"

"He gave your father some pills. I asked him about Geritol, like you said, and he said, 'Sure, why not.'"

"But he didn't say anything like what he thought might be wrong?"

"Not a word. But he didn't seem very worried."

"Well, that's good."

"Sure, why should he be worried? He's not the one missing work."

"Where's Daddy now?"

"Napping again. Snoring away while I do all the work."

"He's sick, Ma."

"Well, I'm sick of him being sick. I hope that effing doctor sends him right back to work."

"I'm sure that's what'll happen. Just one more week."

"Jay, is there a number where I can call you?"

I was tempted to give her the camp number, but it would probably be a disaster when someone answered in Spanish and she wound up screaming at them.

"Well, I'm kinda on the move, so not really."

"When are you coming home?"

"I don't know. I'm working on a deal."

"Well, work it faster."

"I'm doing the best I can, Ma."

- Thirty-Six -

The talk with my mother put an end to my high spirits. Was I really doing the best I could? Couldn't I figure out any way to get to Roger sooner? I tried to come up with a plan, but it all kept coming out the same.

I spent the next morning hacking away at the cane. I was swinging so bad Walter had to stop me.

"Are you trying to chop a leg off?" he said.

I told him about the call.

"Why don't you take the rest of the day off? Before you hurt yourself or someone else."

"Thanks," I said. "I think I'm better off here. Maybe I just had to say it out loud."

"Okay. Just take it easy, get back in the groove."

"Thanks. Thanks for looking out."

"Well, I ain't Brigade 27 leader for nothing, you know."

After that I got my rhythm back for a while. I sang my song and thought of Avis. But thoughts of Dad and then thoughts of Roger came crowding in, my song would disappear, and I would suddenly find myself mashing the cane again. Walter came back and insisted I go back to the barracks or take a walk or do anything but cut cane. This time I didn't argue.

Away from the field, Roger was all I thought about. Was I actually going to see him? Walter had not mentioned him for days, and in my "act casual" mode, I didn't dare to bring it up for fear that I would sound as anxious as I was. Then—assuming that Walter was going to say something like the visit to Roger was still on and it still included me—how I was going to do what I was supposed to do? The idea that I could get him out to a bar and then poison his drink there still seemed like the best plan I could come up with, although I reminded myself to stay flexible in case some other opportunity came along sooner.

As the day off got closer, I moved the poison around. I had originally put it in a rolled-up pair of dirty socks. But then I imagined that some guy in our tent desperate for a pair of socks and digging through everyone's gear would take even a dirty pair. So I moved it inside a rolled-up pair of dirty underwear at the bottom of my duffel bag, figuring it was very unlikely that anyone would borrow dirty underwear. I was judging by my own low standards and hoping that I was close enough to the bottom for it to be a safe choice.

I wanted to take the vial of pills out to look at them, but living in close quarters made that extremely difficult. There was always someone around. A couple of times, I slipped the vial out of the bag and into my pocket and took it to the john where I could examine the pills in the privacy of a stall. But I was so worried that I would drop it on the floor and it would roll out toward the sink and wind up under someone's feet that I stopped doing that.

It was silly to want to look at the pills. They hadn't changed, and looking at them didn't tell me anything that I wanted to know, such as were they really going to work if I really could find a way to slip them into Roger's drink? And what if I couldn't? What did Short One say? Stick a fucking carving knife in his fucking heart. Like that was going to be any easier.

Lying in my bunk, exhausted but only half asleep, trying to envision the scene as it might take place, I thought about what Walter had told me back in St. John, sitting in the bus waiting to board the *Luis Arcos Bergnes*, that if I had gone against Roger, others would have followed me. I didn't know if that was really true. I didn't have any reason to think it was. I'd never been any kind of leader and never tried to persuade anybody about anything, except when it came to romancing. Never about anything like politics. It was impossible to think that I would have done anything other than what I did, which was to clear out.

Somehow it made me hate Roger all the more. He had done this to me. With his stupid talk and his idiotic bomb-making, he had killed Eddie and the others, and because of that, I was in Cuba getting ready to kill him. I found myself blaming him for my having deserted and for being in the Army in the first place. Why hadn't all these political geniuses who hated the war so much and who were so eager to stop it, why hadn't they stopped it before it started? Did they really care? Was it just a chance to shoot their mouths off and pat themselves on the back for being right? Fuck 'em, I thought. Fuck all the big talkers! Fuck their big talking mouths!

"You okay?" said Walter.

He was standing next to my bunk.

"Huh?"

"You were tossing around and grunting. Still thinking about your dad?"

"No, not this time," I said. "It was the war. It comes back to me sometimes. Thanks. Thanks for checking on me."

"No sweat. Oh, hey, still want to see Roger?"

My heart began to pound.

"Oh, yeah, sure. But, when?"

"This weekend. We have a day off, remember?"

"Oh, great. Okay."

Walter walked off and I thought, You don't mind if I poison him when we get there, do you?

- Thirty-Seven -

The buses that had brought us to the camp came back to take the *Brigadistas* to various locations for the day off. One was heading into Havana then on to the beach just east of the city. Another bus was taking some very serious people who had sugar on the brain to see the factory where the syrup was extracted from our cane. There were a couple of other similar field trips, but I didn't pay attention. I knew where I had to go.

Walter had called Roger. He had mentioned I was there and could I come by and say hello. Apparently Roger would be delighted to see me. It was agreed that his apartment would be too hard to find, and that it would be easier to meet someplace well known. Roger suggested the Plaza Cathedral, in the center of Old Havana. From there we could find a place to have a drink or lunch, and then he and Walter would go on to the apartment and I could continue on to the beach.

As Walter and I headed to the bus for Havana, I noticed Avis heading our way from the women's tent. We arrived at the line for the bus at the same time.

"Hey," she said. "Good to have a day off, huh?"

"I never thought it would come," said Walter.

"Yeah," I said.

"Are you staying in Havana or going to the beach?" she said.

"I'm staying in Havana," said Walter.

"Beach?" she said to me.

"Later," I said. "I have to stop in Havana first."

"We're meeting an old friend, well, an acquaintance, really," said Walter.

We were in the bus looking for seats. There was a single seat about halfway through the bus and Walter slid into it. He looked up at me and winked. "I'll let you know when we have to get off."

He nodded for me to continue on after Avis, and I followed her up the aisle.

Juan was sitting toward the back of the bus with Julio and Roberto, who were having a lively conversation with a couple of young women from Brigade 16. Juan was not paying attention to them. He was focused on Avis, staring at her, trying to guide her with the force of his will to the empty seat next to him.

But there were two seats together a little further up the aisle and Avis moved into the one closest to the window as if she expected me to sit with her. Jesus, I thought, she wants me to sit with her, she's inviting me to. I had so wanted to sit with her, to have a chance for an intimate conversation, one that might allow us to talk about something other than work, and this was the perfect moment. Except, of course it wasn't. I had poison in my pocket, Roger on my mind, and Juan staring daggers at me. I wanted to turn and run. Did I really want a jealous machete-wielding Cuban angry at me? But I sat. It was not anything I had planned, and I was more than a little uncomfortable doing it, but I sat.

"You must have gone to the beach a lot growing up in Brooklyn."

"I did."

"Are you a good swimmer?"

"I'm okay, not great. It's like walking to me. I don't remember learning to walk and I don't remember learning to swim. It's just something I always knew how to do."

"Wish I could say the same. Learning to swim was a trauma for me."

"Learn in school?"

"No, my dad taught me. Except he didn't know how."

"Didn't know how to teach, or didn't know how to swim?"

"Both."

The conversation was like a dream come true and I could barely keep my mind on it.

"Are you okay?" said Avis.

"Sorry. I'm … I don't know. Just tired, I guess. But I'm really glad we have a chance to talk."

"Me, too. I wanted to say, well, you've really surprised me. I thought you were going to be nothing but trouble. But you've been great. So I guess what I'm saying is thank you."

"Well, you're welcome. If I've been helpful, I'm glad. I'm definitely having a better time than I thought I would. I guess I've learned a few things."

"Like what?"

"Like it's good to be part of something important. Not to be just worried about myself all the time."

"Cool."

"Yeah. Cool."

"So are you thinking you're going to try and stay here?"

"Here? In Cuba?"

"Yeah. You said that once. That it was a possibility. Is that why you're going to see this acquaintance who lives here?"

The last thing I wanted to do was talk about Roger.

"Gee, I hadn't thought about that. Maybe he could help. But I'm not that far along. I don't know for sure what I'm going to do."

"Is he a Cuban?"

"No, he's American. Someone we knew in New York."

"What's he doing here?"

"He got in trouble and had to get out of the country."

"You don't want to talk about this, do you?"

"No, no. I mean, well, yeah. I mean, it might be better for him if we didn't go into details."

"Okay."

Awkward silence. I had to get Roger out of my head.

"So your father couldn't swim?"

"Yeah. You know that old cliché, blacks can't swim?"

"No, I never heard that." (But of course I had.)

"Well, turns out it's true. Didn't stop my dad, though. He'd drown before he admitted there was anything he couldn't do."

"Huh. My dad would have stayed on shore."

"Your dad couldn't swim?"

"Oh, no, he was a great swimmer. I meant that if there was something he couldn't do he wouldn't bother trying."

"So you're not like him."

No, I thought. I can still get out of bed. I thought about telling Avis what was going on with him, but decided I didn't want her pity. I'm not sure why I thought that, but I stuck with it.

"No, I am," I said. "A lot. I guess I've just been forced to do a lot of things I didn't know how to do, even if I didn't want to do them."

"Like cutting cane?"

"I guess that would qualify."

"You really haven't figured out what you're going to do next?"

"Tell you the truth, I haven't thought about it for days. Too busy cutting cane."

"Right. But today you're off. No cane."

"No cane."

"So, what do you think you'll do?"

"You're really interested?"

"I am. Look, everybody else here is going to go back to doing what they did before. Your life is up in the air. Maybe there's something I can do to help you."

Help me. Yes, please help me. I felt like one of those maniac killers in a horror movie who leaves messages at the crime scenes saying, "Stop me before I kill again." Help me get back to the States, help me see my dad again, help me stop those lunatics from hurting the people I love. Only don't get too close or you might wind up on their list of people to hurt.

"I don't know. There doesn't seem to be much that can be done."

"How much time would you have to spend in jail if you go back to the States?"

"I don't know. Five years, twenty years. Whatever it is, I'm not going to do it."

"Could you go underground? Get a new identity? Become someone else?"

"I suppose. Look, I appreciate your interest and maybe we can talk about this another time. But right now, I can't."

"Sorry. I do want to help you, though."

"Then talk about something else. Where did your father try to teach you to swim? You never did tell me where you're from."

"Chicago. And it was in Lake Michigan where he kept trying to drown me."

"Do you still live there? Chicago?"

"It's still home. But lately I've been in Milwaukee most of the time."

"School?"

"Organizing."

"Brewery workers?"

"No, they've been organized forever. Mostly foodservice industry and hospitality."

"Hospitality?"

"Hotel/motel."

"Cool. Good for you. How's it going?"

"It's tough. People are scared they'll get fired if they join up. Sometimes it happens. Then you go to court, but it takes a long time, and meanwhile the guy or the woman who got fired is out of a salary. You're asking a lot when you ask someone to join a union in a hostile environment."

"Yeah. I remember times my dad went out on strike. It was like the world came to a standstill."

"He's a Teamster, right?"

"Yeah."

"I heard that. Heard you hit Geronimo up with that."

"A little class warfare."

"But you two are getting along now, right?"

"We haven't been out for a beer or anything, but, yeah, things cooled down."

"Well, I thank you for that. Makes my life easier."

We kept talking, about our families, our childhoods, where we went to school, books and movies we liked. Avis's dad was an alderman and her mom worked for the board of education. They had worked their way up through the ranks of the Democratic Party machine, running errands for the local bosses on the South Side, getting out the black vote on Election Day, learning to be in the right place at the right time, waiting for their turn to move up and cash in. As a result, her childhood had been more comfortable than a lot of the kids she grew up with. The machine took care of its own.

Her parents were able to get her into a good Catholic girls' school where she would be away from the trouble of public schools and away from boys. She liked school, liked learning, so she was happy to have the quality education, even though the rigidity of the school drove her crazy. And there was no way she could grow up on the South Side and not experience her fair share of trouble and boys, no matter where she went to school.

As she got older and came to understand where her parents stood in the scheme of things, she rebelled. The rhetoric of democracy and liberation, unavoidable even in the friendly confines of Maria High School, conflicted with their "I've got mine" Chicago philosophy. Her rebellion went from reformation to revolution when she went on to the University of Wisconsin in Madison, where she became an activist in the civil rights and antiwar movements. She went south to work in the voting rights campaign, marched on Washington to end the war, got her head split open by a police baton during a sit-in on campus, and was arrested in the streets of Chicago during the Democratic Convention (while her father was inside the Convention as a delegate).

She worshipped Dr. King, and talked about how he had influenced her decision to turn away from the Panthers and the Weathermen. She was, as I had guessed, in for the long haul, starting with her union organizing in Milwaukee.

We had left the countryside and entered the outskirts of Havana. I wanted the bus to keep driving straight through the city, straight through to Milwaukee, where I would become her assistant, carry her picket signs, make sure her bullhorn had batteries, feed her tea with honey when her throat got sore from making speeches outside in the cold Wisconsin winters. All that and more would I do. I would stay in the background, wear disguises, get a new identity just so I could be there for her, making her life easier as she said I had in the cane fields.

But the bus drove into the heart of the city, slowed as it entered the narrow streets of Old Havana, then stopped. We were at the Plaza Cathedral. A few rows ahead, Walter stood up and called for me to come. I didn't want to. I wanted to stay with Avis, go with her to the beach, play with her in the waves, lie next to her on a blanket in the sun, and walk hand in hand into the sunset. I wanted to believe she felt the same, that I was seeing that in her eyes.

"I hope I see you later," she said. "On the beach."

"I hope so, too."

"Come on," said Walter. I grabbed my things and went down the aisle. I took a last look back before we got off the bus. Avis was smiling at me. It went through my head that I might never see her again. I tried to avoid looking to the back of the bus, but the pull of Juan's hatred was too strong. My eyes shifted from Avis to where he sat glaring at me. Though I was looking all the way to the back seat from the front steps of the bus, I could still see the layer of tears in his eyes.

PART IV
Havana

- Thirty-Eight -

Roger was there, waiting for us at one of the tables set out in front of a café on the south side of the Plaza. He stood up and raised his arm to catch our attention. My hand went to the vial of pills in my pocket. I let them go and joined Walter in waving. The bus pulled away. I looked to see if Avis was at the window, but it was too late. I followed Walter across the cobblestone plaza to the table.

Roger embraced Walter in a great bear hug, then shook my hand enthusiastically.

"Great," he said as we took our seats. "Fabulous to see you both. And Jay! What a surprise!"

He seemed taller than I had remembered, but maybe it had to do with being outside. It occurred to me as we settled in around the table that I had never seen Roger anywhere but in Eddie's house.

His face was a little different, too. His beard less well trimmed, a bit scraggly, more in keeping with the guerrilla fashion mode set by Fidel and Che. He seemed thinner, too, not long and solid as he had appeared in New York, but a little undernourished. Maybe he had less to eat and maybe it was another attempt to fit in with a hungry population. I thought his eyes were different, too, brighter, almost feverish compared to the way they looked in New York. I remembered how back there he would use them almost like a hypnotist. I didn't think he would be able to do that now. Some part of his control was gone.

The one thing that hadn't changed was his clothes. He wore the same outfit as in New York. It made him seem out of place, at odds with the weight loss and untrimmed beard. I couldn't figure out why he hadn't chosen something more tropical. Maybe he did dress differently and had only put these clothes—the charcoal pants, the vest, and the rest—back on so we would recognize him, or to signal us that he hadn't changed, that he was the same person that we knew. I was glad he looked the same. If he had dressed differently, if he had seemed like a different person, I might have found it harder to give him the poison.

And then I realized how hard it was going to be. In fact, it was clearly going to be close to impossible. For one thing, he already had a drink, a tall schooner of beer that he had hardly touched. For another, a waiter was at the table as soon as our butts were in the seats.

"Beer okay?" said Roger.

"Sure," said Walter.

"Sounds good," I said.

The waiter took off and with him went my fantasy of going to fetch drinks and slipping the poison into Roger's drink at the bar. That was my Plan A. There was no Plan B.

"So how goes the cane cutting?" said Roger. "Are you going to make it a career?"

"We're actually pretty good," said Walter. "Although when we started it was a nightmare."

Walter launched into a detailed explanation of our experience with the cane that grew into a narrative of the whole expedition to date. I listened just enough to throw in a remark now and again and laugh at the right places as my mind raced to come up with a Plan B. Have the pill ready to slip into his beer if he went to the men's room. Have the pill ready in case he had a heart attack and I could slide it down his throat while pretending to give him mouth-to-mouth resuscitation. But be careful not to let him blow it back into my mouth. If only the damn waiter would go away so I could get up and go to the bar myself. But there were five other waiters to take his place, their eyes fixed on us like they expected we were going to make a run for it without paying.

I'd fucked up royally. Whatever I was going to do, it wasn't going to take place there and then. I had no back-up plan, and I'd never really *had* a plan. I was always going to wing it and that was all there was to it. The idea that I had a plan was just something I told myself so I could finally fall asleep each night. Something to make me believe I'd get to go home. It was not going to happen.

Walter continued on with the occasional grunted comment from me and questions from Roger. We were both looking at Walter as he spoke, but I could not stop myself from sneaking quick peeks at Roger. As I took one of these brief glances, I saw that Roger was taking a quick look my way. For a moment, neither of us looked away. He widened his eyes, intensifying his stare as he used to do back in Eddie's living room. With the feverish brightness still in them, he looked just crazy. I thought his lips were curling up in a smile, very, very slight but there, and not a happy smile, not a smile that said, "Here we all are and isn't this jolly." It was a smile that said he knew why I was there and that there was no way it was going to happen.

I looked away. He knows, I thought, and a chill went through me. No, he couldn't know. It's all in my head. I'm upset about not having a plan, that's all. I looked back. He was looking at Walter again, but his smile hadn't changed. It was the way he used to look back in New York just before he let loose on someone, destroying their argument with a blast of his Orson Welles voice. Was he going to do that to Walter?

But Roger didn't blast him. Instead he laughed heartily.

"Fantastic! I have to get out and see this place."

"That would be terrific," said Walter. He took it as an honor that Roger would be so interested as to come visit. Walter started to say something about how to arrange it, but Roger ignored him and suddenly turned his full attention to me.

"So, Jay, where have you been since you escaped from New York? And how in the world did you end up here?"

I choked on my beer. I hadn't expected any questions, and of course, the first thing I thought of was the vial of pills in my pocket and my encounters with Short One and Tall One. I looked at Roger. That smile was still there. I felt like he was teasing me, felt again that he knew all about my mission. But that was crazy.

I cleared my throat and launched into a brief repetition of the story I'd told Walter: my trip across America, the move to Vancouver, the commune, hearing about the Brigade, and having the luck to get selected.

"You are a lucky man," said Roger. "Let's hope your luck holds."

"What do you mean?" I said.

"You know, that you get to go back to the States. See your folks. All that good stuff."

"Oh, sure. Thanks."

He was bugging me worse than he ever had back in New York.

"But what about you," said Walter. "How the hell did you get here?"

"Ah," said Roger. "Speaking of luck, I had a bit myself." He turned to me. "Shall we have another round or do you need to run?"

"Oh, no," I said. "I'm dying to hear how you got here."

Roger signaled to the waiter to bring another round. He smiled at me as he did so. I felt like he had read my mind about slipping him the Mickey at the bar. It was impossible. It was all in my head, unspoken, unwritten. I was imagining that he knew, that was all. And maybe he sensed I had something on my mind so he figured to play me along, pretending he knew something, even though he couldn't possibly. I'd never felt so screwed-up before, but I had never sat next to someone I was supposed to be poisoning before. Of course I was going to think he knew. Of course I was going to drive myself crazy whether Roger helped or not.

"You know what happened in New York, I suppose."

"Yes," I said, nodding toward Walter.

"I wasn't so far away from the house that I didn't hear the explosion. I turned, starting running back, and then I stopped. Realized there would be little or nothing I could do. The sound of the blast, the size of it, the amount of explosives in the basement, I knew it had to have been devastating. I was spending almost all my time at the house, but I still had a room in an apartment over on Avenue C. I ran there, not knowing what to do next. So many people would associate me with the house, sooner or later the police were likely to track me down. I had a few dollars saved up, and my roommate owed me about two hundred that I had loaned him to get his car repaired. I made him get it together, told him I had to skip town. He went and borrowed it from someone else and paid me back and I was on the first plane I could catch to Mexico. By the time the morning papers came out, I was in Mexico City."

The waiter had brought the second round. Roger took a long drink from his glass immediately.

"Quite an adventure. Were you always aiming to come to Cuba?"

"No. I was thinking more of heading down through Central America to Peru. I don't know why. I guess I always fancied the idea of going to

Peru some day. See Machu Picchu. The Inca ruins, you know?"

"Yeah, I saw a picture of them once."

"Exactly! I wanted to see *them*, not a picture of them."

"Did you ever get the details of what had happened back in New York?"

"Of course. The news of it was all over the papers there. I was devastated. I felt so guilty. So responsible. If I'd only stayed, I'm sure it wouldn't have happened. I was a fool to run out like that."

I could see Walter squirm a little as he remembered it was his getting the wrong clock that had sent Roger running out. It was great the way Roger could tell us how responsible he felt while at the same time laying the whole thing back on Walter. And poor Walter felt so bad, he couldn't see that Roger was doing it on purpose.

"Did you get to Peru?"

"No. There was a fella there, in Mexico City, a Cuban who had been with Fidel and Che in the Sierra Maestra and all the way into Havana, and then moved on after the revolution was won. We got to talking one night, and he persuaded me that Cuba was the place for me. It hadn't even crossed my mind until he suggested it. Said I could teach English, or work as a translator, maybe do radio broadcasts, or all three, for that matter. Said it was the place to be. The real revolution. Well, of course I had to agree. He hooked me up with the consulate there—he was still pretty tight with the regime—and the next thing I knew I was on a plane to Havana. The rest, as they say, is history."

"And the Cubans took you in with open arms?"

"Oh, they checked me out first. Quite a suspicious lot, you know, not without reason. But when they found out I was a genuine political refugee, wanted by the FBI and all, it put things right on track."

"So something good came out of the explosion, after all," I said.

"Sad, but true," said Roger. "At any rate, it turned out that I was the right man at the right time. There was a need for translators and English teachers. Still want that radio job, which would be fantastic, but there's a long waiting list for that one."

Something clicked in my mind. "But you're not going anywhere, so it could happen eventually."

"I certainly hope so. Not that I'm complaining about the work I have now. It's fine. But that would be something else."

"Wow, it would be. Hey, you know, you got me thinking. You see, when the harvest is over, I don't know what I'm going to do. I'm not thrilled to go back to Canada. The Brigade people asked me if I was thinking about staying here, and to tell the truth, I hadn't really thought about it. But now, well, I don't speak Spanish, but maybe I should start learning."

"Fantastic. You'd be a great asset," said Roger. "And you've got the right credentials. I mean, you'd certainly qualify as a political refugee."

"I guess I would."

"Jay," said Walter, "that would be fantastic."

It was fantastic. Part of the whole madness of my McWilliams assignment had been the idea of getting it done before the harvest was over so I could go back with everyone else. But what if I could manage to stay on? Take my time, get closer to Roger, wait until the right moment, which was sure to come along if there wasn't that pressure of time. And it didn't have to mean waiting a year or anything like that. It could be just another month or two. A couple of get-togethers every week. A friendly drink, lunch or dinner, take in a movie. And then one day, and that day would surely come, he would go to the bathroom, leave me sitting alone with our two half-full glasses of beer. Yes! What a fool I'd been to think I had to get it done so quickly.

But would Short One understand? Would he get that I was still on the case? That I wasn't coming back until my mission was complete? Maybe I could have Walter send a message for me when he got back to Canada, send it to the office in St. John. Something could be done to keep the boys at bay.

Yes. This was a real plan. I relaxed. The vial of pills in my pocket had felt like a container of lead, but now they ceased to exist. I could stop holding my breath. I wasn't going to kill Roger, at least not that day. I felt free. I might get home after all.

"Can you help him?" asked Walter. "You know, introduce him to people, help him find a job?"

Walter was loving this. Leading our small brigade had given him a taste of being a "take-charge, make things happen" kind of guy. I suspect that was something he had always wanted to be but had never found a way to demonstrate before. Now he jumped at any chance that came along where he could show his talent.

"Yeah," I said. "Any help you can give."

"Of course," said Roger. "Love to do it. When will you be finished with the harvest?"

"About four more weeks."

"I'll start talking to the people I know. Put the word out. Will you be able to come back into Havana if I need you to meet someone?"

"Gee, I don't know," I said.

"Of course he can," said Walter. "This is important. Avis will arrange it for you."

"Yeah. Of course. What am I thinking? Sure I can come in if I have to."

"Well, then," said Walter, raising his glass, "a toast to my Cuban friends. *Por Cuba Libre!*"

"Cuba Libre!" Roger and I replied. Then Roger started laughing. It started as a deep, hearty laugh, then suddenly veered toward the hysterical, unrelated, as far as I could tell, to anything that had been said. Tears filled his eyes and for a moment I thought he was going to fall out of his chair.

"What is it?" said Walter. "What's so funny?"

"Oh, nothing, really," said Roger, regaining his composure. "Just that here we all are, a thousand miles from New York, and two out of three are going to be staying here."

As he said it, he gave me that same queer feverish look I'd seen in his eyes earlier. I wondered if he was really as happy about being in Cuba as he claimed. Maybe he felt trapped but couldn't admit that to us. Then that crazy laughter would make sense.

We finished our beers. Now that I had a new, unhurried plan, I wanted to get to the beach and see if I could find Avis. Roger put some money on the table and waved to the waiter. He suggested that, since we were right in front of the Cathedral, we go in and have a look around.

"It's quite spectacular and it's not always open. You must take advantage of the opportunity. Christopher Columbus was buried here, you know."

"Maybe next time," I said.

"It won't take long."

"It's no use," said Walter. "He's got a hot date waiting for him. A little beach blanket bingo."

"Really?" said Roger, turning to me. "Well, you always were a bit of the ladies' man, weren't you? Who's the lucky girl? Are you cutting the cane with her already, so to speak?"

"Our brigade leader, no less," said Walter.

"Well, then, don't let me keep you."

He smiled his old wicked smile, which was somehow more comforting than the other look he'd been giving me.

"Thanks," I said. "For everything. I'll see you again soon."

"Oh, that you will. That you will."

- Thirty-Nine -

I found a taxi and was at the Barucano beach, about ten miles east of the city, in just a few minutes. It was a beautiful day, sunny and warm, and the beach, incredibly beautiful, was crowded with Cubans and tourists, some Canadian, some Russian and East European, and some from Latin America. Music filled the air and people were dancing on the beach. It occurred to me that this was what life was supposed to be like after a revolution.

At first I thought I was going to have a hard time finding Avis, but I quickly spotted the Venceremos Brigade banner, which someone had thought to bring along and plant in the sand. As I got closer, I could see a whole crowd of familiar faces. There were *Brigadistas* splashing around in the ocean, or coming up from the water or heading down to it. Some were lounging on beach chairs, and there was a big group, obviously taking all our lessons on cooperation to heart, working together to build an enormous sand castle.

Down close to the edge of the water were the inevitable Frisbee players, who, as I got closer still, turned out to be the Weathermen, including Beverly in a tiny bikini and Geronimo in a Speedo. They were all laughing, their movements filled with glee, so unlike their usual somber selves. They were, too strange to say, "frolicking." It was like they were back on some ideal campus, with a well-manicured rolling green mall where everything was pure and innocent again.

I spotted Avis just past the Frisbee players, lying on a beach lounge, an umbrella shading her, drinking the Cuban equivalent of a Coke and reading a book. She was wearing a yellow two-piece suit. She looked great. More than great. I stopped walking and just stood there looking at her. I felt like it was one of those moments that you want to go on forever. It wasn't like it was some kind of perfect happiness. I was filled with longing for her, and all the crap that was the rest of my life—Roger, the assassins, the Army—were spinning around inside me, too. But for that moment, looking at her on the lounge absorbed in her book, her beautiful skin, the perfection of a circle of shade cut out of the blazing sunlight, there was the possibility that happiness could be mine. That was all. I picked up my feet and continued on.

I had kind of expected to find Juan hanging around her, but he was nowhere to be seen. I thought he would take advantage of my absence to make a move, but I guessed he was so genuinely in awe of Avis that he couldn't approach her. It occurred to me that it might also be a race thing. Walter, who filled me in on a lot of political things I had no idea about, had mentioned that behind their revolutionary solidarity, white Cubans and black Cubans had a lot of racial shit going on. Maybe the New Man Juan could not imagine bringing Avis home to meet the folks, even if his old man had been with Castro in the mountains.

"What you reading?" I asked, as I plopped down in the sand next to Avis. "Wait, don't tell me. *Das Kapital*. Right?"

"Wrong." She held the front of the book up to me. It was a Dashiell Hammett detective novel, *Red Harvest*.

"Wow. That's a great book. Bloody as all hell."

"You read it?" she said.

"I had a buddy in the Army who was a Hammett nut. Gave me all of his stuff to read."

"Well, don't tell me how it ends."

"My lips are sealed."

"Did you see your friend?"

"Yep."

"Was it good?"

"Better than good." I couldn't begin to explain how good it really was. "As it turns out, he just might be able to help me to stay here."

She swung around on the lounge, putting her feet down on the sand and facing me.

"You're kidding."

"Nope. He's going to talk to some officials he knows. See what he can do."

"Wow."

"Yeah. Wow."

"You don't seem all that excited about it."

"I guess I haven't really wrapped my mind around it yet. I mean, is it really what I want to do? Is it really better than going back to Canada?"

Of course, I couldn't tell her that all it meant to me was that I hadn't had to kill Roger that morning.

"It's a lot farther away from Brooklyn, from my family," I said.

"I guess that's true. But at least it's there if you do want to do it."

"Right. Okay, let's forget about this for the rest of the day. Have you been in the water yet?"

"Just to get my feet wet."

"Then let's go."

I stripped down to my bathing suit and we ran down to the water. I kept going forward up to my waist then dove into a wave. When I surfaced, I saw her back at the waterline, hesitating.

"Come on," I said.

She came toward me, turning sideways as each new wave broke against her, then pushing forward again until she was next to me.

"I had to watch you," she said. "The way you dove in. I want to be able to do that."

"Well, come on. We'll go out and run back in together."

And so we did. We held hands and jumped through the incoming waves, and when we reached the right spot with the right wave coming in, I shouted to her, "Now! Dive!" and let go of her hand and dove forward. I came through the surface and looked around in time to see her break through a few feet away. She shook the water from her head and saw me. Her face lit up in a great smile and we paddled toward each other.

"That was it! That was incredible!"

"You really never did that before?"

"Never. Thank you!"

Below the surface of the water she took my hands. It was the moment when we should have kissed. I could feel she was ready, and God knows

I was. But we both knew that there were a few dozen pairs of eyes in the water around us and on the beach and it was not going to happen. There had been, of course, a fair amount of fraternizing among the *Brigadistas* (and plenty of complaints from the solo barracks mates who had to listen to the sounds of lovemaking coming from the bunks around them). But that was between comrades, peers. I had learned in the Army that rank has its privileges, but Avis was not going to take advantage of that. It wasn't the kind of thing she would do. If we were ever going to take the next step, we would have to find a way to be alone. But it wasn't here or now. She squeezed my hands then let them go and moved away from me.

"I'm going to go back to the book," she said. "It's a very exciting part."
"Okay. I'm going to swim a little."
"But this was great."
"Maybe we can walk up the beach later."
"Maybe."
"Or not take the bus back. Stay and have dinner somewhere."
"We have to take the bus."
"No, we don't. I have a bunch of pesos. I can pay for a cab."
"Jay, I have to take the bus."
"Of course. I'm sorry. I just …Can we sit together again?"
"I'd like that."

She turned and pushed her way through the water back toward the beach.

- Forty -

The rest of the afternoon was wonderful and sad. We spent all our time together, swam again, joined the Weathermen in their Frisbee frenzy—which they had somehow turned into an anti-imperialism metaphor—ate the sandwiches that had been packed for us back at the camp, drank Cuban sodas, and stretched out in the sun and under the shade of the umbrella. We even took a walk up the beach. But it was all chaste, except for some more hand-holding under the waves. It was like being back in the fifties.

I kept an eye open for Juan. He must have been somewhere around, but I never saw him.

Walter showed up late in the afternoon, not long before we had to pack up for the bus ride home.

"How was your day?" I said.

"Tell you later," he said before heading into the water for a swim.

As much as I wanted to hear what he had to say, I wanted still more to be with Avis, no matter how limited our contact could be. As we got in line to board one of the buses, I was relieved to see Juan waiting in line for a different one.

On the ride back to the camp, she talked about the future, her future as she saw it. Everything she thought she might do came out of her belief that there would be a revolution in the U.S. She wasn't crazy enough to think it was imminent, but she did think it could happen in our lifetime, though she admitted we might be pretty old when it did come.

"I know it's optimistic. The country is so tied into the idea of individual success, and the unions have gotten more conservative because of the war. But it's still capitalism, and capitalism will fail. The scary part is that we could just as likely become a fascist country as a socialist one."

"More likely," I said.

"Oh, don't get me started on that. You'll be sorry."

"No, tell me. Do you really think it could happen?"

"Sure. What does it take? You just have to scare the shit out of the majority of the population. The straight white population. Scare 'em about black revolutionaries killing whitey, scare 'em about drug-crazed hippies pulling more Manson-type killings, bring back the commie scare from the fifties. It recycles well, you know. Remember, it worked in the twenties long before Joe McCarthy came along. Put them all together, suspend the First Amendment, suspend the Fifth Amendment. It wouldn't take much. Lincoln suspended Habeas Corpus during the Civil War. What if Geronimo and his pals started blowing up military bases around the country? What if they started killing soldiers? They're crazy enough to do it, you know. It's just what an asshole like Nixon would love. What happens if the war is still going strong when the next election rolls around? What if there are riots that make Chicago look like a picnic? It wouldn't take much. Not much at all."

"I guess you've thought about it a little."

I was paying attention to what she said. But I was thinking at the same time that I had started out looking for a distraction from my Roger assignment, a girl to chase like all the others I had chased in high school and college, for the fun of it, for the challenge, the game. And instead I'd fallen in love. I was pretty sure it was love, because it wasn't like anything that had come before.

"I think about it too much. Instead of worrying about it, I should concentrate on keeping it from happening."

"But you are. I know you are."

"You know?"

"Everything you do, I mean, all the things you've done with the brigade, I'm sure you must be doing the same in Milwaukee."

"You're sure?"

She was laughing at me. She knew why I was babbling.

"You know what I mean."

"I think I do."
"You do like me a little, don't you?"
"A little."
My face must have dropped. She laughed again.
"Maybe more than a little."

For the rest of the trip we rode in silence. We casually let our hands fall against each other, back to back but still touching, gently. After a while, she dozed, exhausted from her hours in the sun. Her head was against my shoulder. Nothing in my life had ever been so good.

PART V
Campamento Brigada Venceremos

- Forty-One -

Walter had been waiting impatiently to tell me about his afternoon with Roger. We took a walk before we went to our bunks that night, and it all came tumbling out as soon as we were off by ourselves.

"I told you we'd been writing," he said.

"Uh-huh."

"It started after he got here. He wrote to me wanting to know what was happening back in New York, mostly what people were saying about him, did they blame him for the explosion, for the deaths."

"Did people blame him?"

"Some did, some didn't. It depended on how they felt about bombing and how they felt about Roger. Anyway, it was all stupid, since nobody really knew what had happened except me and Linda."

"And now me."

"That's funny. Roger asked me today if I'd told you what really happened."

"Did you tell him?"

"No. I don't know why, but I didn't want him to know. Why did I do that? Why did I lie about it?"

"I don't know. I think there's something about Roger always wanting to know everything about everything that makes you want to keep stuff from him. Like it's the only edge you have."

"Yeah."

"What else did you talk about?"

"That's what I was getting to. That's why I was talking about when we were writing. The other thing he wanted to know was what people thought about his being in Cuba. And I remembered that he had asked me if I knew whether you knew he was here. I mean, it was so odd. You'd basically disappeared. How would I know if you knew? But he had the idea that we were in touch."

"Why would he care what I thought, anyway?"

"Well, that's what I mean. Weird. And then today, asking if you knew about what happened and again what you thought about him being here and did I think you were serious about staying. Did I think you really meant it."

"What did you say?"

"What could I say? It was all new to me. If I'd thought about it, I would have guessed you'd go back to Canada."

"Yeah," I said. "Until today, that's probably what would have happened."

I couldn't let Walter know how much this was freaking me out. Did Roger suspect why I was there? Had I said anything or done anything to make him suspect? He certainly was an oddball, but I never took him for a mind reader. Had someone tipped him off? But then who would know except Short One, Tall One, and the McWilliamses? Had they changed their minds about revenge and somehow managed to warn him? But why wouldn't they have just contacted me and said the deal was off?

What about Miss More, Short One's receptionist? She might have known what was going on. But why would she contact Roger? Maybe it was John Lydon, the cowboy from the bus. But I never mentioned Roger by name. Maybe it was Wildflower, maybe it was Ori. Maybe I talked in my sleep. Maybe he *was* a mind reader.

"Maybe he's lonely," I said. "Maybe he just wants to be sure that he's going to have someone to play with. And maybe he's worried that if I do stay, I might not want to be his friend, if I was pissed at him for what happened in New York."

Walter didn't say anything. He looked as if he were trying to make up his mind about something. We kept walking. I waited. Whatever was on his mind was important. At least it was to him. Finally he was ready.

"I was pissed off at him about what happened in New York. I was, I am. But I couldn't say it to him. I know he knew it, that I felt like that, but it was like he was daring me to say it and I couldn't. It was too much to say."

I had no idea what he was talking about.

"Too much?"

"Too big. I can't prove it."

"Prove what?"

"That he knew."

"Knew what?"

"That the bomb was going to explode. He knew it and he just left. He didn't say anything. He made up that bullshit that the timer wasn't working and he got his ass out of there because he knew the bomb was set to explode and he couldn't stop it. He didn't know how, so he took off."

"But why wouldn't he tell everyone to get out?"

"I know. That's why it's so crazy. That's why it's so hard to say. Except I feel it. It's the truth. I know it."

A big chill went through me. It was exactly what Lauren McWilliams had said. Was it possible? When you hate someone, it's easy to believe all the worst about them. But was Roger a murderer because he was a prick? I found myself resisting the idea just because it was so easy to believe it.

"Look, it's easy to believe because Roger is such a self-serving scumbag. But killing you all? Why?"

"Because he didn't want us to know he was a fraud. The great bomb expert and he didn't know how to stop the clock. He couldn't admit to it and let us live to say anything about it."

The expression "dying from embarrassment" popped into my head. Did Roger kill from embarrassment? It also hit me that this was why Linda had told the cops she saw Roger walking away from the house before it exploded. Walter must have shared his suspicion with her, meaning Roger had been willing to let her die. No wonder then that she fingered him.

"Walter, that's pretty far out," I said.

"I know. So I spent the afternoon wanting to put it to him and not being able to. It was torture."

"So he rattled on and you never told him what you suspected."

"If I'm right—and I'm sure I am—he tried to kill me. That's a tough thing to say to someone. I mean, what if he decided to finish the job? I think he's wacko enough to do it."

"So what did you talk about instead?"

"Besides you, you mean? He talked about how great his life is here. He has a car, some dopey Russian job that's like a life-size version of one of those little Hot Wheels that kids play with, and we went for a drive so he could show me his world. How great it is to be part of the revolution. How wonderful the people are. How much he enjoys his job."

"That's good."

"I didn't believe a word he said."

"Really?"

"He's miserable. It was clear. He was trying to be the big know-it-all that he was in New York, but it was just so obvious it was an act. The more he went on, the more pathetic it got. I think he's cracking up here. Which made me think about you."

"Me?"

"Yeah. Like maybe you should think twice about staying here. I mean, really, you might be better off going back to Canada."

"Wow. And I was getting all excited about staying."

"Oh, I'm not saying you shouldn't. But don't jump in on Roger's say so. That's all."

I couldn't tell him I wasn't planning to stay very long and that my plan wasn't to go back to Canada, either. I was going to go home. If I could kill Roger.

"What's his place like?"

"I think it's one of the reasons he might be depressed. It was really drab. I thought he must live in one of those beautiful buildings near the church. You know, historic, colorful. Maybe small, but with one of those little balconies with a fancy cast-iron grille. But he was in a kind of tenement, like an old hotel that had been made over into apartments. It looked like it might have been something nice maybe a hundred years ago, but all downhill since then except maybe for a fresh coat of paint every decade or two. Anyway, he has a living room and a kitchenette and a bedroom. All really small. At least he has his own bathroom."

A living room and a kitchenette and a bedroom and a bathroom. I wanted to know more. I wanted Walter to draw a floor plan, but that would have been way over the edge.

- Forty-Two -

I called home the next evening to see what the tests had found out. It was bad.

"It's cancer," said my mother.

"What do you mean, cancer?"

"I mean cancer. What do you think I mean? He's got cancer."

"Okay, Ma. Don't shout at me. Just tell me what the doctor said."

"I am telling you. He's got cancer. He's dying."

"Awright, Ma. You have to calm down. You have to talk to me. What kind of cancer?"

"Cancer cancer. That kind."

"I mean, is it lung cancer, stomach cancer …"

"In his blood. Blood cancer."

I tried to think what it was called. My mind was blank.

"If he went to the doctor like he was supposed to they could've told him. They could have done something."

Leukemia. That was the word I was trying to think of. My mother kept talking.

"But he couldn't be bothered. He was just tired. He just needed a day off. I told him, but would he listen?"

"Is it leukemia? Is that what it is?"

"Yeah, that's it. Bad leukemia. Very advanced, he said."

"Who said? The doctor?"

"No, the mailman. Of course the doctor."

"Is Daddy home? Is he in the hospital?"

"He's home. He's in bed. They gave him something to sleep. Jay, what am I gonna do?"

"What did the doctor say about treatment?"

"There is none. It's too late."

"But, what are they going to do?"

"The same as me. They're gonna watch him die."

- Forty-Three -

The doctor figured my dad had about three months left in him. There was a calendar in the information post right near the phone. I started calculating, trying to get a handle on things and also trying to make my head stop spinning.

It was March 2nd, a Monday. We'd been in the camp since February 19th, a Thursday, so that made it about a week and a half. We'd left St. John on February 12th. I'd left Pacific Breeze on February 6th, less than a month before. As I figured that out, I realized it wasn't important. I was spinning my wheels. Looking ahead was what I needed to do.

I started over. We were supposed to be in the camp until April 5th. That was a Sunday, five weeks away. Then there was supposed to be another two weeks of a guided tour around Cuba for the Brigade before we shipped back to Canada, then a week on the boat.

Flipping the pages of the calendar, it looked like I wouldn't be back to St. John and Peter Ward's office until April 29th, just under two months. If they had the pardon ready to go, I could maybe have a whole month with my dad.

If the doctor was right.

If they didn't extend the harvest.

If the ship didn't sink on the way north.

If I killed Roger.

- Forty-Four -

I went into countdown mode. In the war, you didn't go there until you passed the halfway point, until you were short. Before that, you didn't think about how long you had to go because it was too long. To start counting too soon was bad luck. You put a curse on yourself.

But here, the halfway point wasn't a matter of days. It was my meeting with Roger and I'd made it that far. My idiot plan had been exposed for the crap it was, but now I had something in mind that, if less specific, was more real. It wasn't a plan of detail, it was a plan of opportunity, open-ended, unfortunately, requiring patience, but real because, given enough time, an opportunity would have to come along.

Except now, patience was harder to come by, even though the calendar hadn't really changed. There wasn't much I could do about it unless I snuck out of camp, made my way to Havana, killed Roger, and figured a way to get out of Cuba immediately thereafter. One of the Brigade women had gone home because of a family emergency back in New York. I had a family emergency, but everyone knew I couldn't go home. I could ask them to send me back to Canada, maybe hint that I was going to risk a visit to my dad from there, but I didn't think I could pull off a story like that. And it would all have to be perfectly timed. I'd have to kill Roger, and ask to be sent to Canada, and be gone within a day or two before the authorities came calling on Roger's American friends in the Brigade.

As unrealistic as it was, this became an ongoing fantasy, and I returned to it time and time again, but knowing it was a fantasy and not going to happen. Maybe I was just rehearsing in my mind, preparing myself for when I really would be there, alone with Roger in his apartment, watching him die from the poison I'd slipped into his drink. I thought about the men I'd seen die back in the war, GIs and VC. I tried to think about Roger dead like the dead after a battle. It was war and people died, horrible, nightmarish. It made me sick and it made me glad to be alive. I imagined standing over the dead Roger and feeling the same.

I thought about Lauren McWilliams and what she thought his death would be like. Did she picture herself killing him? Did she fantasize about making him beg for mercy? Did she imagine shooting him, stabbing him, tearing his eyes out, cutting his balls off? Or did she just want to know he was dead?

Sometimes the thought came of my father dead, but I pushed that away before any details could develop.

- Forty-Five -

Somehow, the days went by. There was cane to cut and Avis to love, even if that was also a matter of waiting for an opportunity in a situation that was finite rather than open-ended. That opportunity was not likely to come before she had to go home, but pursuing it would keep me going. And it helped to keep my mind off both my father and Roger.

I had decided that when we finished in the fields, I would skip the tour of Cuba and press Roger to hook me up with his Cuban contacts. I would ask him to let me crash at his apartment while the job hunt was going on. That would make it easier to find the right moment for doing him in, although it would also make me the chief suspect. I might be able to figure out a way to leave Cuba on my own, in which case I could kill him and leave before the boat ride home.

Out in the fields, I got back into my "Sugar, Sugar" rhythm. I kept an eye out for Juan, who was usually working a couple of rows away. He had gone from giving me the evil eye to ignoring me. I wondered if he had a plan in mind, a fantasy that involved his machete and one or more of my body parts.

Back in the war, there were guys in our outfit who hated each other, and there was always the chance that in the heat of battle a bullet might get sent in the wrong direction. There were always rumors circulating about that kind of thing happening. It was never clear if the stories told were genuine or myths, and I never saw it myself.

There were stories about Brigadistas in the First Brigade who had cut their comrades, but those were always accidents, not willful acts. In our Brigade, people had cut themselves, but no one had cut anyone else. I was hoping it would stay that way. And after all, Juan had little reason to go after me. Sure, Avis and I had spent a lot of time together on our beach outing, but since then, I had hardly spoken with her. Maybe that was why he had retired the evil eye. In fact, Juan actually stopped by our tent on his bicycle to ask me to work with one of the other members of Brigade 27 who had lost his swing. He was quite civil and I thought maybe his New Man-ness had overcome his jealousy.

- Forty-Six -

Our routine was interrupted by the announcement that we were going to have visitors. A crew of North Vietnamese soldiers was coming to work alongside us cutting cane. I got a lot of attention following the announcement. People wanted to know how I felt about being confronted with "the enemy." I said I thought it was a great chance to speak up for peace, and everyone seemed satisfied. When we were alone, though, Walter wanted to know more.

"What about your nightmares?" he said.

"I don't have nightmares."

"What about last week? You were definitely having bad dreams about the war. You said so."

"Look, that was about combat. I spent plenty of time with the Vietnamese without any problem."

"South Vietnamese."

"It doesn't matter. North, south, they're all the same people. Don't you pay attention at the antiwar rallies?"

"But the Vietnamese who are coming are soldiers."

"As long as none of these guys comes at me with a bayonet, I think we'll be fine."

I wondered if anyone was checking with the North Vietnamese to see how they felt about me. As it turned out, they had. Before their bus arrived Avis sought me out.

"The leaders want you to meet with the Vietnamese."

"How come?"

"They want to take pictures. Revolutionary solidarity."

"I don't think I can do that."

"How come?"

"'Cause I can't."

"Why not?"

"Look, I don't have any problem meeting with them. But I can't be in a picture."

"Okay, no one's going to make you take a picture if you don't want to, but can you tell *me* why?"

"'Cause that's like collaborating."

"Collaborating? Like collaborating with the enemy?"

"Okay, maybe the word is fraternizing. Whatever. And I don't think of them as 'the enemy.' I hope they win. It's their country and we should get out and all that kinda crap. But I have buddies back there, and I don't want them to see any pictures of me shaking hands with guys who are trying to kill them. I mean, it's war, that's what you have to do, and when it's all over someday, then we can all shake hands and say hell of a good fight and all that crap. But not till the shooting is over. Is that so hard to understand?"

"But that's the whole point. It's supposed to be about ending the fighting now."

"Hey, if you're back in Milwaukee organizing the cooks or whatever, would you want a picture going around of you and McDonald shaking hands before the contract got signed?"

"McDonald?"

"The guy who owns McDonald's."

"Kroc."

"What?"

"The guy who owns McDonald's is Kroc."

"Okay, Kroc. Would you want a picture with him? Would anyone trust you if you did that?"

"Okay. Forget the picture. But you'll talk to them, right?"

"Oh, yeah. But I swear, if anyone tries to take a picture, I will go fucking ballistic. Will you make sure that is understood?"

"If anyone tries to take a picture, I will personally take the camera and smash it. Okay?"

"Okay. Thanks."

In fact, that was what did happen. The Vietnamese (forget North and South) came a few days later and we met and that was cool. As it turned out, there were some Viet Cong in with the regulars. They had a translator along with them, a young guy who went to school in the south then went back up north to join with the regular Army rather than be in the Viet Cong, who had a much tougher time of it.

They knew I'd been there and had fought them and killed them and it was war. Nothing personal, even when it turned out we had been in a couple of the same battles. In fact, it got kind of interesting, talking about it from both sides, like those Civil War veterans (our Civil War, not theirs) from the North and the South who met up in the years after and had some kind of nostalgic reunion. Time heals all wounds, especially if you're alive to see the scars.

The rest of the Brigade was impressed by this show of comradeship between us. But it was short-lived. The Vietnamese had a political officer with them, an older guy named Sang, and he was having none of this fraternization. He shut his guys down before we got to exchanging addresses and phone numbers.

The Vietnamese worked in the field and ate with us and there were pictures taken and I wasn't in any until I was. It wasn't anybody from the camp, Avis having made sure they had their marching orders. But a photographer had come over from Havana, and he was the guilty party. And, true to her word, Avis smashed the camera. Well, not really. But she took it away and removed the film and exposed it. The guy was quite pissed and made a stink about it, but she took the heat, and the Cuban directors, who had never been happy about my refusal, stood behind her.

The Vietnamese wanted to know what was going on.

"Can you explain?" said Avis.

"Not really." Most of what I could say in Vietnamese I'd learned in a whorehouse, and I didn't think it would be welcome.

"I mean through the translator."

"Oh. Sure."

So I told the Vietnamese the same story I had told Avis. It was soldier talk, you had to keep faith with your comrades. The Vietnamese talked it over among themselves and it looked to me like all of them understood, all but Sang. For him, as the translator explained, the cause took precedence over the smaller loyalty to the platoon. It was just such loyalties that sapped the strength of the revolution from within. Such loyalties were understandable, and, in a capitalist society, no doubt admirable. But they had no place in a revolutionary socialist society and must be overcome.

The soldiers all nodded in agreement. It didn't look like they were buying it, but clearly Sang was the big cheese and any disagreement might lead to some unpleasant consequences back home in Hanoi.

"Well, okay," I said. "But I'm still not taking any pictures."

It might have consequences right there in Cuba for me, it might interfere with my getting a job or being able to stay after the Brigade left; maybe they'd give me the bum's rush and toss me out the next day. But I couldn't come around.

I can't say that I had a lot of support. There were a couple of other veterans in the Brigade and they understood, but most everyone else, doing their best to be good revolutionaries, bought into what Sang had said.

"Hey, man," said my close personal friend Geronimo, "the man is right. The revolution comes first."

Others argued with me along the same lines. I didn't argue back. I just said no. Avis and Walter stayed out of it, which was something. I don't know if they agreed with me or the others, but they knew I wasn't going to change my mind.

For the rest of that day, I was pretty much shunned except when somebody decided they had a different way of saying what everyone else had said, some way that was finally going to make sense to me. By evening everyone had given up.

- Forty-Seven -

The next morning started out the same, with everyone except Walter keeping any contact with me to a polite minimum. People were genuinely confused. I figured that they understood where I was coming from because they all had more or less the same feeling. It was like what we all had come to agree on as kids, that squealing on your friends was wrong, no matter what your parents or teachers or other adults might tell you. Not wanting to let my picture be taken was on a par with not squealing.

But we were all trying to be New Men and Women. So maybe our parents were right all along. Maybe you *were* supposed to squeal. Only it wasn't squealing anymore. It was socialist rectitude. The problem was, just about everybody had read *1984*, and the whole thing reminded them of Big Brother. So I wasn't being shunned, I was just being avoided because I was a pain in the ass, spoiling the easy joy of being socialist revolutionaries just by coming to Cuba and cutting cane.

I didn't mind too much. I hadn't come to Cuba to be a New Man. I'd come so I could get back to the good old USA, pick up my life, as unsocialistic as it may have been, and make peace with my dad. I was actually having a good day cutting cane, singing my song, thinking about Avis, not bothering to count minutes or hours because I knew they were ticking away and I would be another day closer to getting on with my real mission.

And then my real mission showed up. Roger came to camp to cut cane. He arrived on a bus with a group of teachers from the school where he taught English. Walter and I and the rest of Brigade 27 were at the machete rack picking up our blades before heading out to the field we were working that day.

He spotted us as he disembarked. "Hello, boys!"

His greeting shook us both. There was something ominous about his being there. Walter told me afterwards that he felt like Roger had come to finish the job he'd started in New York, of getting rid of Walter. For myself, I feared once again that he had read my mind, knew why I was in Cuba, and had come to do unto me what I was supposed to do unto him.

"Roger!" was all Walter could say.

He was grinning madly as he joined us. He was still wearing his heavy boots, but he had discarded his usual urban look for a peasant outfit of loose-fitting cotton shirt and pants. In addition, he had on a wide-brimmed straw hat. It was weird. It looked like he was wearing a costume, yet at the same time he seemed completely at ease in it, as if he dressed that way all the time.

"I've been recruited at last. The whole damn faculty is here, ready to do our part for the *zafra*. It's ten million tons or bust!"

He picked up a machete and swung it in the air. Everyone jumped away from him. Juan shouted at him in Spanish to put the blade down. Roger, still grinning, put it back against the rack then raised his hands up, palms forward.

"*Dispenseme*," he said in an exaggerated fashion, mocking Juan for being so serious.

Juan lectured him for a minute in Spanish about how dangerous it was to fool with the machetes. The other instructors, Julio and Roberto, arrived in time to catch the end of the lecture and note who was on the receiving end. Juan said something to them that I couldn't catch, but that I was sure amounted to "watch out for this clown," then he turned and headed out to the field. As he passed me and Walter, he asked if Roger was a friend of ours.

"He used to be," said Walter.

"See you later, boys!" said Roger as we followed after Juan.

"What the hell," said Walter as we walked to the field.

"Yeah," was all I could say.

It was almost impossible to concentrate that morning, especially after Roger finished his training and came out to the field with the other teachers and Julio and Roberto, who were sticking with them. Evidently, none of the new recruits had shown much aptitude for cutting cane.

The single exception was Roger. He went to work with a lusty passion, swinging away with strength and accuracy and rhythm. It was as if he had been born to cut cane. Maybe it was a great release for him, considering that his life at the school didn't involve a lot of physical activity. Still, to watch him work was especially astonishing for me and Walter since back in New York it had seemed like he hardly ever left the plush armchair in the McWilliams library that he had staked out all for himself.

I was particularly disconcerted about what lay ahead. I had never considered that I might have a difficult time handling Roger if it came to a confrontation. Again, his attachment to the soft comfort of the McWilliams easy chair led me to think of him as a pushover. Watching him slice his way down a row of cane stalks put me in a terrible mood.

At the morning *merienda*, Roger came over to join us as we sprawled under one of the shade trees that edged the area we'd been working. He plopped down next to Walter, who introduced him to our brigade. Jerry, Walter's friend from Virginia, asked how they knew each other.

"We were in the revolution together in New York," said Roger, giving Jerry his best devil's leer.

"Oh," said the pugnacious Jerry, "I didn't realize New York had had a revolution."

"Then you must lead a very sheltered life," said Roger, and he burst out laughing. I knew the laugh was completely bogus but Roger turned in one of his Orson Welles performances and made it seem genuine. Jerry had been ready to respond, but the laugh was just hearty and long enough to put an end to the conversation. Jerry rolled his eyes and settled back with his cup of yogurt. Roger stopped laughing, but a big shit-eating grin stayed on his face as he turned his attention back to me and Walter.

"So this is how you boys have been spending your days. Plenty of fresh air and sunshine, great exercise, good companionship, and lovely views." He winked at us and nodded his head toward where a couple of the women in our brigade were stretched out on a bed of leaves.

Walter was losing it fast.

"Roger, those are our comrades. So none of your bullshit, okay?"

Roger played the offended innocent.

"Walter, whatever do you mean? I'm merely pointing out that you've landed in socialist heaven."

I thought about what Walter had said about Roger being miserable. It seemed like he'd decided to take it out on us. "Roger," I said, hoping to turn the conversation, "have you talked to anyone about my staying?"

"Ah, yes indeed. You see, I too, have comrades." He sneered at Walter as he said the word.

"So, what's happening?" I said.

"I think you are in like Flynn, my boy. I've spoken to a certain colonel in the FAR—that's the Fuercias Armadas Revolucionarias to you—and there is a need for teachers."

"Won't I have to speak Spanish before I can teach them English?"

"Well, you'll need a few words, but mostly it's up to them. Anyway, most of the cadets speak some English already. It's about teaching them what to call military things. Rifles and bullets and so on. They have a training academy right here in Havana where the cadets live while they study. I guess it's like their West Point. You might even be able to get rooms there and free eats in the dining hall."

"Really? But why do they want to know what the English words are?"

"I don't know. In case they want to defect, probably."

"Huh?"

"I'm kidding. Honestly, I have no idea why they would want to know unless there are training manuals in English or something like that. I know they have Russian teachers because they have Russian manuals for some things, so that could be the reason for the English."

I didn't know why I was asking or why I cared. It was not like I saw it as a long-term assignment.

"Well, whatever," I said. "What's the next step?"

"They want to meet you, but not, of course, until the *zafra* is done. What is that? Another three weeks?"

"Just about," I said.

"What about the Isle of Pines?" said Walter.

"What about the Isle of Pines?" said Roger.

"We're supposed to go there after the *zafra*," I said. "Then we get a tour of the island before we head home. But I can skip that. I want to get to work right away. If I'm allowed to stay, I can always go there another time."

"I guess," said Walter.

He was very disappointed for me. Or maybe he just hated the idea that I was choosing to go with Roger, as if it was another victory for the slimy bastard. I felt bad for him and for myself. I wanted to go, I had earned that trip. And it would be more time to be with Avis. I can't say I didn't care. But I had my priorities.

"I'll tell you what," said Roger. "You'll come crash at my pad while you get squared away with the job. And who knows? Maybe there'll be a chance that we can hook up with your group before you actually have to get started on your job."

"Yeah," I said. "Crash at your pad. That's great! Thank you!"

Act natural, act natural, act natural.

- Forty-Eight -

Roger and the other teachers stayed for three days. As cutters, the Cuban teachers improved from terrible to mediocre. A few had worked in the field as kids and the revolution had given them a chance to go to school and create new lives for themselves. Maybe they found it ironic that the revolution had also sent them back to the fields. I wondered if they were doing a poor job to avoid having to stay and cut more. But the danger of being identified as slackers would have kept them from trying that. They were just lame.

It was unnerving to have Roger so close. The first night, I lay in my bunk wondering if there would be a way to kill him while he was in camp. I imagined getting him alone in the fields or sneaking into his tent and slitting his throat in the middle of the night. But it still left me with the problem of getting home faster. With a murdered American in camp, there was no way I was going to get a flight back to Canada.

So Roger lived and I waited. He cut well, but the work was still exhausting and he was happy to sleep as much as he could. He sat with us at dinner and joined us at the *meriendas* and never stopped talking, mostly about himself. Brigade 27, taking their cue from Walter and Jerry, ignored him. But he hit it right off with some of the other *Brigadistas*, especially—no surprise—the Weathermen.

I watched them go off together and it was not hard to figure out what they were talking about. After dinner, they would gather at a table in the far corner of the dining hall. I saw Roger drawing and assumed he was teaching them how to put together a bomb. Walter saw it, too.

"Maybe I should explain to them that they shouldn't be in the same room with him when he actually puts one together," said Walter.

"I don't know," I said. "Maybe that's something Geronimo should learn for himself."

Geronimo was genuinely excited by meeting Roger. He stopped me the next morning on the way out to the fields.

"Roger's fucking great, man!"

"Yeah," I said. "I knew you'd like him."

I was in a little bind, as I didn't want to put Roger down since it might get back to him and I needed to stay on good terms with him. Until I could kill him, that is.

- Forty-Nine -

Roger left and I went back to countdown mode. I was hoping for a routine, a sameness, that would make the time go faster. But the pressure to reach our goal made things more intense and didn't really help us cut faster. We were all working hard now, and most everyone had gotten into a rhythm. But it was getting pretty clear that we were running behind, and, from little bits we picked up from the Cubans, the entire *zafra* was going to come up short of the ten-million-ton goal.

I felt bad about this. I hadn't come to Cuba to make that thing happen, but over the weeks we'd been there, it had become my life just as it was everyone else's. I still didn't care about the politics or learning how to be a better revolutionary when I got back to America. That was for Geronimo, and for Walter, and even for Avis, although to my mind she was as good a revolutionary as you could be. I still didn't know if I was going to get back to America, and I wasn't interested in being a better revolutionary if I wound up back in Canada.

But I found myself caring that the people, I mean the Cuban people, were trying to make something happen. This was important to them, not just some hype from their government, but a real thing, a national thing, a revolutionary thing. It mattered to Juan and to Roberto and to Julio if we made ten million tons, and it mattered to the Cubans who worked in the kitchen and around the camp and who worked in the fields with us, and so it mattered to me, too.

The rest of the socialist world was pulling out the stops to make the thing happen. We kept getting new teams arriving from Korea (North, of course) and from Africa—Angola and the Congo, I think—and from countries in South America. I don't know if these were government groups or groups of revolutionaries who had to sneak their way to Cuba the way the Brigade had had to go to Canada in order to come to Cuba. But they were there, and once they got their machete training, were out in the fields cutting away.

Each time a new team arrived, it was a little disruption from the flow, as we had to have some kind of solidarity celebration. But even those events got to be part of the flow over the next couple of weeks.

The biggest disruption to any routine was the unexpected arrival in the camp of Fidel. We knew that he had come to cut cane with the first Brigade, and everyone was hoping against hope that we, too, would get to stand shoulder to shoulder with the man himself. It turned out that he was there to inspect some cutting machines, not to cut with us. But when word got around that he was there, hardly anyone could resist heading over to the field where he was. A couple of people started chanting, "Fidel, Fidel," and in seconds we all joined in. He turned and waved to us, and, his business with the machines finished, he came over to where we were standing at the edge of the field.

It was pretty electric. This was Fidel, the leader of the Cuban Revolution, the guy who defied the U.S., one of the most famous people in the whole wide world. He was a big guy physically, at least six feet, and husky. You could almost feel his weight as he approached. Not in a bad way, he was very natural, as if he had absorbed the power that had been given to him, made it his own and held it with ease. I guess it was self-confidence.

I didn't really know a lot about Fidel back then. I knew he was in his forties, but looking at him, he seemed younger, more like in his thirties. I knew he came from a good family, had led a revolt that failed, been sent to jail, then exiled, and had come back to Cuba with Che and led a rebel army in the mountains that eventually beat the regular army. I knew Batista was the guy before him and that he had been a dictator. No one said so, but it was pretty clear to me that Castro was now a dictator, too, but popular, still the revolutionary leader, still wearing his fatigues to remind everyone that he was the one holding the fort against threats from the U.S., which had, after all, tried to invade the country and overthrow him and the revolution.

Fidel drained a tall glass of water, then started talking, a little in English but mostly in Spanish with the camp director Javier translating. He talked about the importance of the harvest, the difficulties and the challenges. He explained that he had never cut any cane himself until after the revolution when he realized that, since it was the heart of the economy, everyone was responsible for making sure it was a success. He thanked us for our courage in coming to work with and for the Cuban people. He went into some detail about the cutting machines he was inspecting. He talked about the international revolutionary movement, about international socialism, about the faults of capitalism, and about the new men and women that were emerging in Cuba. He talked and talked and talked, but it was all fascinating. Like I said, I didn't know much about him before, but in the hour or so that he went on and on, I understood how he could lead a revolution and how he could dare to stand up to the U.S. He was simply a huge guy.

Finally, one of his aides persuaded him that he had to be somewhere else and was late. We all followed him back to his car by the front gate. He shook hands with a bunch of the *Brigadistas* and embraced some others, and with a wave of his hand, he shouted, "Venceremos!" and left. Then everyone talked excitedly about what we had just experienced, and finally we went back to work.

I was one of the people who shook Fidel's hand. Pushing myself forward to do some celebrity kind of thing is not normally something I would have done then or since. But it was a special occasion that day, my twenty-first birthday, and I decided to give myself something to remember it by.

No one knew it was my birthday. There was no reason anyone would. Walter didn't know it, and unless Avis checked the Brigade records for some reason, there was no reason she would know. My parents had no idea where I was. Neither did Wildflower or any of the guys from my platoon (even if they would have remembered the date), or any of my cousins or the kids I grew up with.

That day, I thought about the guys from my block, the guys my age that I had grown up with and gone to school with grade by grade. For us in New York, turning eighteen was a bigger deal than twenty-one, because you could drink legally and have a real driver's license. (Not to mention getting drafted.) But twenty-one was still a landmark, more about being a grown-up than just a teen who could go into a bar without getting tossed. Free, white, and twenty-one was an old expression that still had a hold.

I was white and now I was twenty-one, but I wasn't free and I didn't know when I would be. It occurred to me that the McWilliamses probably felt free and, with their money and power, they probably were. Probably all their rich and powerful friends were free, too. Eddie could have been free, too, if he'd stuck with his parents, but he felt trapped by his own privileges and threw away his freedom and then his life. Fidel was free and threw it away, but he survived his revolution, and, sitting at the top of the heap now, was free again. Maybe freer. But he still came to cut cane. Eddie was more like Che, born free, turning away from it, and dying in the effort to spread it to everyone. In her own Chicago way, Avis was like that, too.

If I could kill Roger and get back to the States, would I be free? I hadn't thought about it much before, but turning twenty-one put it in my head. Mostly, I'd been focused on seeing my dad and not having to go back to Vietnam. Besides that, I hadn't thought much about what I would do. Maybe I could go back to college, or, after my father was gone, I might go back up to Canada, back up to Pacific Breeze and see how Wildflower and Ori were doing. Maybe there were other communes, or maybe I'd track down John Lydon and see if he could use a hand on his ranch.

But first I had to deal with Roger.

- Fifty -

There was one more week of cutting to go when we got another day off to go to the beach or do whatever might please us. It was kind of a surprise, since we were so close to the end, but then again we had been going at it so hard one day after another, it made sense to give us a breather before the final push.

The big question for most of the *Brigadistas* was whether to go to the beach or sleep all day. The big question for Walter was whether or not to see Roger again.

"I mean, what's the point? I can't stand the creepy scumbag anymore. He tried to kill me."

"You *think* he tried to kill you. We don't know for sure."

"I know. Why do I want to have a drink with him and chit-chat about old times? What do I say? 'Hey Rog, remember the good old days when you tried to blow me into little pieces? Wasn't that a swell time?'"

"I agree. If I were you, I sure wouldn't do it."

"But what about you? Shouldn't you see him? I mean, you have a lot at stake."

That was exactly what I wanted to do, and I was looking forward to seeing Roger without Walter there on the chance that I might be able to take care of business right then and there.

"I guess so," I said. "Although I can't wait till he gets me set up with his contacts, and then I won't have to deal with him anymore, either. But are you okay with contacting him for me? Would it be better if I just went ahead and called him myself?"

"I'd love that. But what are you going to say? 'Walter doesn't want to play with you anymore because you tried to kill him'?"

"I don't have to say anything."

"Of course you do. He'll ask where I am, why I didn't come."

"I could say you're sick. Too sick to get out of bed and you needed to save your strength for the last week of the *zafra*. You'll see him when the tour comes through Havana the week after."

"But what if he decides you guys should go to the beach and we run into each other? Or he goes to the bus with you and spots me there? I'd feel so stupid."

"I could tell him you've got a hot date and you weren't giving up a minute with her since you could see him the week after. That way, if he came to the bus, it would make sense you were there."

"That way he'd be sure to come to the bus just to get a look at her and make some leering remarks if he got the chance. And you know him. He'd make sure he'd get the chance."

"Well, I could skip the bus ride back. Go out to dinner and drinks, miss the bus, and get him to drive me back here."

"Could you stand to be with him for that long?"

"I might as well get used to it. Especially if I'm going to crash with him until I get the job thing straightened out."

What I was thinking was that I could get him drunk and slip him the poison. Or if I couldn't give him the dope then, I could insist on his driving back to the camp, and when we reached some dark part of the road, I could beat his brains in. Then I'd drive to the Havana airport, leave his body in the trunk of his car, and fly back to Canada. I just had to remember to bring my passport with me. And the poison, of course.

- Fifty-One -

After work, I used the camp phone to call home. I'd been calling once a week since the tests results came back, willing my father to get no worse, willing his three months into six months or more, willing him toward a medical miracle, a total recovery for no reason other than that he couldn't die. According to my mother, he had been getting progressively weaker. I wondered if he had accepted the three-month verdict as a route he had to follow, and had set about turning each corner along the way at a steady pace so as to arrive back at the garage on schedule. It would be just like him to do that.

"Where are you?" said my mother.

"Still in Canada."

"You sound different, like it's a different phone."

"Yeah, it's a different Canadian phone. How's Daddy?"

"Weaker every day. Mostly he just lies in bed except when he sits in his chair in front of the TV. Sometimes I can't tell if he's awake or asleep. He doesn't want to eat."

"Can I talk to him?"

"Jay, you know—"

"Tell him he has to."

"I did. He won't."

"It's not my fault this happened."

"What are you talking about?"

"Nothing. Just being stupid. Forget it."

I spent the rest of the night before the day off going back and forth between fantasizing about killing Roger and fantasies of showing my dad the pardon. Walter had called Roger and told him we were coming in, and they agreed that we'd meet in the Plaza again. Walter and I had agreed that I would get off and he would keep going, and I would handle Roger. If Roger insisted on seeing Walter, I'd tell him that I didn't want to, that we'd been getting on each other's nerves and I really needed a break from being with him twenty-four hours a day. It would be up to me to put my foot down if Roger tried to force his mischief upon us.

I'd been looking forward to sharing the bus ride with Avis again. It was about the only positive thing I could cling to. The furious pace of the past few weeks had not left us much time to continue our flirtation, and the bus ride promised a chance to spend time with her, blocking out all the crap that was otherwise eating me up. But because of the demands of the *zafra* quota, she had been spending more and more time out cutting cane and less and less at a desk or in meetings and so felt compelled to take advantage of the day off from the fields to catch up on her administrative work. She was sympathetic to my disappointment.

"I know," she said. "I was looking forward to it, too. But I have reports I have to produce for the Brigade Central Committee. I have to do them before we go home."

"God, I'm being dumped for the Central Committee. Is this how Mrs. Lenin felt?"

"Mrs. Lenin was probably *on* the Central Committee. It was likely the only time she got to see her man."

"Does that mean I have to join the Central Committee if I want to see you?"

"You'd fit right in. They're all crazy, too."

"You sure you can't come?"

"Positive."

"Well, okay. But you owe me time, then."

"And you will have it. I'm looking forward to the Isle of Pines."

I hadn't told her yet that I wasn't going. I was hoping that somehow I would be able to make that trip even though I knew it was almost completely impossible. But until I knew absolutely one hundred percent that I wasn't going, I didn't want to say anything.

The day off came. Walter and I sat together on the bus into Havana. I noticed that Juan was not there. I wondered if he was on one of the other buses or if he'd stayed behind to try for a little private time with Avis, maybe changing her typewriter ribbon for her. I sure as hell would have.

We rode in silence most of the way, our faces buried in a couple of paperbacks that had been circulating around the camp. I had *The Teachings of Don Juan*, which Walter had recommended to me.

"You tend to be too literal," he said. "You need to open yourself up to the mystery of life."

I didn't want to remind him I'd seen the mystery of life come spilling out of someone's guts more times than I cared to count. As we neared Havana, Walter finally spoke.

"Do you think I'm doing the right thing? Am I being a coward?"

"You'd be a coward if you gave in and went to see Roger. So, no, you're definitely not being a coward. People do too many things because they think they have to."

"What about you? Aren't you doing it because you think you have to?"

"I'm doing it because I have to survive, not because I don't want to seem unsocial or offend Roger. In fact, as soon as he gets me a job, I'll make sure to offend him. I'll do it twice, once for me and once for you."

"I just don't know …"

"Look, just go to the beach and enjoy your day off. Get drunk and work on your tan so you'll be all beautiful for when you get to the Isle of Pines."

PART VI
Havana

- Fifty-Two -

The bus pulled out of the Plaza, leaving me behind. Roger was at the same table, out of his peasant garb and back in his old outfit. He stood and waved. He was smiling, but he looked puzzled, too.

"Where's Walter?" he said when I reached the table.

"Walter's in love."

"What?"

"Says he'll see you when the Brigade comes to Havana after the *zafra*'s over."

"Ah, love rears its ugly head. But he should have brought her along."

"Walter's still in the courting stage. He needs to stay focused."

"And what about your honey? Why didn't you bring her?"

"She's stuck in camp doing paperwork."

"So, just the two of us then." He laughed.

"What's so funny?" I said.

"I knew it would wind up just the two of us. But I thought it would come later."

He gave me one of his dramatic big eye looks.

"Later?"

He dropped the look and laughed again.

"When you come to stay with me, old boy."

"Oh. Well, it came now."

"Well, then, let's have a drink."

He signaled to a waiter. It was the same one we'd had before.

"Beer?" he said.

"Sure."

"Hungry?"

I was. He told the waiter to bring us beers and menus.

"Did you want to do that? You know, a chance to practice your Spanish?"

"Beyond *cerveza*, I would have been lost."

"Well, who knows? Maybe that's all you'll need."

"You think?"

"I can't say I remember you drinking much else. And anyway, rum is rum and vodka is vodka and whiskey is whiskey, so I'd say you're all set."

"I don't know. What was that word you said for menu?"

"*Menu.*"

"Oh."

"And taxi is *taxi* and telephone is—big difference—*telefono*."

The waiter came back.

"*Gracias*," said Roger to the waiter. Then he turned to me.

"I know," I said. "'Thank you.' Now tell me what's on the menu."

"*Arroz* is rice and *frijoles* are beans—*negro* is black."

It was my turn to laugh.

"I know all those from the camp."

"Well, as I keep saying, you know all you need to."

"Is there anything more than rice and beans?"

"*Conejo.*"

"What's that?"

"Rabbit."

"Rabbit?"

"Not bad, roasted. Tastes like chicken."

"That's it?"

"Hard times, old boy. You chop your ten million tons of sugar cane and next year we'll have chicken."

"Rabbit, it is."

Roger gave the waiter the order. He took out a pack of cigarettes and offered me one. They were the same Canadian brand I'd been smoking in Vancouver. He swallowed some of his beer, wiped his mouth, and sat back in his chair.

"So, ready for your great adventure?"

"Which one is that?"

He laughed again. We hadn't been together five minutes and already he was driving me crazy. He was so irritating, I felt like I wanted to kill him. Then I remembered I *could* kill him, that I was *supposed* to kill him, and I actually became less irritated. You prick, I thought, you're going to make this easier for me, aren't you?

"Your great Cuban adventure, of course," he said. "Not just six weeks of self-righteous cane-cutting you can hold over your comrades when you play movement one-upsmanship back home. I mean the real thing, becoming one with the people, becoming a New Man."

"Is that what's happening for you?"

"Of course it is. I'm newer than ever! Isn't it obvious?"

He laughed his devilish laugh again.

"I don't know. You seem your same sweet self to me."

The big shit-eating grin suddenly disappeared from his face and he became serious.

"We never did get to know each other very well. That was too bad. I thought you had something on the ball, unlike the rest of Eddie's pack of nitwits."

"Nitwits?"

"Not all of them. Eddie was smart, though his sincerity clouded his judgment. Walter's smart, too, only he's got his head up his ass. But the rest of that crowd, just children parroting the party line. You know what I'm talking about. You saw it, too. I know you did."

Of course I did. But I wasn't going to say it to him. I didn't know what to say. This was hardly the conversation I was expecting to have.

"I really wasn't thinking about that. I mostly had my own head up my own ass."

"Well, of course. You were in a unique situation. For the others, it was more like an extracurricular activity, the left wing equivalent of being on the football team or the cheerleading squad. Hence all the chants. 'Ho, Ho, Ho Chi Minh, the Viet Cong are gonna win!' They might as well have been shaking pompoms and twirling batons."

"I think it was more than that. I think Eddie was more than that."

"Of course. The exceptions that prove the rule. I grant you that. But for ninety-nine percent of the revolutionary movement, it was just the current form of college highjinks, an add-on to sex, dope, and rock and roll. None of the others had anything nearly as serious going on in their lives as you did."

"What about you? What was serious in your life?"

His serious attitude vanished as quickly as it had arrived and he laughed again.

"You see, that's what I'm talking about. You know exactly the right thing to say."

"And the answer is …?"

"What was serious in my life back then? Let me see …"

He leaned back in his chair and put his hands behind his head and made a thoughtful face. I think it was the first time I'd ever seen him pause to think before he spoke.

"I suppose I was most serious about … pussy."

I expected the big self-satisfied laugh to follow, but instead he just looked at me with the most honest expression I'd ever seen on his face. In fact, it was the only *truly* honest expression I'd ever seen on his face.

"You weren't serious about the revolution?"

"One can't be serious about that. It's too depressing. Besides, the revolution was just something people talked about. There isn't going to be any revolution. Not in the U.S., anyway. You know that."

I did know it. I just didn't like him saying it.

"You sure argued a lot for something you didn't believe in."

"I didn't say I didn't believe in the idea of revolution. But the reality of it, a real revolution? Not in the U.S. At least not a political revolution. Sexual revolution, women's rights, civil rights, even the fucking faggots will get their rights. It will all come despite all the fuss. But capitalism will go on, the government will go on, the establishment will go on. Nobody really wants that to change."

I thought of Avis.

"That's not true. Lots of people want that to change."

"Yes, 'people.' There are always 'people.' But you can shout 'power to the people' all you like, power will stay where it is."

He leaned across the table and whispered in a conspiratorial manner.

"That's why I say, 'Pussy to the people.' Better yet, 'Pussy to me.'"

He threw his head back and laughed again. It was going to be a long day.

"You talk like a reactionary. What would Fidel say if he could hear you?"

"Fuck Fidel," said Roger. "And the boat he sailed in on."

"I don't think you want to say that too loud."

"I do want to. I want to shout it. But it could cause something of a mess if I did."

"You really don't like Fidel?"

"Oh, I'm just tired of all the Big Brother stuff, is all. Don't make too much of it. A slight libertarian streak in me, that's all. Ever read *Left Wing Communism: An Infantile Disorder*?"

"Is that a Mickey Spillane?"

"Lenin, you dolt. One of his best. I've got it back at the apartment. I'll lend it to you."

- Fifty-Three -

Our lunch came and we ate.

"How's the rabbit?" said Roger.

"You were right. Tastes like chicken."

"There are some spots where tourists can eat well. Tourists and anyone who has a lot of money. By the way, you do have money, don't you?"

"I brought all I had from Canada. I never had a bank account to leave it in."

"Wonderful. You can pay when we go to one of the tourist places. And it may come in handy for your job application."

"I have to bribe somebody? Sounds a lot like how things work in Brooklyn."

"The world's pretty much the same all over."

"I thought Cuba was supposed to be different."

"It is, but then it isn't. One thing I've found in my travels: every place is different, at least on the surface. But underneath, believe me, they're all the same."

I knew what he said was true, but the fact that he said "believe me" almost made me doubt it.

"Have you traveled a lot?" I said. "I don't remember you ever talking about it."

"Not a lot, though maybe more than most."

"Where have you been?"

"The usual European highlights, Middle East, a bit of Asia, a bit of

Africa, Mexico, of course. Canada."

He said it casually, but an expectant look went through his eyes, as if he were telling me the punch line to a joke. He started to laugh again but held back. I was curious.

"Is Canada funny?"

"I'm sorry. I didn't want to laugh. I was just thinking that for you, it's either here or there. And you don't really want either."

"No, I really don't."

"I guess you'd kill to get back to the States, wouldn't you?"

I felt like my hair suddenly stood on end. I had just put a forkful of rice into my mouth and I chewed it slowly. He swallowed some beer. I finished chewing.

"Wow," I said. "I guess maybe I would."

"After all, you've killed before in order to survive. Why not again?"

I fought against the urge to put my hand on the vial of pills in my pocket.

"Did you have someone specific in mind?"

"No, but I'm sure we could find someone if we had to. Latin tempers run hot. Even in a communist country. Even among New Men."

"Yeah. One of the New Men in the camp is ready to use his machete on me whenever I talk to the woman he's crazy about."

"The same one you're crazy about?"

"Yep."

"I'd watch my back then, old boy. This New Man business only goes so far."

"What about you, Rog? Would you kill to get back to the States?"

He didn't wait a second to answer.

"In a blink of the eye. Maybe even faster."

- Fifty-Four -

We'd finished eating and switched from beers to Cuba Libres. The afternoon was hot and there was no breeze. I wished I was at the beach where I could strip down and dive into the life-giving waves. Instead I was sweating through my clothes as I listened to Roger's deadly litany of all that was wrong with Cuba, the revolution, and his life. Walter had said he didn't believe Roger's account of what a great life he was leading, and he was clearly right. I didn't think Roger had gotten drunk on two beers and a couple of rums, but his tongue was definitely looser than he may have intended. Still, this was Roger and I was on guard in case it was all an act and any moment he was going to slide away from his own troubles and start picking away at me to reveal my own.

"It's not difficult getting pussy here. There isn't a hell of a lot else to do except screw, and plenty of hot and horny daughters of the revolution and liberated convent girls ready to take wing. Sure, there's plenty of goddamn revolutionary saints and goddamn Catholic ones still around, but mostly it is slut city, like that parade of liberated college girls at Eddie's. God, that spoiled me forever. Well, you know what I mean."

"They knew what they were doing, all right."

"Exactly! I mean, they weren't all great. Did you ever fuck Maureen? No? Well, she was pretty hopeless. Thought a blow job meant she made her lips into a little circle and let you do the rest. What a dolt. But most of them had fucked their way from Abington Square to Avenue C and back again and could give you a ride worth remembering. And the ones who were playing at being lesbians! Jesus, what good times! Did you ever double up with Ruthie and Johanna? What a scene that was. Damn, just thinking about them gives me a hard-on."

We ordered another round of drinks. Between the sun and the booze and Roger's rambling, I was feeling the need for a nap. But he seemed to be just getting started. I thought about taking the poison in my pocket just so I wouldn't have to listen to him anymore.

"The problem is, there's not enough variety. After a while, one Cuban slut's the same as the next. I never thought I'd live to say it, but I'm getting pussy-bored."

"That's a drag."

"Oh, but I shouldn't be telling you all this. I should be telling you how great it is here and what a swell time you're gonna have. With the same old pussy day after day. Shit."

The waiter brought the drinks. Roger raised his glass in a toast.

"Well, the hell with it, I say. A short life and a merry one. Here's to you."

We drank. Or rather, he drank and I sipped.

Someone called out to Roger from across the Plaza.

"*Hola!* Roger!"

A man in uniform came toward the table.

"How fortuitous," said Roger. "This is the very fellow I was going to introduce you to when you came back after the harvest."

Roger stood up and I did likewise. The officer arrived at our table. He looked to be in his forties, short but very trim in a white uniform, with a bold black mustache that looked like it should have a rank of its own. "Colonel Enriques, what a delight. May I introduce the young man I was telling you about, Señor Jason Cardinale. Señor Cardinale, this is Colonel Francisco Enriques, Director of Military Education for the Cuban National Forces."

"Good to meet you," I said as I shook his hand. I was thinking that I should point out to Roger that my name was not Jason. That Jay was what my family called me instead of Joseph so as to distinguish me from all the other Josephs in the family and neighborhood. But why bother?

"My pleasure," he said.

"Won't you join us?" said Roger.

"Only for a moment. I must be to the Academy in a little time."

We all sat. The waiter was already at the table, having seen the colonel arrive, and Roger ordered him a Cuba Libre.

"No, no, my friend," said Enriques. "I am about business today." He changed the order to coffee.

"You enjoying Cuba, I hope?" said Enriques.

"I am today," I said. "It is very pleasant to have a day away from the cane fields."

"Yes, you are in the Venceremos Brigade. You are a great person to help the Cuban people in so many ways."

"It is a worthy cause, though my help is only a small thing to do."

I had instantly switched to the polite conversation I'd been taught to use when dealing with Vietnamese village leaders and other officials. I don't know that I ever much used it there, but as soon as the colonel got to the table it popped into my brain.

"You are too modest," said Roger. "The Brigade members have jeopardized their safety by coming here. The U.S. government may prosecute them, and the *gusanos* have threatened their lives."

I had heard about the threats in camp, a hot topic of discussion. The government stuff was real, as some congressmen had brought it up. The *gusano* stuff was, as far as I could tell, only a rumor. Lefties were always talking about attacks on different groups by these right-wing Cuban exiles, but I never met anyone who'd actually been attacked. It was always something they'd heard fourth-hand. Maybe it was true, that there had been attacks, but it wasn't anything I knew for sure.

"I will try to make it up to you," said Enriques. "You have certainly earned a better fate."

"If I can continue to be of service," I said, "it will be my pleasure."

His coffee came and we toasted.

"To the True Revolution," said Roger.

"*Salut!*" we said back.

"The true revolution," said Enriques, looking at me. "You understand?"

I had no idea, but I said yes.

"Thank you, my friend. Muy gracias. Your courage and dedication will not be forgotten when the great day of victory has arrived."

He stood and held out his hand. I stood and shook it.

"Duty calls. But we will meet again very soon."

Roger had stood and he shook hands with Enriques, as well. The colonel stepped back, came to attention and saluted us crisply, then did a parade ground turn and marched off.

"That was weird," I said.

"He's a bit of a strange duck. I think he had a head wound during the revolution."

"We didn't really talk about my job."

"Plenty of time for that. I wanted you two to meet first."

"You knew he was coming? I thought it was a surprise."

"Oh, I meant that he actually showed up. Not the most reliable chap."

It sounded like typical Roger bullshit. He just couldn't resist playing games. We finished our drinks.

"Well," said Roger, "what should we do next? Still have a day to kill."

"Let's get out of the sun. I'm getting dizzy."

"Want to go back to my place? You can stretch out on the couch and take a siesta."

"What about you?"

"I could use a snooze. We can nod off for a couple of hours then hit the streets when it's cooled down a bit. I'll give you the walking tour of Old Havana, show you the sights and we can still have time for another round of drinks before you have to get back on your bus."

It was an appealing scenario. But he was being so chummy, little alarm bells started going off in my brain. I didn't trust him to begin with, and this seemed just too cozy and convenient. What was he up to? Did he know somehow why I was there? Was he asking me back to his place so he could kill me? As evil as I thought he was, that still made no sense. He couldn't know. That was just my own guilty conscience talking. Because what I was thinking was that if we went back to his place, maybe I could kill *him*. Maybe we would have another drink or just some water, and then while he was asleep, I could slip the poison into his glass and when he woke up, thirsty with sleep, he would finish the glass that stood there on the table and I would be done with it.

At the very least, I would see his place, see what the layout was for later when, if I didn't kill him today, I'd be staying once the *zafra* was complete. If I didn't kill him today. If he didn't kill me today.

"A nap sounds good. And I'll get to see your place."

- Fifty-Five -

It was an exhausting half hour's walk to Roger's apartment. We passed through some shabby neighborhoods that looked even worse than they were in comparison to the well-preserved part of Old Havana that was kept up for the tourist trade. In some areas, the streets were completely torn apart, with houses leveled, while other streets were a varying combination of dead and alive.

"It reminds me of Bed-Stuy," I said.

"They're in the middle of reconstructing the barrios. A lot got done right after the revolution, but the work's been on again, off again since then, depending on how much money is available."

"Sounds like New York."

"As I said, every place is different except it's the same."

Despite the rundown housing and broken streets, there was a vitality to the place. Houses may have been dead, but the people were alive, coming and going with purposeful energy, even joy. That, too, reminded me of Bed-Stuy and the Spanish parts of South Brooklyn, and even some of the rougher parts of Bensonhurst where I'd grown up. In one vacant lot, there were little kids playing baseball just as I had done before I got onto the school teams.

But there was something odd, too. People stared at us. That wasn't unusual; we clearly were not from the neighborhood. But on every block, there was someone who eyed us the whole time we were on their street. One old lady, leaning out her window and smoking a cigar, her skin like leather, especially gave me the creeps the way she glared as we went by. It was the same look the waiters had given us at the Plaza the first time we went there, with an expectation in it that we were going to do something wrong.

Roger's building was as depressing as Walter had said, and his apartment smaller even than Walter's description had led me to believe, so small that Roger would already have to be dead not to notice that I was trying to kill him.

"Make yourself at home," said Roger. "I'm going to take a leak."

I thought about making a run for it before he returned.

"You look upset," he said as he came out of the bathroom. "Envisioning your own life in a place like this?"

"I guess."

"Welcome to the Seventh Ring of Hell. Eternal punishment for those who commit violence against others."

"Eternal? You must have a good lease."

He laughed his big laugh.

"You are good. I knew it. I always knew it."

"Seriously. Do you ever get to move? Is there a waiting list for bigger places? Is it like in New York? Can you slip a super some key money to move to the top of the list?"

"I've been told I'm lucky to have this."

"I'm sorry, man. I don't mean to put your place down."

"Believe me, there's nothing you can say that I haven't said myself. You can stretch out on the couch if you still want a nap."

I didn't want to stay there another second. Was there any chance I could kill him if we did take our naps? I didn't see how I could give him the poison. It would have to be something else. I'd have to hit him in the head or smother him in his sleep. And I'd have to do it without making any noise since you could hear every sound that was made throughout the building. Then again, the sound of two men fighting might have blended in with the rest of the racket that was the life of the building. And if I smothered him in his sleep, maybe there would be no sound at all.

"Sure," I said. "You going to sleep?"

"You bet. Siesta time for me. Then we can get up in a couple of hours and see what the afternoon still holds."

He went into the bedroom. As I began to stretch out on his sofa, he stepped back into the living room carrying a pillow. He stood there holding it in two hands, just the way I envisioned holding it before I shoved it down on his face, then he tossed to me.

"Of course, if there was something you had in mind, something you were planning to do …?"

"No. I'm completely open. Let's play it by ear."

"All right then. So long as you have time to kill …"

He smiled like a crocodile and went back into the bedroom, leaving the door open. I lay back on the sofa wondering again if he was a mind reader. Through the door, I could see him as he sat on the bed and pulled off his boots then stretched himself out, lying on his back. He had a clock next to the bed, and I could hear it ticking over the collection of voices that carried through the building and up from the street.

I felt wiped out physically and my brain was a foggy mess, but exhausted as I was, there was no way I could fall asleep. This was the moment I'd fantasized, or one of them. Roger was there, presumably asleep, and all I needed to do was take the pillow he had so generously given me, tiptoe into his room, and put an end to his miserable life and get my own back. Wait five minutes, I thought, give him time to fall into a deep sleep, then do it.

I began to count the seconds but kept losing track of where I was as other thoughts pressed in. Was he really asleep? Was this some kind of set-up? He'd made so many cracks that made it seem as if he knew what I was up to, how could he not be waiting for it, ready to turn the tables on me?

Every thought I was having, I'd had a dozen times before. He knows, it's a trick, he's ready, smother him, hit him in the head, stab him with a knife, strangle him, I'll have to fight him, maybe I can still use the poison when he wakes up—there was not a single new thought except one. Could I really do it? Up to that moment, it had always been how and when. Not since up on top of Mount Tzuhalem, when I had decided not to do it, not since the moment the seersuckers had jumped me in the commune vines and threatened my friends and family if I didn't, not since then had I thought about whether I'd actually go through with it when the moment came.

I couldn't do it. I couldn't go in there and kill him. It was the sad, simple truth of it. It didn't matter how many people I'd killed before. It didn't matter that I'd never see my father again. It didn't matter what the seersuckers said. I couldn't kill Roger, not in cold blood, no matter what the consequences.

And as I assured myself that was so, I sat up on the sofa and swung my feet to the floor and gripped the pillow in two hands, just as he had done before he tossed it to me. Without a sound, I was on my feet, holding the pillow waist high, pressed up against my body, ready to swing it into action, treading heel to toe, looking for a safe spot to put my foot down, like I was back in the jungle looking for trip wires, sneaking forward toward the bedroom door, sneaking forward to attack, wary of an ambush.

With each step, I told myself I wasn't really going to do it. I was only going to take another step, I was only going to peek into the bedroom, I was only going to stand there and look at him and imagine what it would be like to do it if I was going to do it. Which I wasn't. Which I couldn't.

It was a weird combination of my first patrol and my last, telling myself I really wasn't in Vietnam, telling myself, "This is not really happening," while at the same time thinking, It's an ambush, get ready, any second now, look for the signs …

I stopped in the doorway, looking for the signs, wondering how I could be sure he was sleeping, part of me tensing for the fight, part of me thinking this couldn't be real. I took a step into the bedroom and was at the foot of the bed thinking, Now, do it now.

I nearly jumped out of my skin when he spoke.

"Is it time?" he said softly.

"Time for what?" was all I could think to say, barely able to get the words out of my throat.

"Time to rise and shine."

"No," I said. "Not yet."

"Right. I didn't think it was time yet."

My brain, frozen for a moment, began to function. "I was looking for another pillow."

"Of course you were. That lumpy old thing's not good for anything. But I'm afraid that's all I've got. Sorry if it won't do."

"It'll have to."

I could still jump, I could still get on top of him, have the lumpy, inadequate pillow over his face before he could react.

But I didn't. And then it was too late.

"You know," he said, "for a moment there I thought you were going to jump me."

"Jump you?"

"Yes. I thought maybe you'd gone homo after all those months in Canada."

"Nope. Still straight."

"Good for you. No offense, old man."

"None taken. Anyway, it's your loss I'm not queer. Might have been the best fuck you'd ever get in Cuba."

He laughed and for once it sounded sincere.

"I *will* miss you," he said.

"Am I going somewhere?"

"I mean eventually. One of us has got to get away. We're not both going to die on this goddamn island."

"I hope not. Anyway, I'm going back to sleep."

I retreated back to the couch and stretched out again, tucking the pillow under my head, which felt like it was spinning around on my shoulders. I didn't know if I had really been going to kill him or if I would have stopped. I had been cool and alert, with all my senses at their peak the way I had always been before a battle. For me, the rage, the blood lust, only came when the shooting started. When Roger spoke, I should have flown at him, with the pillow over his face or my hands around his throat and my mind and body both bent on nothing but murder. I would have been better off if he had had a gun and taken a shot at me instead of talking. I might have been best off if he had shot me and killed me and put me out of my misery.

I felt miserable. The moment had come and I had failed. I felt like I was every useless thing my father had ever called me. This time I'd let him down for good. I was close to tears and my head began to pound. There would be no pardon, he would die hating me.

What's more, I was sure I'd tipped my hand. Before, I could only think he was psychic with all his odd remarks, that I was reading into them because I felt guilty and exposed. Now, I thought, I really was exposed, standing in the doorway to the bedroom holding the pillow up with two hands. Whether he did or didn't suspect something before, he must suspect me now. And if he does, and he cuts me off, ends the job business, crashing with him, getting me settled in Cuba, how will I ever get another chance at him?

And even if I did, even if I was wrong and he didn't suspect anything, I had to suspect myself of not being able to go through with it. At the moment I needed to act, I had hesitated. In the war, with bullets zipping past, with mortars and grenades exploding, I had always moved forward. I had obeyed my training. The road to survival lay through the enemy, not away from him. With Roger, I realized, I believed I could survive without attacking, despite all the cowboy talk of "it's him or me." But how? How was I going to survive without getting rid of Roger?

- Fifty-Six -

I must have fallen asleep because the next thing I knew, Roger was standing over me holding a pillow in two hands, looking for all the world as if he was about to smother me. For a second I thought it must be a dream, but then he spoke and I knew it was real.

"If you want to sleep some more you can have my pillow," he said. "I'm awake now."

"No," I said, sitting up quickly. "I'm awake."

"Want some coffee? I brew it Cuban style."

"Yeah. That'd be great."

"I don't think I have any milk, though."

"That's okay. Black with sugar is what I like."

"Yes, so Walter told me."

"Huh?"

"Your enamorata, the woman in the camp. The one with the paperwork."

"Avis."

"Yes, the rara Avis."

"Walter told you she was black?"

"In passing. Not a big deal. Anyway, I hope I get to meet her when the Brigade comes through Havana on their tour post-*zafra*. Who knows? Maybe you'll have a job by then and your own place. We can have a housewarming. Bring you fondue pots or some Cuban equivalent."

I was astonished. I was sure after the pillow business he would want to get me out of his life. Instead he was bringing me fondue pots.

"My cousin Susan got a fondue pot when she got married."

It was a moment before it came to me that I'd said it out loud. I wondered what else I might have said out loud without being aware of it.

"I'm sure she must have been very pleased."

"We used it once. It was good."

"Terrific. We'll be sure then to invite the Swiss embassy staff to the party. By the way, we should go by there, the Swiss embassy, I mean. Good place to know if you ever have any trouble here."

"What kind of trouble?"

"The usual stuff. If you get caught screwing some official's wife, or someone decides you're a spy, or if you kill someone."

"Right. The usual."

"The Canadians are good for that, too. They might even think of you as one of their own. Did you ever apply for citizenship while you were there?"

"Thought about it, but no."

"It's a great country. I guess you saw a lot of it, traveling from Vancouver to St. John. You said you took the bus across, right?"

"Yeah. It was swell."

I was wishing I was back on that bus. Or on the bus back to camp. I was so miserable at being with him another minute, I was almost wishing I was back in Vietnam. Not quite, but almost.

The water boiled. He made the coffee and handed me a cup where I sat on the couch, and put his own cup down on the small table that stood in front of the couch. He didn't sit.

"Got to take a leak. Be right back."

The bathroom was next to the kitchenette. He went in and closed the door, leaving me suddenly alone with his coffee cup and the poison pills in my pocket. It was sort of an ambush in reverse, the enemy surprising you by turning around so you could stab him in the back. I was completely lost.

I could hear him peeing in the bathroom, a loud, healthy stream. It sounded like he was pouring a bottle of beer directly into the bowl. I stared at his cup. I had seconds to act. I reached into my pocket for the pills. It occurred to me that I should have had a dry run, practicing opening the vial quickly and quietly, pouring out the contents, and unsticking the poison pills from the bottom in as short a time as possible. Too late now.

I popped the lid off the vial and poured the harmless aspirins into my hand. There were a lot of them, more than I remembered from when Short One had poured them into my two hands when he first gave them to me. A couple spilled over onto the floor. I bent to reach them and a couple more spilled. Roger's stream came to an end. It was all I could do to pour the pills I still had back into the vial before he came out of the bathroom.

"What's that?" he said.

"Pain killers. The VA gave 'em to me. For the pain."

"That would make sense. Pain killers for pain. I didn't realize you were still hurting."

"On and off. Maybe the walk here stirred things up."

I picked up two of the pills I'd dropped and looked around for the others. He came over to the couch, bent down and picked up the others.

"Look just like aspirin."

"They do, don't they? But stronger."

"Glad to hear it. I forget. Where was it you were shot? In the leg?"

"In the side. And I wasn't shot. I was stabbed with a bayonet."

"Of course. Now I remember."

He handed me the pills and I slid them into the vial.

"You have a lot left."

"They gave me a lot and I haven't taken them for a while."

"Can I see the prescription?"

I hesitated. Could I really hand him the poison that was supposed to kill him? But I couldn't think of any reason to say no.

"The cane cutting must be difficult," he said as he examined the label. "I mean if walking here gave you a pain."

"Yeah, it does. But I got used to it. Anyway, it's worth it. Getting me out of Canada."

"Of course."

He turned the vial over. It was almost as if he were looking for the pills taped to the bottom. I didn't think he could see them through the colored plastic, but it gave me a chill. All the while his face was twisted with that wicked smile I hated so much. I thought for sure he knew there was poison in the vial and he was trying to decide if he should keep it or give it back to me. After a very long few seconds, he tossed the vial back to me.

"You must let me try one sometime. If I come to cut cane again, I mean."

 "You got it," I said as I slid the vial into my pocket.

"Can you take them and drink? Because I'm ready for another beer."

"I can drink. What about the coffee?"

"You can finish yours. I didn't really want it anyway."

I took a sip. He took his cup, went into the kitchenette, and poured it in the sink then washed the cup. There was something about how he did it, like he was putting on a show for me, that made my head ache. I had an urge to take him by the throat and strangle him until his smile came out his ears. It occurred to me that if I did that I might succeed, having failed in my first two feeble attempts to kill him, and going by the theory that the third time pays for all. But I was past acting. I didn't know if I was capable of killing him, but I knew that it wasn't going to happen that day.

- Fifty-Seven -

We walked back to Old Havana by a different route than the one we'd taken to his apartment. Roger never stopped talking the whole time. As we went along, I was again aware of the watchful eyes on every street.

"Why are people staring at us?"

"They're the neighborhood watchers. Keeping an eye out for counterrevolutionaries."

"Really?"

"Castro has lots of enemies."

"But why are they watching us?"

"Look like spies, I suppose."

He continued on with the guided tour of the landmarks of his new life, the store where he bought his vegetables, the store were he bought his meat, the best Cuban-Chinese restaurant in the neighborhood, a bar where the prettiest hookers were to be found. Although most of the travelogue was about him, he would occasionally point out some place where a significant event of the revolution had taken place.

I was only half listening, and maybe not even that much. Most of my attention was on what had happened, or not happened, in Roger's apartment. I think I was trying to convince myself that it wasn't that I couldn't go through with killing him, but instead that I didn't really have the chance. He was awake when I was going to smother him and he came out of the bathroom too quickly when I was going to put the poison in his coffee. And then again, he didn't even drink the coffee, so it would have been a waste of one of the pills. I was better off having missed the chance.

So I told myself as we walked along. But the thought would not go away that I simply didn't have it in me to go through with the whole deal. Was it just Roger? Was there something about him that put me off, that scared me and kept me from believing I could do it? Would it be impossible for me, no matter who I was supposed to kill? What about the whole plan? What about my dad and getting back to America and the pardon?

Did it really matter if my father died thinking I was a hero and not a deserter? He'd be just as dead either way. But it did matter. I couldn't say why. It just did.

I think it was the sound of Roger's voice that convinced me I wasn't done yet. It was so annoyingly self-confident, so clearly full of shit no matter what he was saying, and so unconcerned that this was apparent to anyone with half a brain. I would kill him just to shut him up, just to reduce the asshole population by one. I knew I had thought that before and failed, but it didn't mean I couldn't try again. I thought of the Vietnamese who never stopped fighting because they hadn't won yet. A thousand years they'd been fighting to get other people out of their country, the Chinese, the French, and now us. I thought of Fidel, busted in 1953 and coming back against all odds to drive Batista out. All I had to do was put a pill in a glass of water.

Maybe I could still do it that day. We were headed for a bar. Maybe there would be another chance. I interrupted the travelogue just as he was describing where he had his laundry done.

"Where are we going?"

"Thirsty, old man?"

"Yeah. And hot and tired, too."

"I have just the place for us. El Floridita. You know, the place where Hemingway hung out."

"No, I don't know."

"You do know who Hemingway is, right?"

"Yeah, of course."

"And you know he lived here."

"What do you mean? In this neighborhood?"

He laughed, a sort of combination real and too-jolly-to-be-real pretentious laugh that I hadn't heard before.

"No, he had a house outside Havana. We should go there sometime. It's a national shrine."

"But you're saying he lived in Cuba?"

"Yes. Famously so. For about twenty years, I think."

"He's dead now, right?"

"Yes. Blew his brains out."

"Yeah, I remember. I learned that somewhere. Shotgun."

"Right."

"Was that here?"

"Back home in Idaho, I believe."

"Why did he do that?"

"He knew he'd lost it as a writer and couldn't live with the fact."

"Wow. That's tough."

"You might say so."

"I read one of his books. In school. *The Old Man and the Sea*."

"Yes. That's the one set here in Cuba."

"No kidding? I don't really remember it much. I think I thought it was boring."

"It is sort of a book for older readers, not schoolchildren."

"The old man hooks a fish and it's too big for his boat, right?"

"Something like that."

"But he's stubborn and won't let it go."

"Right."

"Yeah. Not a book for kids. Although I knew some fishermen over in Sheepshead Bay who would've done the same thing. So I guess it made sense."

"Did your teacher make that connection? I mean, to real-life people the students would have known?"

"I don't think so. It would have been more interesting if she had. But, no, she just stuck to the book."

"Too bad."

"So, we're going to a place he hung out?"

"Yeah. There's even a statue of him there."

"You're kidding. Sounds touristy."

"It is. Very touristy. Which means there'll be white women there."

"White women?"

"Women who aren't Cuban."

"Oh."

"Canadians, Europeans, Russians. Lots of blondes. Real blondes, I mean."

"You like blondes?"

"Not especially. But as I said, what I do like is variety. And blondes—"

"Real blondes."

"Exactly. Real blondes are a distinct minority."

"Have you been to this place before?"

"Yes, but, I'm somewhat embarrassed to say, without any luck."

"I'm shocked."

"Yes, it is surprising. The problem seems to be that these women travel in pairs, if not trios and quartets. One man can't approach them without getting shot down. But two men, well, that seems to make everything all right."

"Ah."

"Exactly. A handsome young American who's both a hero and a deserter, and in the Venceremos Brigade. My god, I'll be lucky if they pay any attention to me at all."

"But I'm not in the market."

"I'm not asking you to marry one of them. Just chat them up while I circle in for the kill."

"I don't know …"

"Listen, my friend, I've seen you work. You're a ladies' man if ever I saw one."

"That was different."

"No, that was the same. These women coming to Cuba for a holiday are just a slightly older version of the teeny-bopper radicals back at Chez McWilliams. They will eat you with a spoon. Please, I'm so horny I'm going to bust if I don't have some decent pussy soon. Be a sport. All you have to do is help me cut one out of the herd and then you can be off to your bus and back to your beloved rara Avis."

"Aw, jeez."

"There you go, old boy. That's the spirit!"

I couldn't believe this was what the day had turned into. From near murder to picking up girls together. I'd come to believe that Roger was on to me, that somehow he knew what I was there for. Now it seemed as if everything I had taken as sinister was innocent, he didn't suspect a thing, and all those double entendres about "time to kill" and "jumping him" were just throwaway remarks because what he was really thinking about the whole time was steering me into this little adventure at the bar. I can't say that it made me want to kill him more, but it didn't make me want to kill him any less. I thought back to that last conversation in New York, about wanting to work together. Is this what he'd had in mind?

- Fifty-Eight -

As expected, El Floridita on a late Sunday afternoon was filled with tourists. The place was neat, with pictures of celebrities all over the walls, but the thing that was the focus of attention was the life-size statue of Hemingway there at the end of the bar. I'd have to say it was one of the weirdest things I've ever seen in my life. Was this supposed to make people think they were not only in the bar where he hung out, but were actually there with him?

We were barely in the door when Roger zeroed in on a pair of good-looking blondes at the far end of the bar. The girls, Tish and Barb, were Canadian, from around Winnipeg, in their twenties, drawn to Cuba by the heroic image of Che and the relatively low cost of the vacation package deal they'd gotten from a local travel bureau. Their tour had brought them, their long legs, short skirts, and light blouses, to the bar.

Roger introduced us as a pair of American exiles on the run from the law, said that I had come to cut cane with the Venceremos Brigade, and, like them, had come down from Canada. He made us sound like Butch Cassidy and the Sundance Kid and it worked like a charm. We bought them drinks, which I paid for.

The girls were drinking beer.

"We can drink beer till the cows come home, if you know what I mean," said Barb, the taller of the two. She told us she was a nurse, an emergency room RN.

"You mean you won't get drunk on beer," I said.

"Give the man a cigar!"

Roger went at them full speed ahead, giving them the deluxe Roger treatment, a barrage of politics, philosophy, and cultural commentary. I hardly said a word. Mostly, I stared at the Hemingway statue. Tish, who told us she worked at a day care center, was eying it, too.

"It is a bit queer, though, don't you think?" she said. "I mean, what are you supposed to think? That he's still alive and sitting there?"

"That's the idea," I said.

"Well, I don't care who knows it," she said, "but it gives me the willies. Why is it there at the bar? Why couldn't they put it outside like a proper statue? Or just put a plaque up on the wall? You know, 'Hemingway drank here' and the dates and all. I mean, they have all those pictures up of him already so why not just a plaque?"

"I think that after a couple of double daiquiris, you forget it's a statue," I said. "And after a couple more, you start talking to it, and after another few, you think it's answering. Then when you get back home you can tell everyone you hung out with Hemingway. And you're so convinced of it yourself, they believe you."

"But what if someone points out that he's been dead for ten years?" said Barb.

"You tell them that's just a rumor."

"I still think it's extremely queer," said Tish.

"It's just capitalism," said Roger. "The bar owner feels cheated because Hemingway's dead. I mean, he was only about sixty when he shot himself. If he was still alive, he'd only be about seventy, so he could still be sitting there, drinking his Papa Doble, telling his tales, bringing in busloads of thirsty tourists. Since he's not, they put in the statue."

"Well, you have to give them credit," said Barb. "It certainly is working."

"They should add a statue of Che Guevara," said Tish. "Double their business."

"Add one of Fidel and triple the business," said Roger.

"But he's not dead," said Barb.

"Not yet," said Roger, smiling his wickedest smile. "But you never know. Might as well have it ready. Another round?"

We kept drinking and talking. The girls wanted to know about the Brigade, so I got to talk for a while. They were impressed, and out of their sight, Roger was giving me an appreciative nod, letting me know I was doing a good job of reeling them in. I had mixed feelings about it. It definitely felt good to have the attention of these two pretty girls, to be flirting, engaged in the kind of game where I was at my best. Even though I was talking about the Brigade, it was the romance of it, not the politics.

And the girls were flirting back, into the game as much as I was. But nagging at me was the whole rest of the afternoon with Roger, the presence of murder in my mind, and his presence reminding me of why I was really there in Cuba—not to cut cane and not to be standing in this tourist bar trying to get laid.

On top of that, it was getting close to my bus time. Despite thinking that the cane was not why I had come to Cuba, I felt an urgency not to miss the bus that would take me back to the camp. In part, it was a sense of guilt toward Avis, since I was supposed to be in love with her and here I was putting the make on the Canadians. But it wasn't just that. As I described the camp and the work of cutting and the politics of the Brigade to Tish and Barb, I realized how much it had, for however long it might last, become my responsibility, had become, in fact, my life.

Still, as I talked I kept thinking about how I could work this out so I could get laid and still get back to the camp for the next day's cutting. Standing at the bar, smiling and laughing and trying to be clever, my mind was boiling with the battle taking place between my heart and my head on the one side, and my dick on the other. I felt like I was in one of those cartoons where the guy has a devil on one shoulder and an angel on the other, each whispering into his ear, telling him what he should do. In my case, the angel was Avis and the devil, of course, was Roger.

The devil had his allies in the Canadian blondes. They were both very pretty, their conversation was clever, and they talked about their work with sarcasm, but in a way that made it clear they cared deeply about what they did.

I could feel my dick taking control, a dick feeling so strong it was overriding my hatred for Roger, turning him from enemy to comrade. Some dumb sense of male loyalty had kicked in for no better reason than that we were two guys standing at a bar talking to two pretty girls, making it my concern that he get laid. More purposefully, I wanted to keep him happy and confident in me for the next time we were together, which is when I was now planning to kill him, one way or another, whatever way was possible and whether he saw it coming or not.

So I was able to reason that the action at the bar was, in fact, part of my job, the one I had come to do. Once again, Roger seemed to be reading my mind, because as soon as I had convinced myself that staying there was the right thing to do, he jumped into the conversation. It was as if he had kept himself quiet until I had managed to work out the decision he wanted from me, as if he understood that if he had spoken, the sound of his voice would have sent me to the other side.

"My God, Jay, I just remembered, you have to catch the bus back to camp."

"Damn," I said. "I'm having such a good time I didn't even think about how late it was getting."

"Oh, no," said Tish. "You don't really have to go, do you?"

"I hate to do it, but it's a very long walk if I don't get my ride."

"What an idiot I am," said Roger. "I'll drive you there."

"You have a car?" said Barb.

- Fifty-Nine -

Roger's car was stowed in a garage not far from his apartment. The plan was, we would walk there, stopping along the way for more drinks and dinner, then drive out to the beach for a late-night swim. The girls were excited at the chance to experience the "real" Cuba, as Roger put it. Before we left El Floridita, Roger convinced the girls that they had to at least try a Papa Doble, the double daiquiri that Hemingway invented there. The bartender looked relieved that we had finally gotten them off beer. We toasted Hemingway and then, on our way out the door, we stopped to pose with his statue, snapping each other's pictures with Barb's little Kodak and having one of the waiters take a picture of the four of us together.

Roger launched into guided-tour mode as soon as we hit the street. He gave the girls a slightly more entertaining version of the spiel I'd heard. I was only half listening, feeling a little loopy from all the alcohol, which was much more than I'd had since the night in the Singing Brakeman with John Lydon. I had told the girls about my bus ride, but hadn't mentioned John by name, just that I had had drinks with an old cowboy. Also, I was a little preoccupied looking for the neighborhood watchers.

As we walked, I reflected on the fact that I had not wanted to use Lydon's name in front of Roger. Despite all our cozy camaraderie at the bar, I didn't trust Roger with any information that he could somehow use to hurt anyone I knew. I was sorry, in fact, that he knew as much as he did about Avis, and hoped there wasn't more Walter had told him that Roger had not fed back to me.

Despite little cautions like not mentioning John's name, I felt my plan to lock in Roger's trust was going well. I was charming with the girls, contributing my share of laughs to the afternoon, but deferred to him as the older, wiser, more knowledgeable Cuban hand. It was hard to say, seeing as how it was Roger and he was always putting on an act, but I thought I felt some kind of genuine appreciation coming back from him. As he had said earlier in the day, the thing he was serious about was pussy, and I was giving my all to support his habit.

After about twenty minutes of walking through the evening chill, the girls were ready for another drink and a chance to use a ladies' room. We stopped at a bar that Roger knew and where he was known, which impressed the girls. Roger wanted to order more daiquiris, but the girls insisted on beer if we expected them to walk any more.

Another twenty minutes on the street put us close to Roger's place. We were all hungry, and Roger suggested we eat at the Cuban-Chinese restaurant he'd pointed out to me earlier. It was a cuisine they didn't have yet in Winnipeg, and the girls were excited to try something new. Roger gave them the lowdown on how it had evolved and what a big thing it was in New York.

While he talked, I was remembering my favorite places, like Asia de Cuba, and the people I went there with and what life was like back then, which, after all, was only a couple of years earlier. Maybe it was the booze, maybe it was the walk through dark city streets, maybe it was the flirting, maybe it was all of them together, but I suddenly felt in a way that I had not until that moment, that the past was past and how it could never be the same again. It wasn't just that we were all different, but that *I* was different. The whole world had moved on, and wherever I was going to come out from this thing with Roger, I was going to be in a world that didn't exist yet.

"Is that your favorite, Jay?"

Tish was talking to me.

"My favorite?"

"Your favorite Cuban-Chinese dish."

I was eating sautéed Chinese vegetables with—what else?—rabbit.

"Sort of, except usually it's chicken not rabbit."

"The rabbit is good."

"You've had it before?"

"Of course."

"Right, of course."

"You looked like you were lost in space there."

"Sorry. It's just been a rough couple of years, and eating Chinese again made me, I don't know …"

"A little nostalgic?" she said.

"Yeah, I guess that's the word for it," I said, even though it wasn't nostalgia at all. The nostalgia had disappeared in the seconds before she spoke. I was looking forward now, not back.

- Sixty -

We finished dinner and had coffee. Tish and Barb were properly impressed by the food, and with a couple more beers in us, everyone was feeling good. While we ate, Roger had focused his attentions on Barb, and Tish had shown her preference for me, so things were shaping up for the rest of the night.

    I wondered if Roger had a plan, like him taking Barb to his place and leaving me with Tish in their hotel room. I supposed it was even possible that the girls each had their own room, but I would have bet on them sharing. Maybe Roger was thinking of us all together in his place, him in the bedroom and me in the living room, or at the hotel with two double beds in the one shared room. Maybe he hadn't thought about it at all or had some other vision beyond my ability to imagine.

    I was hoping there would be a way to work two separate spaces. I liked privacy when I was having sex. I took no pleasure from having a conversation with another guy who was fucking another girl across the room, or in the next bed, or in the same bed. Most of the women I'd been with, the sex was the culmination of a courtship and it happened somewhere that the girl and I were alone together. But there had been some nights in high school and college when, after a party, after drinking bottle after one-dollar bottle of Yago Sangria and smoking dope for hours, I'd wind up in a place with a girl where there was another couple or two or three and we were all fucking. It wasn't ugly, exactly, but it wasn't my romantic ideal and it wasn't what I wanted with Roger and the

Canadians.

I paid the bill and we headed out to the garage for Roger's car. There was a little market open next to the garage, and Roger sent me in to buy a bottle of rum and some Cokes and some towels if they had any. He had the car out of the garage and waiting at the curb when I came out of the store. Roger's car, a big heavy Russian Moskvich, was as Walter had described it, like a giant version of a child's toy car. Barb was in front with him and Tish was waiting for me in the big back seat.

There were a few big clouds scattered overhead, but otherwise the night was clear and the moon was near full. We had gotten past the first chill that came when the sun went down and could ride with the windows open. But it was still cool enough to give Tish a reason to cuddle up against me. Up front, Roger was actually letting Barb speak, interrupting her twisted tales from the emergency room to make a wisecrack or ask a question. The devil, I thought. He's reeling her in like a pro, although there was no question but that she was going willingly.

I had my arm around Tish and she had her head against my chest and her hand on my thigh. One of Barb's stories made us laugh out loud and we looked at each other as people do when they're close together and laughing together and we kissed. The first kiss was a sweet kiss and the second was serious. I squeezed her shoulder and she pressed her hand down on my thigh and after a few seconds we relaxed away from each other.

"Almost there," said Roger.

Tish laughed, almost a giggle. "He read my mind."

"He does that a lot," I said. "Be careful what you think."

We emerged from an overhang of palm trees and there was the beach stretched out alongside the road. It was Barucano, the same beach where the Brigade had gone. For a moment, I envisioned the buses still being there and coming upon my comrades circled 'round a bonfire roasting marshmallows and singing camp songs. Avis would be there, and all the Weathermen, and Walter. Not only them, but Miss More and Short One and Tall One and even Wildflower and Ori. It would be like an all-star California beach movie. And I would show up at the bonfire with Tish, the new girl in town, and sparks would fly. I was amazed that I could think something like that and put it down to the amount I'd had to drink and the impact Tish was having on my hormones.

Roger parked the car and we went out onto the sand. The tide was going out and the beach was wide and the moon was large and low out over the horizon. There was no one else in sight. As soon as my feet were in the sand I knew I was making a mistake. My movie fantasy dissolved, and all that was left was the presence of Avis in my mind. Maybe if we had gone to a different beach, I might not have felt the way I did, but we hadn't and here I was where I had walked with her and swum with her, and where our hands had touched beneath the waves.

I knew that Tish could tell something had come over me. It was too much to hide. It wasn't the first time in my life that I'd been with one woman while thinking of another. I'd been on the other side of it, too, with a girl who wished in her heart I was someone else. Either way it wasn't anything good. But it was one of those things you could live with, even take some pleasure from, unless you were desperately in love with the person whose mind was on another. Then it was torture. Self-inflicted, but still a knife in the heart.

Tish was not about to stab herself out of love for me and seemed ready to get as much pleasure as she could out of the situation. We walked slowly, falling well behind as Roger and Barb ran down to the water's edge.

"Nice moon," she said.

"Beautiful."

"Are you coming back to Canada? I mean, after you finish cutting sugarcane?"

"I'm not sure. Roger says I should stay in Cuba."

"Is she here? The girl you're thinking about."

"What makes you think—?"

"I work with children all day long. I can't afford to miss sudden mood changes."

"Right now she is. But she goes back to the States with the Brigade."

"And you can't."

"Probably not."

In the moonlight, we could see Roger and Barb down by the water and hear their laughter. They peeled off their clothes and raced into the water, diving under a wave, then back out and then in again.

"They're being awfully bold," said Tish.

"The water's pretty warm."

"You've been in?"

"A couple of weeks ago."

"Do you want to go in?"

"I don't think so. It's still going to be cold coming out."

I really wouldn't have minded a swim, but I was feeling that the ocean belonged to me and Avis and I couldn't share it with another. But I also didn't feel it was right to keep Tish out if she wanted to swim.

"Did you want to go in?" I said.

"I'm not much of a swimmer. But I wouldn't mind getting my feet wet. I don't get to the ocean too often."

As we went toward the water, Barb came splashing out roaring with laughter and raced off down the beach with Roger close behind her. We came to where Roger and Barb had left their clothes and the bag with the drinks and the towels. The bottle of rum was out of the bag and we could see that it had been opened. I picked it up and offered it to Tish, who took it and drank then handed it back to me. I drank, too.

We dropped our shoes and waded into the surf. It was colder than I had remembered from my last time in.

"I'm awfully sorry about your girl," said Tish. "I know what it's like."

"You have someone?"

"That's the problem. I don't have him. It's one of the fathers. He came to pick up his little girl one day and we hit it off. A little too well, I'm afraid. It was a stupid thing to do."

"I'm sorry."

There were more clouds, and the moonlight that had been steady came and went.

Tish said, "I want another drink."

We went back to the clothes and the bottles and sat down close to each other on the sand and passed the bottle between us.

"Are you thinking about her?"

"No," I said, "I was thinking about you."

Down the beach we could hear Roger and Barb. Their laughter had changed to something more like roars and grunts and it was pretty clear they were screwing. Tish leaned toward me and kissed me.

"Please, fuck me. I need you to fuck me."

She kissed me again and started to unbutton my shirt. Early on in the evening, when my dick was running the show, I'd been looking forward to just such a moment. I felt a twitch, but most of my desire for sex had disappeared when the spirit of Avis rolled in on the waves. And worse yet, looking out over the water, I thought back to all the times out fishing with my father, and from there to thoughts of his lying in bed refusing to get on the phone with me. It would be hard to feel less romantic.

Tish kept kissing me and pulling at my clothes, saying, "Come on, come on." I hoped if I did it, too, kept kissing and got her naked, then everything would be fine. But I knew it wouldn't. I'd been in this place a couple of times before, with a woman who wanted me when I didn't want her. Most often, of course, it had been the other way around, but I did know what it was like to try to please someone when my heart wasn't in it.

We got naked and Tish did what she could and I tried to help, but it just wasn't going to happen. After a few minutes, we stopped and lay back together in the sand.

"I'm sorry," I said.

"No, I'm sorry. It was foolish of me to insist. I don't think either one of us really wanted it. I was thinking about that husband, thinking 'I'll show him, I'll show that bastard.' That's not a very romantic place to start from. Now I'm glad we didn't do it."

She leaned over and kissed me, very sweetly on the mouth. We were relaxed now, and it was better than anything that had come before. For a moment, I thought she was going to start in again, and I thought if she did, this time it would work between us. But she took her mouth away.

"Although if you do come back to Canada," she said, still leaning over me, "I'd certainly like to try again."

In the dark we could hear Roger and Barb coming toward us. We sat up and started to sort through our clothes, but were still naked when they arrived. The sky was more cloud than clear by then, but some of the moonlight still broke through.

"Well, you naughty lovebirds, what has been happening here?" said Roger as he plopped down on his knees next to us. He was wet and so was Barb. They must have just been in the ocean.

"Where's the rum?" said Barb. "I'm freezing."

She dug around through the clothes and found the bottle and took a big drink, then handed it to Roger.

"Just a short one for me. I have to drive, you know."

PART VI *Havana* 227

"We should go soon," I said. "Beat the rain."

"Right," said Roger. "We don't want to get wet."

Barb laughed.

We were all dressed in a minute or two, exchanging items and the bottle until everyone had their own clothes and a good buzz. The girls lagged behind for a bit as we headed to the car.

"Go on," said Barb. "We've got some business before we get in the car."

"Women," said Roger as we put some distance between ourselves and the girls, then, like them, stopped to pee along the side of the path. "Still, I can't complain."

We got to the car and he started the engine to let the car heat up before we took off. We had a cigarette while we waited.

"Still want to go back to the camp?" he said, talking over his shoulder to me in the back seat.

"I don't want to, I have to."

"Too bad. Barb is coming home with me, so Tish will have the hotel room to herself."

"I have to go to the camp."

"Of course, Tish could spend the night with me and Barb."

"Fuck you, asshole."

"Just kidding. I'm sure she's had enough for one night."

The girls had come and were getting in the car, Barb in front again, Tish with me.

"Everyone comfy?" said Roger. He started to drive without waiting for an answer.

"Is there any rum left?" said Barb.

I handed her the bottle.

"How does the pirate song go? Yo-ho-ho?"

"Yo-ho-ho and a bottle of rum, sixteen men on a dead man's chest," sang Roger.

Barb joined him and they sang together, trying to make up more lyrics beyond the opening line. Tish and I spoke softly together in the back seat.

"You okay?" I said.

"Of course."

"I'll miss you," she said.

Cuddling up tight to me, she whispered very close and quiet in my ear, "I will miss you, but otherwise I'm so very glad to have the room to myself. I can wait until tomorrow to get her detailed description."

PART VII
Campamento Brigada Venceremos

- Sixty-One -

It was raining when we reached the camp. Tish and I had been saying our goodbyes the whole way there. I hadn't told her the truth about why I was in Cuba, but I wasn't lying when I said that if I wound up coming back to Canada, I was coming to her. I took her address and promised to write and let her know my plans. She wanted to write me, but I said I didn't know yet where I'd be that I could receive any mail.

I had told her more about John Lydon and that I had a notion I could give him a hand on his ranch. She thought that would be great and wondered if he could use two hands, or if there were enough people around Red Deer to support a day care. It was happy fantasies like that all the way to the gate.

Roger stopped the car so we could all get out and have proper hugs. There was a guard on duty at the camp gate, and I waved to him to let him see that it was me and everything was okay. Then I saw the bicycle next to the guard station. It was Juan who was on duty that night. I don't know what he thought at first when he saw the two blondes get out of the car. Maybe it was another Bay of Pigs, only with Sweden leading the invasion. But looking over Tish's shoulder as I gave her a final hug, I could see the nasty grin that twisted his face. The "New Man" was about to become the "New Gossip."

Just before he got back behind the wheel, Roger said, "Thanks, man. You stood up like a champ. Can't wait till we're roommates proper."

I waved as the car drove off, and then turned and slogged on through the mud, past Juan and into the camp.

"*Buenos noches,*" I said to him as I went by, as cheery and innocent and wide-open, nothing-to-hide as I could be.

The best news as I reached my tent was that Walter was asleep and I wouldn't have to give him a rundown of the night until the morning. All I wanted now was a few hours' sleep before the wake-up cry of "De pie!" that would start us on the big final two-week push to the end of the harvest.

- Sixty-Two -

Walter was all over me that morning as we grabbed our quick breakfast and walked out to the field. He even rearranged the team assignments so we could work together and keep talking. I gave him a step-by-step account, leaving out, of course, my fumbled attempts to kill Roger.

I also fudged the details of what happened on the beach with Tish, making it sound like she wasn't interested in having sex with me, so we had just waited, talking about Canada, until Roger and Barb reappeared. I was hoping that Walter's gossiping would offset whatever tale Juan might spin out based on the goodbye hugs and kisses he'd observed at the gate.

Walter interrupted constantly, asking a million questions. He was most surprised when I told him about Roger's put-down of the crowd at Eddie's.

"That son of a bitch," said Walter. "He was egging everyone on and he didn't really mean it. You don't think he was just putting you on, do you? Playing one of his games?"

"I think he meant every word of it. He's just a scummy bastard. Clever as shit, but just a fucking devil."

"He *is* the fucking devil. I'm so glad he hates it here. He really does, doesn't he?"

"No doubt about it."

"Good. I hope he has to stay here for the rest of his life and he hates every miserable second of it and he never gets laid again."

"I hope so, too."

"But you still think you're going to stay here?"

"I'll give it a try. If I don't like it, then I'll head back to Canada or see if I can get to Europe somehow."

"I hope you do that. Really, I think you'll be better off. You know, there'll be an amnesty someday. I mean, once the war is over. You'll be able to come home then. It'll be easier if you've been in Canada and not Cuba."

"Yep."

"And it'll be easier to keep in touch with people from Canada. And I can come up and see you. Hell, you never know. After we get back to the States, a lot of us might have to move up to Canada."

"All true."

I didn't want to shoot down his happy-making fantasy. I hadn't told Walter about my father, so he had no idea about the urgency of my need to get back into the U.S. I wasn't about to tell him now.

I'd never been happier in the cane field than I was that morning. We worked hard and it felt clean and honest after the long hours with Roger and my own dirty work, even if I hadn't gone all the way with it. I thought about Tish, too, and that made me feel good. I hoped I would see her again, and I hoped she would find someone who could love her with all the love she deserved.

I thought about my own love on and off throughout the day, although I didn't see Avis until dinner. I caught her eye across the dining hall where she was sitting with the other camp leaders. She gave me a look that I suppose could be called ironic, as if she were saying, "What have you been up to, my bad little boy?"

We finally got to speak after dinner and I found out the look had not been ironic at all. She was just pissed at me. I was sitting on a bench outside the meeting hall, pretending to read *The Teachings of Don Juan* while waiting for her to go by. When she did finally show up, she kept walking, even though I knew she had seen me. I hurried after her.

"Hi. You got a minute?" I said.

"I'm in kind of a hurry."

"Come on. Please. Just a minute."

"I don't have a minute. I'm late."

She kept walking. I stayed with her.
"I didn't do anything."
"I'm sure."
"You don't understand."
"And I don't care to."
"You're not being fair."
"I don't need to be fair. There's nothing to be fair about."
"Yes, there is."
She stopped walking.
"I don't want to make a scene. Please go away."
"I have to kill Roger."
I don't know why I said it. I never meant to share my mission with anyone. But it just blurted out by itself.
"You probably should. Now go away."
"No, really, I have to kill him. That's why I'm in Cuba. That's why I'm here."
"You're here to cut cane. Just do that and I don't care about anything else. Okay?"
"I was hired to kill him."
"You're being ridiculous."
"How do you think I got in the Brigade?"
"I know how you got in the Brigade. Some bleeding heart paid off the committee."
"Right. But why?"
"Because he's a fucking bleeding heart."
"No. Because they had to get me here so I could kill Roger."
"They. They who? The CIA?"
"No, this rich couple. But the guys working for them could be CIA. They're really creepy—"
"The CIA. Come on …"
"Look, I don't know. They could be FBI. That's not the point."
"You know, you could just apologize. You could just say, 'I picked up some blonde bimbo and fucked her and I'm sorry.' You don't need the fucking CIA."
"She's not a bimbo and I didn't fuck her and I'm here to kill Roger so I can get a pardon and go home to see my father before he dies."
"Don't give me the father business. It's pathetic to use him as an ex-

cuse. You should be ashamed of yourself."

She turned away.

"I love you."

"Oh, for Jesus' sake. Will you just go away?"

She walked away as fast as she could. I didn't follow her.

- Sixty-Three -

From that point on until we were done cutting, I was more or less a zombie. I woke and cut and slept and cut some more. I don't remember eating, and I don't remember much of anything else except Avis avoiding me and Walter trying to console me.

"She'll get over it. Just give her time," he said.

"I don't have time to give. Once we're done here, I'll never see her again."

"You don't know that."

"Yes, I do."

An occasional fantasy would break through the gloom. I would get my pardon and go back to the States and knock on Avis's door in Milwaukee and she would greet me with open arms. I didn't have to explain anything to her. Somehow she knew I'd told her the truth and that I had killed Roger and that it was a good thing to do and she welcomed me like a hero. It was kind of Hollywood, the tears, the hugs, and all of that.

I tried to battle the sense of time dragging by, giving myself over to the work. It helped a little. I found I couldn't use "Sugar, Sugar" any more to help me work. It had been fine when I was looking ahead to winning Avis with a sense of confidence that it was something that could really happen. But now that that seemed only possible when I was in a fantasy, the song just reminded me of what I had lost.

I started singing blues songs instead, and all the hurting love songs and breakup songs I could remember. They gave a rhythm to my feeling sorry for myself and the work got done. The days were still long, but at least they went by.

I wasn't alone in wanting the days to go by faster. It was clear that most of the *Brigadistas* were eager to get on to the two weeks of beach and touring and put the long days of hard labor behind them. Not everyone had risen to the challenge of the fields, but most had, working long hours with their bodies and not their minds. Only a few had ever had to work like this at any time in their lives. As students or as dropouts who went from job to job or worked part-time, the majority of the *Brigadistas* lived their lives by their own schedules, cutting classes if they felt like there was something more interesting to do, then making up the work with an all-nighter before the exam.

This was completely different, this not being able to call the shots about how you spent your time. Maybe the great lesson of the Venceremos Brigade was that you couldn't cram for the *zafra*. It would be a stretch to say this made the *Brigadistas* into the New Men and New Women that were the Cuban ideal. But it seemed clear to me, after the weeks spent together, that my comrades had gone through some kind of change and seemed the better for it.

It was like what I had gone through in basic training, learning to somehow be more alert, more aware, maybe even more alive. Like in the Army, there were some who didn't get it, some who had their heads up their own asses so far they were never going to see the light of day.

As the end of the harvest came closer, the *Brigadistas* were talking more than ever about what it had all meant, which meant that they would all pretty much get it all wrong, either making too much of what had happened or too little. I was surprised when Walter turned out to be one of those who made light of the experience, since he had so obviously changed. He was more focused, more determined about himself. I thought there was no question but that he was aware of the change. But maybe he wasn't, or maybe he didn't like the change, or maybe he didn't want to admit that there had been that much about him that *could* change.

"I am so glad it's almost over," he said. "I mean, I'm glad we could help bring in the harvest, but all this bullshit about how much it changed us is ridiculous. We're no different. We're just going to go home and be the same assholes we were, and probably worse. I can just hear Geronimo telling everyone what a real revolutionary he is now that he worked side by side with the Cubans and the Vietnamese."

I didn't bother to correct him, but I could see that even Geronimo and most of the other Weathermen were different, still cocky but maybe less cocky about what they thought and more cocky about what they could actually do.

"This was great, man," said Geronimo, as we sat next to each other during a *merienda* a couple of days from the end of the harvest. "You know, all the street action we did in Chicago is nothing compared to what we did here. This was like, real. I'm thinking I might get a job when I get home. See what that's like."

With the Army, I had been through this kind of thing before, and it wasn't so much new to me as it was a revival of feelings that had slipped away. So much of my attention had been focused on the whole Roger business that I hadn't really noticed it until these last days when I saw it in the rest of the Brigade. For me, it was a balancing act, trying to meet that need to do for myself but at the same time trying to do for the Brigade. Again, like being in the war.

Now I had a new story to go along with my "Me Before and After Vietnam" story. Now I could add "Me Before the Brigade and After." Looking back, I thought I hadn't been concerned about owning things and I hadn't seriously planned a future around possessions and goals. I knew I wasn't a hippie, but even though I didn't think of myself as being especially materialistic, either, I could see how much of an American I was, how much I was given over to small pleasures, things that were sold to me on television and the radio, things that were important to have, places it was important to go because other people thought they were important. Clothes and records and food. A new car I yearned for. A groovy bachelor pad, in my wildest fantasies, high up with a view and a great stereo system and the best whiskey money could buy. All the things money could buy.

But the work in the field, the talk with the Cubans and the Vietnamese and even with the other *Brigadistas*, and especially Avis, had done something to me. It wasn't just love that made me want to be more like Avis, doing what had to be done to stop all that idiocy in myself and the country.

I didn't know if I would still think that way if I could go back to the

States. There was a part of me that was as cynical, if not more cynical, than Walter. And part of it was romantic, imagining working side by side with Avis, being dedicated, living simply. But I knew something was coming that would be new and different.

- Sixty-Four -

The days passed and the last full day of cutting came. We still had some field work to do the next morning, a Sunday, then it would be time to clean up, pack, and get ready for the tour. I called Roger to let him know which day I'd be in Havana. He said he could hardly wait.

"Ready for another visit to El Floridita?"

"Sure," I said. "Whatever you say."

There was a party that last night in camp. I didn't want to go. I wanted to be left alone and not have to see Avis and not have to hear about how great the two weeks off were going to be. But I went because it was easier to go than argue with Walter about it.

The *Brigadistas* were giddy with joy and rum, which had been portioned out so that there could be one serving for each of us. Something great had been accomplished and they were part of it. I felt it, too, and would have been glad to give myself over to the moment as completely as the others. Instead, I stood along the side of the meeting room where the party was in full swing, with music, dancing, and the smell of rum mixing with cigar smoke. I stared at the band with a smile frozen on my face while in my head I ran through scenarios of killing Roger. Envisioning it from the outside, seeing myself doing it as if I were a third person observing and not one of the two in the scene, somehow made it seem more real to me.

That would be yet another division in my life, like there was "before the Army and after" and "before the Brigade and after." Next there would be "before killing Roger and after." Soon there would be "before Dad died and after." I wondered if there would ever be a "before Avis and after."

What I knew for sure at that moment was that there was a "before drinking that rum and after." I'd only had my one allotted glass, but it had gone straight to my head. I went outside to get some air.

I sat on the bench outside the meeting hall. It was a good night, clear and cool. Over toward the southern horizon there was a comet. It had been in the sky for a few nights. Someone had told me it was called Bennett's comet, which I guess was the name of the guy who'd discovered it. I wondered what it was like to discover a comet, to be an astronomer whose job it was to stare into space. I thought about all the dopers I knew who qualified for a job like that. What kind of life did Bennett live? Did he sleep days and stay up nights? I knew dopers who did that, too. There weren't supposed to be any dopers in Cuba. There must have been some, of course, but they had to be undercover because the government was against drugs. So instead they had rum. Cuba Libre and Papa Doble. Would the government ban those, too?

Walter came out and sat down next to me. He had a full glass of rum.

"Want some?" he said. "Jackie didn't want any and gave me hers."

"Sure," I said.

He took in the night, the cool air, the smell of the jungle, the comet on the horizon.

"This is fucking great. I can't wait to get home and tell everyone about it."

The rum had eased his cynicism, but I wasn't going to say anything that would make him back off. I wanted Walter to go home and tell everyone that the revolution was a success, that there was another way to be, that there were New Men and New Women, and that things could actually change, people could actually change. Suddenly it was so important for me to believe it, wanting to believe it about myself and to believe that one day Avis would change and understand what I had told her was true.

- Sixty-Five -

It was supposed to be a short work day. We went out to the fields as usual. There was still cane standing in several fields, but we stuck to those we had already worked, cleaning up all the loose ends, doing some burning where it was needed, making sure anything worth harvesting had been gathered in, making sure no machetes were left lying around. I had one of my "back in the war" moments, feeling like I did after a firefight, when we went over the field looking among the dead for anyone still alive.

I wondered what would happen to the cane in the fields we hadn't been able to reach. Were other Cuban crews going to come in after us and attack those? Were there more foreign brigades coming to help? Was there another Venceremos Brigade forming up back in the States, getting ready to head to St. John and the boat ride to Cuba? I hoped that would happen, but I also found myself thinking how great it would be if we were the last ones, part of a small group who had done something that nobody else would get to do. It suddenly hit me: I was the asshole who'd been seduced.

When we were done, we went back to our tents and changed out of our work clothes for what we thought was the last time. Dressed in our clean outfits, we were ready for a relaxing Sunday. Some people wondered if there would be another party and more rum that night.

Then word came to get back into our work clothes. Fidel was coming. There had been a rumor that he would show up near the end of the *zafra* to cut with us and the Vietnamese and Koreans and the volunteers from Africa and South America, but as it got down to the last couple of days, we all assumed it was just a myth.

This time the myth was true. Fidel arrived with four bodyguards and another guy who later turned out to be a translator. They used the directors' tent to change, and came out in work clothes and headed to one of the far fields that we had not gotten to. A representative from each of the small brigades was picked to go work side by side with *El Jefe* while the rest of the Brigade were spread out in the other fields.

Walter picked me to go with Fidel.

"Are you sure?" I said. "A lot of the other brigade leaders are just going themselves."

"I'm sure. I've had enough glory for one lifetime. Besides, working side by side with Fidel could be a good thing to have on your résumé when you're job hunting in Cuba."

It was a pleasure to watch Fidel out in the field. He had a great athletic swing and looked like cutting cane had been his life's work. I remembered someone saying that Fidel had been a baseball player, a pitcher, and had been scouted by the majors. It wasn't the same motion as throwing a fastball, but it took the same balance and it was a full-body effort. Anyway, he looked great and did a great job.

Watching Fidel cutting cane, I thought of Lincoln, famous for splitting rails. They had that physicality in common, but otherwise how different they were. Lincoln was from the people. He was a poor kid and he was the American Dream, going from nothing to being president. No matter how much cane he cut, Fidel would always be *for* the people but not *of* the people. He was no New Man. He was too big for that, too much a hero. Lincoln was those things, too, and maybe even a saint, but he was more like Jesus. In the end, just a simple guy.

Did Fidel ever think about Lincoln? I couldn't say, because when I got to cut alongside him, we skipped the philosophy and talked baseball. I told him I'd heard he played baseball and that, judging from his swing, he must have been a good hitter.

"No," he said in English. "I threw a good fastball, but I couldn't hit one. Did you play baseball?"

"In high school," I said. "But I couldn't hit a curve ball."

"Were you a pitcher?"

"Third base."
"The hot corner."

The translator was working next to us and interrupted to ask Fidel what that meant. Fidel explained in Spanish.

"Ah, *sí*," said the translator. "*Rincon caliente.*"

"Sí, "I said. "Rincon muy caliente."

As I spoke, I swung at a cane stalk and made a perfect cut, the best I'd ever done. The cane stalk flew up, heading toward Fidel. My free hand shot out and grabbed it in the air before it could hit him, and I laid it down neatly next to the last stalk I'd cut. Fidel looked startled, then started to laugh. The translator, who had also been startled, began laughing, too, and so did I. I noticed that the other *Brigadistas* were all looking our way. I had made Fidel laugh.

- Sixty-Six -

There was another, bigger, party that night. This time, the rum was not portioned out and spirits ran higher than ever. Fidel had stayed through dinner, a big outdoor buffet which I guess was in his honor, and then sat down to talk for about two hours, downing a tall glass of water before he started answering questions with lengthy, very thorough answers. When the questions finally ended, or rather, when his aide reminded him that he had other places to be, things to do, he got up, mingling a while longer and shaking hands before he took off.

He spotted me in the crowd around him and made his way through to shake my hand.

"Maybe someday we will be in the field together again," he said. "But in the ball field not the cane field."

Then he laughed and gave me a big bear hug and headed for his car.

"That was fucking incredible," said Walter.

"No shit," said Geronimo.

I looked around for Avis, hoping she had seen what had happened. I spotted her up front, among the camp directors who were escorting Fidel out of the hall and back to his car. She turned and our eyes met. Her look was cold. A hug from Fidel had not redeemed me.

The party went on long into the night. I got drunk again. Images of Fidel, Roger, Avis, my dad, Wildflower and Ori, Tish, and cowboy John Lydon churned through my brain. What if I didn't stay? What if I gave up on the pardon and seeing my dad and just headed back to Canada?

I could return to the commune or I could find Tish and see what would happen.

People kept approaching me, wanting to hear firsthand about my sudden friendship with Fidel, and I repeated it all in detail. If I hadn't been drunk and exhausted, I would have started making up details just to keep myself from being bored. Instead, I kept trimming it until it sounded like a news radio report. I said this, Fidel said that, the translator said the other, we all laughed.

Pretty girls invited me to dance, hoping that coupled off in the intimacy of the dance floor I might reveal some secret detail about Fidel that would then be their secret, too. But even if I had a secret to reveal, the music was too loud and the dancing too vigorous for any intimate exchange. After the dancing, they would say let's go outside for some air, hoping we could wander off to the privacy of the volleyball court. But the party had spread, and short of heading into the woods, there was no place to go to be alone.

After a couple of walks outside, I excused myself, grabbed a couple of cups of rum, and snuck out the door hoping to escape to my tent, lie on my bunk in the dark, and give full attention to my drunken fantasies. Outside the meeting hall, I ran into Avis, who was about to come up the three steps into the hall. We looked at each other for a moment before I spoke.

"Oh, hey. Would you care for some rum?" I said.

"No thanks."

"Okay." I drank down the cup I'd offered her. "One left. Sure you don't want?"

"Sure."

She started up the steps into the hall. As she brushed past me, I took a step back and fell down the steps, landing sprawled out on the ground. I looked up and she was standing over me.

"You okay?"

"I spilled my drink."

"No kidding. Can you stand?"

"Why?"

"Come on."

She got behind me and sat me up, then gripped me under the arms and lifted up.

"You strong," I said.

"Yeah, I strong. But you could help."

"Okay."

I don't know that I helped, but I was on my feet, although I probably would have fallen if she let me go. She started walking me toward my tent.

"Wait. Forgot my drink."

"You're kidding."

"Okay."

I sort of walked, leaning on her as my feet shuffled forward. As gone as I was, I knew how much I liked touching her arms and shoulders and smelling her beside me.

"I love you."

"You stupid shit."

"Yes. But I love you. I never loved anyone but you."

"Right."

"You've got my love cherry."

"Shut up or I'll leave you right here."

"Where?"

"Keep walking."

"Okay . . . Love you."

"Stupid shit."

"After I kill Roger, I come to Milwaukee."

"Right. You do that."

"Okay."

I started singing. "Sugar, honey honey, you are my candy girl, and you got me wanting you …"

The next thing I knew I was in my bunk. I could feel her taking my shoes off.

"I love you," I said.

"You dumb shit, I love you, too."

She kissed my forehead and then there was a dream, although I don't remember what it was.

- Sixty-Seven -

I woke up with the worst hangover of my life. I wasn't the only one.

"Oh, Jesus," said Walter. "Just shoot me. Put me out of my misery."

All around us we could hear moaning, hacking coughs, and deep sighs. It continued through breakfast, packing, and onto the bus. I was pretty much side by side with Walter all morning, but conversation was slim, given our condition, until we were on the bus. By then we were several aspirins and many cups of coffee toward recovery.

"I think I feel almost human," said Walter. "Speaking of which, what should we do when I get back to Havana?"

"I don't know. Is there any way you can call from the island and let me know you're coming? Then we can meet somewhere if you don't want to see him."

I was making conversation about something I hoped would not be happening. I wanted to be long gone by the time Walter got back from the Brigade's vacation trip to the Isle of Pines. I wanted to kill Roger as soon as we got back to his place that night, and get to the airport and haul ass out of Cuba on the first flight to Canada they had.

"I suppose there'll be a phone on the island. If not, I'll call when we get back to the city."

"I guess that will have to do."

"I don't want to leave Cuba without seeing you again."

"Yeah. We'll make it work."

"Yeah."

I envisioned Walter calling Roger's number and getting no answer because Roger was dead and I was already back in Canada or on my way to Switzerland or wherever else I might go to get out of Cuba before the law got on me. I could feel the tension throughout my body as I began to gear up for what I had come here to do, while he was letting go of all his tension of the last few weeks.

"You nervous?" he said, sensing the anxiety screaming out of me.

"What do you think?"

"I'm really sorry you have to go through all this. It's just not right."

"It's nobody's fault but mine. I'm the one who deserted."

"It's not your fault. It's Johnson's fault and Nixon's and all the creeps that got us into this stupid war."

"But they're not the ones stuck in Cuba."

"Well, Johnson's stuck in Texas. That's something, anyway."

The bus was slowing to a stop in the Cathedral Square. I got up and lifted my bag down from the overhead rack. Walter stood up with me.

"I guess this is it," said Walter. He reached out his arms and we embraced. "Good luck. With everything."

The bus had stopped and I went down the aisle saying goodbye to the Brigadistas I'd worked with over the past few weeks. Geronimo was seated near the door. He got up and embraced me, too.

"Hey, man, it was great working with you. Hope I get to see you again."

He put out his hand and gave me a power shake like the black guys would do in Vietnam. It was awkward and silly, but I responded as seriously as I could.

"Right on, bro. You keep on truckin'."

PART VIII
Havana

- Sixty-Eight -

I got off the bus and it started up. There were two other buses right behind, and I watched them go by, looking at the windows as they passed. There were faces I recognized and some people waved. But I didn't see the face I was looking for. I felt more than alone. I felt disconnected.

I looked toward the tables in the square, expecting to see Roger seated where he'd been before. He wasn't there.

"Did you have a tearful farewell?"

It was Roger, standing a few feet away. He'd been on the other side of the bus.

"Were you hiding?" I said.

"I was being delicate, old boy. Allowing you your final moment of romance."

"You're a sensitive soul."

"Yes, I am. Which is why I need some pussy."

"I guess you're over Barb."

"Who? Oh, Barb. Yes, I'm afraid she broke my heart and now I need to mend it. With some fresh pussy."

"Back to the Floridita?"

"No. I thought we'd try a new hunting ground. The Hotel Capri."

"Sounds fancy."

"It's a trip and a half. Old gangster place from the fifties. Casino, a bar and swimming pool on the roof, mob heaven."

"But not anymore. I mean, they all left with Batista."

"Sadly, yes. Now it's a new mob, commissars and *Fidelistas*. And of course, our beloved tourist pussy."

"Of course."

"It's a fine crop, lounging by the pool in their lovely bikinis. We can have lunch up there and assess the talent. Do you have a swimsuit in your bag?"

"I do."

"Then let's be off. I'm parked just off the next street."

"No walking today?"

"In your honor. I figured you'd have your gear."

"Have you talked to Colonel Enriques?" I said, as we walked to his car.

"Of course, old man. The job is yours. It always was."

"Really? Wow. That's terrific. Thank you."

"Not at all. You were made for it. A perfect fit."

"You think?"

"I don't think. I know."

"But what exactly am I supposed to do?"

"Please. No more talk about work. That can all wait until tomorrow. Today is for pleasure."

- Sixty-Nine -

And so it was. The hotel had seen better days, but it still had a kind of cheap glamour, the kind that passes for elegance if you don't know any better. My mother would have been dazzled. What I liked best were the Cuban girls who ran the elevators and called out "*Arriba*" to let you know they were ready to close the door and take off for the roof.

We changed into our swimsuits in the men's room then settled in at the bar and ordered Cuba Libres. Just as Roger had said, we could see the girls stretched out on their lounge chairs all around the pool. But you could also look beyond the girls out over the city. The Capri was seventeen stories high, and except for other hotels, like the Nacional just a couple of blocks away, there weren't many buildings that stood that tall. Mostly it was a low city that spread out to the east, west, and south as far as I could see. To the north was the sea.

For a moment, I was taken back to Mount Tzuhalem, where, what seemed like a lifetime ago, I had decided I could not and would not come after Roger. How long had it really been? Three months? How long since I'd last been in the U.S.? How long since I'd seen my family? How long since the McWilliams's house had blown up? How long since I'd deserted?

I looked at Roger, who was looking at the girls. He seemed intensely happy. As usual, he seemed to read my thoughts.

"This is the life, hey?"

"Well, it's a life."

"My God, you are hard to please."

"Sorry, but I'm kind of at loose ends."

"I told you, not to worry. Just trust old Rog that everything is going to be exactly right tomorrow. Do you trust me? Come on, do you trust old Rog?"

"All right."

"And you believe that tomorrow everything is going to be exactly right?"

"Yeah."

"Come on, say it."

"Tomorrow is going to be exactly right."

"Good. Now help me pick out some pussy."

Of course, I didn't trust him, but what else was there to say? Besides, I wanted to think that tomorrow *was* going to be exactly right. Just not the way he thought. It was going to be exactly right for me, though. This time I was going to see to it. The *zafra* was over and I was tired of waiting.

But first I'd have to help him get a girl. I wanted him to be happy, relaxed, and satisfied, without a suspicious thought in his head. I was going to be his best friend.

"What about them?" I said, nodding toward a couple of blondes lounging a short distance from the bar. I was assuming he still wanted a blonde.

"Just the pair I was thinking of. And speaking of pairs, just look at the knockers on the one on the left."

"It doesn't look like there are guys with them."

"No, I've been watching them since we got here, and no husbands or boyfriends in sight."

"Which is not to say they don't have some back in their rooms, or out playing golf, or fishing or something."

"Always the possibility. Adds a bit of danger to what might otherwise be a pathetic little game."

"Why, Roger, how philosophical of you."

"More psychological than philosophical, I'd say. But thank you, dear fellow."

"So what do we do? Send them a drink?"

"My goodness, you are eager. Don't tell me your rara Avis was not meeting your needs."

"Let's just say she's on her way to the Isle of Pines and I'm here."

"Well, aren't you the filthy beast."

"That I am. So, drinks?"

"Yes, but flowers first."

He turned around on his stool and spoke to the bartender in Spanish, then turned back to me.

"And now we wait."

We ordered another round of drinks and tried to guess what nationality the girls were. Roger said it was most likely they were Russians.

"Look how happy they are. You can feel their relief all the way over here. If they were back in Leningrad or Moscow, they'd still be under twenty feet of snow. I'm guessing a trade mission. They don't look like agricultural types. Maybe they're here peddling vodka. That would be great, swapping vodka for rum and plenty of free samples back in their suite."

I was thinking Norwegian. They both looked an awful lot like Francine Heggesta, who I used to hang out with on Fourth Avenue over by the Verrazano Bridge my last year in high school, and who was my date for the prom. Other than Wildflower, Frannie was probably the easiest to get along with of any woman I ever knew.

A wave of desire to be back in Brooklyn, back with Frannie, back in time, came over me. It was so much better then than now, sitting on top of an ex-gangster hotel in Havana with a guy I was planning to kill and all the crap that went along with that story. I was up against it and had been for a while, in fact, almost since I had last seen Frannie, right before I went off to basic training. But I wasn't done yet. I'd made it through six months in Vietnam and having a bayonet go through my side and every crazy thing that had happened since.

The word came to me: *Venceremos*. I would win. I would see Francine Heggesta again. I would see my dad. I would see Avis. Venceremos.

After a few minutes and a third round of Cuba Libres, a waiter came around from the far side of the bar carrying a tray that held two small bowls with flowers floating in them. He placed the bowls on the little table between the girls and said something to them and looked in our direction. They followed his glance. Roger lifted his glass and saluted them. They laughed and waved for us to join them.

We pulled up a couple of chairs.

The girl closest to Roger said something to us in Spanish. I picked up "*gracias*" and "*flores*," but the rest went by too fast for me to follow. At least, I thought, Roger was wrong. They're Latins, not Russians.

Roger answered her in Spanish and I wasn't sure what he was saying until the end when he said, "*Nosotros no somos Cubanos. Somos Norteamericanos.*"

"Americans?" said the chatty girl, switching to English. Both girls laughed. "We love Americans!"

"Are you Cuban?" I said.

The girls laughed again.

"You are being funny, no?" said the chatty girl.

"I don't think so," I said. "You're not Cuban?"

"We are Russian."

Damn, I thought. He was right again. I wondered if he would be right about them peddling booze.

"What are your names?" said Roger.

"I am Tatiana," said Chatty, "and this is Anya."

"And I am Onegin and this is Vronsky," said Roger.

The girls laughed so hard they actually did spit takes. Roger looked at me to see if I understood the joke. Clearly I didn't, so he explained.

"Tatiana is the girl in *Eugene Onegin* by the great Russian poet Pushkin, and Anya is Anya Karenina, whose lover was Vronsky." Roger leered at them as he spoke, a broad, comical leer, and the girls laughed even harder.

Roger asked them what they were doing in Havana and they explained they were stewardesses, working for Aeroflot and on a layover between flights. Damn, I thought again. They do peddle booze. Only they do it at 30,000 feet.

Anya told us they'd come in from Moscow via Paris that morning and were unwinding by the pool before crashing for the rest of the day.

"Are you brothers?" said Tatiana. "You look like brothers."

"Of course we are," said Roger. "And you are sisters."

"Of course," said Tatiana.

"And you are good communist sisters?" said Roger.

"Yes," said Tatiana. "And you are good capitalist brothers?"

"Of course," said Roger.

We all thought this was very funny and laughed heartily. The waiter

PART VIII Havana

arrived with our drinks. Roger made a toast in Russian. I had no idea what he said, but he said it very well. We all drank. It was my fourth Cuba Libre and I was dizzy.

The girls laughed and said something in Russian.

"What's going on?" I said.

"They're complimenting me on my accent."

"What did you say?"

"Just an old Russian toast. *Za lyubóf*. To love."

"To lub," the girls repeated, raising their glasses high. Roger spoke in Russian again. One of the girls, Tatiana, answered him and they went back and forth. It was so interesting to watch them go at it that it took me a few seconds to grasp what was going on. Roger was speaking Russian. Not just a toast or a phrase like some old revolutionary slogan he might have picked up somewhere along the line. He was rattling on at length like he was a native.

"You speak Russian," I said.

He left off talking to Tatiana and turned to me.

"You noticed."

"Yes I noticed. Where did you learn Russian?"

"In college. What did you learn? Not Spanish, I know."

"But you're good. Nobody learns that well in school."

"What can I say? It's a gift."

He turned back to Tatiana and said something that made her laugh. I thought it was about me. Anya laughed, too.

"Did he say something about me?" I said to her.

"Yes. He say you very good boy, but it is enough you speak English."

"That made you laugh?"

"It was how he say that."

"What else is he saying? I mean what are they talking about?"

"He ask if she believe in love at first looking."

"At first looking? Oh, okay. What does she say?"

"She say 'no,' what she believe is sex at first looking."

"Wow."

"Yes, 'wow.' You believe in sex at first looking?"

"With you, yes."

The words were out of my mouth faster than the thought not to say them. As I began to stutter an apology Anya stood up and put out her hand to me.

"Me, too. Come to the room and fuck me."

Tatiana broke off her conversation with Roger and said something in Russian to Anya, who laughed. Roger laughed, too.

"What?" I said to him.

"She told her to take it easy on you. You're just a boy."

"Tell her she can go fuck herself."

"Hey," said Tatiana, "I can speak English, you know."

"Okay," I said, "go fuck yourself."

She laughed and then we all laughed. Anya picked up her glass and drained what was left of her drink. I did the same. She belched and we all laughed again.

"Come," she said.

What the hell, I was thinking. What the hell. The *zafra* was over, Avis was gone, Walter was gone, the Venceremos Brigade and the camp were gone, the cane was gone, Fidel was gone. It had all been too wonderful, a poor boy's dream, and it was all over. All that was left was Roger. Roger and murder. I was furious. I felt screwed. I could feel a rage in my gut burning through to my skin. I wanted to explode. Get it over with.

We were at the elevator. Anya was about my height and built solid. She put her arms around my neck and pulled me close and kissed me, deep and wet. I kissed back. We were still mouth-to-mouth when the elevator doors opened.

"*Bajando*," said the elevator girl.

Yes, we were going down.

Two floors below, we got out and staggered arm in arm to her room. She found a key in the beach bag she carried, opened the door, pulled me inside, and kissed me deep again. There were a couple of beds in the room and we collapsed onto one of them, tearing away at each other's clothes. But it wasn't sex, at least, not for me. It was that rage. I was aching to just let everything go, to stop being good, to forget about the fucking revolution and ten million tons of sugar and New Men, and here was the exact right woman—maybe with a rage of her own—here she was at the exact right moment.

We were all over each other with our hands and arms and mouths and legs and feet. I wasn't sure if we were wrestling or fucking. Not that it mattered. It was what it was. And then it was over and we fell back side by side on the bed.

I almost jumped back up again. Roger and Tatiana were on the other bed, naked, she on her hands and knees and he behind her humping away. I was astonished that that I hadn't heard them come in. I didn't want to keep watching them but wasn't sure where else to look. Anya saved the moment by lighting two cigarettes and handing me one. She got out of bed still naked and went over to the dresser and brought back an ashtray and a bottle of vodka. She sat back down and took a swig, then handed me the bottle. I drank and gave it back to her. She took another swig, handed it back to me, then dragged on her cigarette, all the while watching the action on the other bed.

I stopped trying to look away. I'd already gone of the deep end and was drowning in misery and vodka and a bellyful of rum. Roger was there in front of me, naked, distracted, grasping life with both hands and his dick, close enough for me to stab, to strangle, to crack over the head with the bottle of vodka in my hand. Close enough to kill. So close, but—

Anya took the bottle from me, took another swig, and shouted something in Russian to Tatiana who grunted something back to her.

"What did you say to her?"

"I tell her not to stop until his balls fall off."

"What did she say?"

"She say what about her poor pussy."

"Will you cunts shut the fuck up?" said Roger.

Anya drank some more of the vodka and passed it to me. There was still time to reach over and bash Roger's skull in. I hesitated. Anya took the bottle back again and drank deep then got up and took a step over to the other bed. She bent over and kissed Tatiana on the mouth, a big wet kiss just like the one she had given me. I noticed that at the same time she had started to rub herself. She left off kissing Tatiana and turned back to me, reaching between my legs.

I stood up quickly before she could pull me up. She led me to Tatiana and put my fading erection in her friend's mouth. Tatiana began to roll me around inside her mouth with her tongue. Then Anya walked around behind Roger and gave him a hard slap on the ass.

"Yeah!" said Roger. Anya slapped him again, then got behind him and began to hump him in rhythm with his humping Tatiana.

"Oh, yeah!" said Roger.

Tatiana got her hands on my ass and pulled me into her face, rocking my hips back and forth. I grabbed her head with both my hands and pulled it forward. Anya took another drink, emptying the bottle, then tossed it on the other bed, grabbed Roger by the hips and began humping him harder and faster. He picked up his pace to match hers. It went on like that for another minute until Roger was ready to come.

"Oh, yeah," he said. "Yeah, yeah, oh yeah, Jesus Fucking Christ yeah!"

As he started to come, so did Tatiana. She opened her mouth setting me loose, threw her head back and broke free of my hands. I leaned back away from her as she shouted in unison with Roger, but in Russian. I imagine it was very close to "yeah, yeah, oh yeah," although I am pretty sure she never called on Jesus.

Roger fell forward on top of Tatiana. Anya leaned back away from him and slid off the bed and stumbled onto the other bed and stretched out. I slid off the bed and swung myself over next to Anya. She began to snore. I heard more snoring and looked to the other bed. Tatiana was snoring, too. Roger rolled off her and stood up.

"There you go," he said. "We fucked their brains out."

I stood up, too.

"I'm starving," he said. "Let's get some lunch."

He started dressing. I followed his lead.

"I'm dying for a good steak," he said as he pulled his pants on. "Let's go to the National."

"They have steaks? You mean rabbit steaks?"

"I mean real steaks, great steaks. Rich-tourist, Grade A steaks flown in from Argentina to make all the hungry Russian big shots happy. And it's my treat."

He finished dressing and was out the door without a glance back at the sleeping girls. I took one last look and went out after him.

- Seventy -

The dining room was elegant, with big chandeliers and potted palms and tall urns sitting on taller pedestals. We weren't dressed very fancy and didn't have reservations, but Roger handed the maitre d' a large denomination and we were seated in a far corner of the dining room among a group of empty tables near the kitchen.

"I thought you were broke," I said.

"Ebb and flow. Today is flow. I need a martini. How about you?"

"Sure," I said, "more booze is just what I need."

I was still dizzy from the sun and the heat and the drinks at the bar plus my hangover from the night before and all the drinking I'd done in the room with Anya. I'd been one step removed from myself since I'd gotten off the bus, my every choice on the wild side, and despite knowing better, I didn't feel like stopping. Maybe I didn't need a cool head for what I had to do. Maybe some instinct was telling me I needed to be unhinged.

Roger ordered the drinks and studied the menu.

"Yes, steak, baked potato, and salad. Right there in black and white. What do you say? Is that a lunch?"

"Sounds more like a dinner, but sure. Why not?"

The drinks came and Roger gave the waiter our order. He picked up his glass and held it out for a toast.

"To brotherhood, universal pussy fucking brotherhood."

"Brotherhood," I said, picking up my glass and clinking it against his. We drank. I felt a burning chill go through me from my throat down to my tailbone.

"Did you see how I plowed that bitch? Did I fuck her or what?"

"You fucked her royally. She's no doubt dreaming she's been fucked by the tsar."

Roger roared out a laugh. People at tables across the room turned to look.

"Oh, you are too much. Do you know how much I like you? Well, you may not, but you will. I promise, you will come to appreciate me, no matter how you felt before."

"How did I feel before?"

"Oh, save that for later. The deep, serious conversation. I'm drinking a martini, contemplating a steak, and feeling well fucked. You must be feeling well fucked, too, after that ride you had with the madwoman. When she slapped me on the ass, I swear I reexperienced my birth. Thought it was the fucking doctor slapping the life into me. And when she shoved your dick in Tatiana's mouth! My God, what a fantastic woman! Maybe we should go back and wake them up. After we eat, of course. But I would like to fuck that humping bitch. Jesus, I'm glad she didn't have a dildo. She probably would have shoved it right up my ass and buggered me from here to Christopher Street."

"Thank God she fell asleep," I said.

I tried to stay with him, but my mind was stuck on what he had said about how I felt about him. What the hell was he talking about? If he knew I hated him, why all the camaraderie? Was he that hard up for a playmate?

"We should go back just to see what other tricks she has up her sleeve. But I do love her for setting you on her friend. She bonded us."

"Bonded us?"

"Sure. Double-teaming Tatiana. That's a bonding experience. Don't you think however long you live, you'll never forget it?"

"I guess so."

However long I live. He said it casually, but it felt loaded. Roger always sounded as if he was saying something more than the words that came from his mouth. But this time, I felt like something really big was coming.

"You guess right. I need another drink."

He spotted the waiter and signaled him to bring another round.

"Yes. Bonded. Brothers. *Hermanos.* Forever. You know, I always felt that we had something in common. Shared something. Not like all those twits at Eddie's."

"Yeah, you said that before."

"That's right. When you were leaving Eddie's house. But don't you feel it? How much alike we are? Didn't Tatiana ask if we were brothers? Didn't you get that all the time at Eddie's?"

It seemed so superficial, thinking we were alike because we looked a little bit alike and we fucked a woman together. But he was serious. And he was talking about something else. The vodka was making me dizzy again and the waiter was putting another one in front of me. The urge to get a grip came back to me. There was no more time for letting go. But what the fuck. Maybe I was setting it all up so that I'd fail. Maybe, no matter how determined I had been in the camp and on the bus, I knew deep inside that I couldn't do it. Maybe, but I wasn't ready to give up.

"How are we alike? I mean besides being the same height and fucking Tatiana. I mean, I really don't know."

"We're both killers. That's how. Whatever way we're different, that makes us more the same than all the differences combined. It's as simple as that."

"You're a killer? I didn't know."

"Sure you did. You know I killed Eddie and the others. I'm sure Walter must have told you."

I got another chill, but not from the martini. Suddenly my mind, my body, everything came together. The cards were on the table and I had to see how it was going to play.

"Walter told me what he thought. But that doesn't mean it was true or that I believed it."

"But you did, didn't you? The truth, now. You did believe it."

"Suppose I did. Does that make it true?"

"No. What makes it true is me telling you it is."

"You're saying you killed them?"

"Yes."

"Accidentally."

"No. Purposefully. Quite, quite purposefully."

"You meant to kill them? Is that what you're saying?"

"It's exactly what I'm saying."

"But that's crazy. Why did you do it?"

"Ah, good question. Why did I do it? I suppose I didn't have to. But I wanted to. I was sick of all their revolutionary pretensions. And I suppose I was sending a message, too."

"A message? To who?"

"To all the other little pretend revolutionaries. Play with fire and you'll get burned."

"Why the hell should you care?"

"I'm coming to that."

"Why are you telling me this?"

"I said we were the same and I meant it. But we do have our differences. You, for example, are more civilized than I am. I'm telling you something incredibly outrageous, but instead of standing up and kicking the table over, as our emotional friend Walter might have done in your shoes, you lean in and talk softer. A natural gentleman despite your untamed Brooklyn background."

"I'm too drunk to do that. If I was sober I might have done that or more. I might have reached across the table and strangled you."

"Yes, strangled me, or punched me, or at least thrown your drink in my face. That's a nice drunken measure you might have taken."

"I still can."

"Yes. Or you can wait till later and poison me."

I opened my mouth, but all that came out was a dry clicking sound.

"Yes, poison me," said Roger. "With those pills you've been carrying around since you left Canada."

"*Sus bistecs, señors.*"

It was the waiter, standing in front of me, putting our plates down on the table. I almost jumped out of my skin. He'd walked right up to us, in plain view, but I hadn't seen him, so focused was I on the maniac sitting across from me. I had completely lost sight of where we were, the other people at the tables around us, their talking, their eating, and all the other sounds of a restaurant in the middle of lunch service. All there was was Roger and the table between us and the poison in my pocket.

The waiter was gone as quickly as he had come. I watched him cross the room toward the bar on the side opposite us, passing among the other tables that were as far away from me and the world I was in as was the moon. Roger cut into his steak and took a bite.

"Umm, delicious. Exactly what I was craving. Eat some, while it's still hot."

"You know?"

"About the poison? Of course."

"Everything?"

"Everything. Please eat. I hate to eat alone. One of the worst things about this whole fucking assignment has been all the times I've had to eat alone."

"You know the McWilliamses and Ward and Georgie."

"I don't actually know the McWilliamses. Though I did have a yen to meet them. Still, it might have been a bit awkward for them to know about my part in all this. They really thought you were coming here to kill me."

"But I *was* coming here to kill you."

"Well, no. You *thought* you were coming here to kill me. What you were doing was coming here to bring me the poison from Howard."

"Howard?"

Oh, yes, Ward. That's the name he used with you."

"He's not Peter Ward?"

"Oh, yes, he's Peter Ward. Only there is no Peter Ward. You're not eating."

"Peter Ward is Howard. And his friend Georgie?"

"Oh, Georgie is Georgie. Though he usually goes by his middle name, Gordon."

"And you know them."

"If you're going to be this slow about everything, you might as well eat. Really, old boy, I can't stand to see your steak just sitting there untouched."

"You're CIA."

"Ah, you're picking up speed. But, no. At least, not anymore."

"Not anymore?"

"More of a free agent now. Independent contractor."

"The Russian. That's how you know Russian."

"Please eat."

"You know all about their plan."

"My plan, old boy, my plan. Credit where credit is due. After all, they never would have thought to pick you as the courier."

"You picked me?"

"I knew you'd be perfect. Your combat experience, wanting to square things with the old man, and you really are quite resourceful. Plus your appeal with the ladies. I really wanted that, too. I never considered anyone else. I told you we were meant to work together."

My head was exploding. Nothing seemed real. The tables, the lights, even the people were like two-dimensional cardboard cutouts, like stage scenery.

"Why am I here?"

"I told you. To bring me the poison. You have no idea what a fucking problem it is to get your hands on some poison down here. There's plenty around, of course, but the secret police have too many fucking spies. Go near the stuff, even in the most out-of-the-way voodoo location, and you're done for. Believe me, it's easier to get a gun."

"You needed poison and I brought it to you."

"Yes. I did have some to start with, of course. But I lost it in Mexico. I'll tell you about it someday. It's not a long story, but a bit embarrassing."

"You came here to poison someone."

"Of course."

"All that stuff about Peru and hooking up with someone in Mexico who steered you to Cuba and the Cubans checking you out."

"Oh, that last part was true. But everything before was a set-up to get me in."

"Just so you could poison someone."

"It's my mission."

"Who are you supposed to poison?"

"Really, old boy. Eat your steak. Your brain needs protein."

"Jesus Fucking Christ. Are you talking about Castro?"

"Of course, fish would be better. Brain food. You can order the broiled swordfish if you prefer, and we could take the steak home in a doggie bag. Shall I call the waiter?"

"Enough with the food already! You're crazy. Castro?"

The room had disappeared again, almost as soon as the waiter left the table. Roger's mention of the waiter brought it back. There were maybe a hundred other people in the room, maybe two hundred, but certainly a lot. Were any of them sitting with a madman? What would they do if I started shouting it out loud? "This guy here says he's going to kill Fidel!

Call the *policía!*"

Once again, Roger was reading my mind.

"There's no one to turn to here, old boy. I doubt there's one in a hundred in this room who would miss the bastard."

"But he's Castro. He's the fucking president of the country."

"He's a fucking totalitarian dictator, you mean."

"Yeah, but he's a person." I knew it sounded really stupid, but I was thinking of the big guy with a beard cutting cane and talking baseball with me just the day before, not the guy who put his enemies in prison or just bumped them off.

"You were a soldier and you killed the enemy soldiers. Did you stop to check if it was a private or a general when you had him in your sights?"

"That was war."

"This is war."

"But I shot at them and they shot back."

"Oh, and don't you think he has his little assassins making the rounds of Latin American countries? African countries? What about in the U.S.? Who do you think was behind Oswald?"

"I thought it was the CIA."

"Well, it might have been. But it might have been Castro, too. Alas, we'll never know for sure."

It wasn't just the idea that he was going to kill Castro. It was his *Roger-ness*, his cold-blooded humor about the whole thing that was making me crazy.

"You can't kill Castro."

"I can and I will. Well, sort of. I won't do it myself, of course. Just make sure it happens. With the poison you brought. And which you won't mind handing over to me now."

"No."

"Look here, old man, stop worrying about Castro and start worrying about yourself."

"Why should I be worrying? Are you planning to kill me, too?"

"In fact, I'm supposed to."

"What?"

"That's what I want to talk about."

"Killing me?"

"*Not* killing you. I don't want to. That's what I've been trying to tell you."

"You're supposed to kill me?"

"Relax, old man. I'm not going to do it. And I'm not going to let the colonel do it, either."

"The colonel? Colonel Enriques? That little jerk? Why the hell does he want to kill me? And don't tell me to eat my fucking steak."

"Forgive the cliché, but you know too much."

"Too much! I don't know anything."

"Oh, but you do. More than you realize."

"But—"

"Listen, the colonel is on his way here, so let me finish before he arrives."

"He's coming here? Why is he coming here?"

My voice squeaked as I said it. I could hear myself coming unhinged. And why not? Roger had confessed to murdering Eddie and the others, he was planning to kill Castro with the poison I was supposed to use to kill him, he knew I was supposed to kill him, but he still wanted us to be brothers, Colonel Enriques was planning to kill me because I knew something I didn't know I knew.

"He's coming here because we planned to meet here and then take you someplace quiet and shoot you."

"But what do I know that I don't know I know?"

"The other week when you were here. The colonel thought you were part of the plan—"

"I am part of the plan. I brought the poison."

"Please stop interrupting. And, yes, you are part of the plan, but he thought you *knew* about the plan. When I told him you didn't, he decided that you might piece together the things he said about the real revolution and realize he was behind the plot to kill Castro."

"The colonel is going to kill Castro? With my poison?"

"That's the idea."

"Why did you tell him I didn't know about the plan?"

"That was an error on my part, I admit it. A bit of hubris, bragging about how I'd duped you, picked you out, recommended you to Howard, and set the whole thing up. It was such a good plan, I couldn't help but boast. My sincere apologies, by the way."

"But who am I going to tell? Who would believe me, anyway? And if he thinks Castro should die, why doesn't he want credit for doing it?"

"Look, despite what I said before about the people in this room being happy if Castro bit the dust, there are an awful lot of Cubans who'll miss the fellow. Better to let the blame fall elsewhere and be the loyal *Fidelista* who steps in to continue the revolution. At least, that's the colonel's plan."

"And what's your plan?"

"We'll get to that. Now give me the poison."

I could feel the vial in my pocket, pressing against my thigh. I wished I could make it disappear. I wished I could make myself disappear. Sitting there in that civilized dining room with cosmopolitan sophisticates all around me, I might just as well have been up a tree with a pack of wild dogs snapping at my feet. But why? It was just Roger talking to me, telling me I was trapped. That seductive son of a bitch with his talk of bonding and brotherhood had persuaded me I was stuck. I'd had enough of listening. I'd had enough of sitting. I stood up.

"Where are you going?" said Roger.

"Sweden."

"What?"

"The Swedish embassy. You told me to go there if I was in trouble."

"Jay, please sit down. If you walk out now, you'll only make things more difficult."

"Yeah, and I wouldn't want to make things more difficult."

"At least give me the poison."

"Screw you."

"Wait," said Roger.

I headed to the door without looking back. But looking forward, I faced Colonel Enriques, who was just entering the dining room. I didn't recognize him immediately, as he was dressed in civilian clothes.

I kept walking. The colonel was walking, too, coming directly toward me. His face lit up in a great warm smile, and he spoke loud enough for the diners at the tables around us to hear him.

"Ah, Mr. Cardinale, my friend. So good to see you again."

He had his arms spread open, and I thought he was going to throw them around me and hug me. But then he looked past me to Roger, and whatever he saw made him change his mind. Instead of a hug he put a hand on each of my upper arms, his grip firm.

"Let go," I said.

"Let us sit and talk," said the colonel, tightening his grip.

"Screw you."

I kneed him in the balls. He managed to suppress a cry, whimpering instead. He let go of my arms. I brushed past him and out through the entryway of the dining room through the lobby of the hotel, walking as fast as I could without drawing attention. As soon as I got outside, it hit me that I should've stopped at the desk to ask where the hell the Swedish embassy was.

There was a doorman greeting guests as they came and went. He was ignoring me, probably because I looked more like a panhandler than an important personage, as anyone staying at the Nacional would have to be.

"Excuse me," I said in English. "Do you speak English? *Habla usted ingles?*"

"No."

Not even a "No, señor." Just "No." He went back to proper clientele. I thought about stopping and asking one of them. Maybe I'd get lucky and stop the Swedish ambassador himself. But looking back into the hotel, I could see Roger and the colonel coming out of the dining room as fast as the colonel's jangled balls would allow. I'd worry about directions later.

- Seventy-One -

I took off running down the long driveway, no longer caring about drawing attention. I ducked through a space between the bushes that lined the sides of the entry road, running back toward the hotel, keeping low, hoping that they would think I was still going forward. I heard a car passing on the road on the other side of the hedge. It sounded as if it were moving fast. I hoped it was them.

    I skirted around the side of the hotel and came to a delivery area with a driveway that led to a smaller street. I hurried down that street to the first corner, turned there, then turned again at the next corner. I was trying to zigzag away from the hotel.

    I turned down what I thought was a one-way street where I would be facing the oncoming traffic—only to find that cars were parked in both directions and the traffic was actually coming from behind me. Bad mistake. Rolling to a stop right where I stood was a big black car, Roger in the passenger seat and Enriques behind the wheel. I started to run in the direction I'd come from, thinking they'd have to chase me in reverse, and smacked into a small elderly woman, knocking her down and nearly going down myself.

    It was all the time they needed to get out of the car, guns drawn. The colonel punched me with his free hand, driving his fist between my legs, sending a crippling pain from my groin to the ends of my fingers and toes and a flood of tears to my eyes. He shoved me toward the back of the car. The trunk was wide open.

"Get in," he said, shoving me again and kicking me when I stumbled. As the lid came down, I could see Roger helping the woman to her feet. A moment later, the car doors slammed shut and the car lurched forward. I guessed we weren't going to the Swedish Embassy. My mind shot back to Cowichan Bay, leaving the post office with Short One and Tall One and seeing the Lincoln parked by the diner. I knew then that I was going to be taken for a ride in a big black car. It had just taken a few months longer to happen than I'd expected.

- Seventy-Two -

Between the pain in my balls and the panic of being locked in a trunk, I lost it. Curled up in blackness, I cried and moaned without embarrassment. I cried all the tears I had. When there were none left, I started coming around.

I still had the pills in my pocket. Was there some way for me to barter them for my life? No, they would open the trunk and after they took them from me, the colonel would shoot me dead. It crossed my mind to take the pills myself. Why should I let Enriques kill me? Imagine his surprise if he opened the trunk and I was dead and the vial was empty. He'd probably shoot me anyway if I did that. I could do it, lying there in the dark. Get it over with. Save Fidel. Then these would be my last seconds alive.

It occurred to me that I'd been there before, facing death in the dark, the odds high against surviving but somehow, back there in the jungle, I'd made it through. I wasn't done yet. I started feeling around to see what I could find that might be a weapon or a defense. As I did, the car slowed, made a turn, and stopped. I heard the doors open and close and felt the weight of the car shift as the two men got out. A moment later, the trunk opened.

"Get out," said Enriques.

I shielded my eyes with my left hand, trying to adjust to the light as I climbed out of the trunk.

"The pills," said Enriques.

Roger was standing a few feet away. He had a gun out.

"Do it, Jay. Listen to the colonel," he said.

We were at the camp. I was right back where I'd started from that morning.

PART IX
Campamento Brigada Venceremos

- Seventy-Three -

We had driven in as far as the barracks tents. Except for the wind in the trees on the edge of the camp, it was quiet, more quiet than it had ever been when the Brigade was there.

Roger was nodding at me as if to say, "Give the pills to the colonel and then we can get on to my plan." At least, that was what I wanted to believe he was saying to me. I held out my hand and opened my palm. Enriques took the vial. As he did, his angry expression gave way to a sneer.

"*Gracias*. The true revolution thanks you."

"Let me have them," said Roger. "I'll give him the pill."

"You're going to give me a pill?" I said.

"Make it look like suicide, you know. Everyone else off to the beach then home to the States while you're stuck here in Cuba. An act of despair. I'll tell everyone how despondent you were when we had lunch and how you took off on me, I knew not where. You made it back here and overdosed on the painkillers you had for your wound." He turned to Enriques again. "Let me have them, Colonel. We'll go to his tent and have him lie down and wait for it to work."

Was this Roger's plan, to give me one of the non-poison pills and I would pretend to die? If so, it seemed awfully lame. Was I going to die before my father?

"No," said Enriques. "What if something should happen with the pill I will use tonight? If Fidel does not drink the water I give him. You say there are only three pills. I want them all."

"But, Colonel, we agreed. An American shot dead, even one as unwelcome as Cardinale, could stir too much interest."

"Yes, but two dead Americans will look like they had a falling out and killed each other. Or perhaps you are *maricón*, and it is murder and suicide for your sad love."

Roger realized what Enriques was about to do and turned his gun and fired. But the colonel fired a split-second sooner, and Roger's shot went wild as he flew down backwards from the impact of the bullet that had hit him in the gut. The gun fell out of his hand and lay on the ground next to him.

"Hands up," Enriques said to me. "Now kick the gun away from him."

I raised my hands and stepped around Roger, who was writhing on the ground and grunting, and kicked the gun. It slid about ten feet away across the dusty earth. I stared at it with my hands in the air.

"Now, pick him up and carry him to the barracks where you sleep."

"*Qué pasa?*" said another voice from behind the colonel.

It was Juan. He had come running out of the workshop, machete in hand, at the sound of the shot. The colonel turned and fired at him. He missed. Raising the machete over his head, Juan charged. The colonel fired and missed again. He was rattled. But he took aim with his third shot, and this one stopped Juan in his tracks. He spun around and crumbled to the ground, his machete well short of the colonel.

The colonel turned back to me. I had Roger's gun. He fired and I fired back and we both missed. He scrambled behind the car and I ran for cover behind the information post just to the side of the tents. I tried to catch my breath and figure out what to do. I had a gun and had only fired one shot. At least I was pretty sure I'd only fired once. Roger had fired once. The colonel had dropped Roger with a single shot, fired three times at Juan and at me once.

Was Roger still alive? I looked around from the side of the information post. He wasn't moving. I suppose I was leaning out too far because Enriques fired again. I felt a stabbing pain in my right side. I screamed and dropped the gun. Blood was spreading over the front of my shirt. He fired again, I think three times. It occurred to me that he had more than one gun. I picked up my gun with my left hand and fired back more or less in his direction.

I wondered if Juan had been the only one at the camp. If anyone else was there, they were being very smart about staying out of sight. I thought that I should get myself out of sight, as well. I was bleeding, and, based on my scream, there was a good chance that the colonel would come after me to finish me off. If he did, he would probably succeed. The woods at the edge of the camp were not far off. I fired a couple more shots and took off as fast as I could run. He shot at me as I ran and missed.

I was in the trees, bleeding and in pain. I kept going as fast as I could through the mix of tropical bushes and trees. I stumbled a couple of times but stayed on my feet. I was conscious of the gun in my hand and trying hard to keep a grip on it even though feeling dizzy from all the alcohol I'd consumed earlier, the lack of food, the punch to my groin, the loss of blood, and a general state of panic. As I ran, I wondered if I had any bullets left. One? Two? Three?

I stopped for a moment to get my breath and to listen. There was only the wind. I took out my handkerchief, and, lifting my shirt, started pressing at my wound surprised to discover I hadn't been shot after all. Enriques's bullet must have hit the corner of the information post and shattered the wood. What I had was one big splinter and several smaller ones that looked to be a mirror image of the bayonet scar on my left side. It hurt, but not the way a bullet would have and with a lot less damage.

I needed to get a grip and fast. I was safe, even if only for a few moments, I wasn't shot, and maybe my scream had been a good thing—if Enriques thought I was hurt worse than I was.

I pulled out the big splinter and as many of the smaller ones as I could get my fingers on. I was bloody from the scratches, but the bleeding had already stopped. The cuts were painful, but they were a long, long way from being fatal. My prospects for surviving seemed better than they had a couple of minutes earlier.

Then I smelled the smoke. I would have thought that with the rains we'd had, the woods couldn't go up the way they did, but it only took a few minutes for a line of fire to spread out in both directions along the side of the woods where I'd come in. It looked like Enriques had started several small fires and they were burning into each other. Maybe he'd seen the blood on the ground behind the information post. From that and the way I'd screamed when I was hit, he may have figured I was pretty far gone already. He might trust the smoke and flames to finish me off, or he might be circling around to meet me as the fire drove me forward.

I decided to take my chance with the fire. There might be a place where the line was broken. There were several thin streams and creeks barely wider than a foot or two across but enough to make a passage through the flames. If I could get through to the camp, there might still be a first aid kit in the infirmary. And there might be other people there, come out of hiding after the colonel drove away. I turned back toward the camp.

It was probably a stupid thing to do, but I had more luck than brains and found exactly what I had hoped for. Fires were burning on either side of a small stream, leaving just enough space for me to get through. I came to the edge of the woods where it bordered the camp. I was up past the end of the barracks, about fifty yards or so from where I'd gone into the woods. Looking down the length of the camp, I could see Roger and Juan on the ground, but the colonel's car was gone. He had gone to look for me on the other side of the woods. I finally checked the gun. One bullet left.

Staying in the woods, I circled around to the back of the infirmary, opposite the point where I'd gone in. I held my breath and went out into the open and around to the front of the infirmary. The door was not locked. Once I got a bandage on my wound, I could check out the camp office to see if any of the phones worked.

I put some antiseptic on the cuts and bandaged the biggest one, then took a bunch of aspirin. I worked quietly, keeping an eye out the window. The colonel had not returned. It was time to look to Juan and Roger.

Juan was dead. The colonel had hit him right in the middle of his chest. He must have died immediately. Looking down at him, a young guy lying in his own blood in the dirt, I thought of the young guys I'd seen in Vietnam also lying dead in the dirt. They were in uniform and so was Juan, in his cane-cutter uniform. They had died on a battlefield and so had he. The cane, though, was not his enemy. The battle this New Man fought was not with the cane but with the past, the past of ambitious old men like Enriques.

Roger was alive. He was lying face down, the ground around him soaked with blood. I turned him over and he groaned and opened his eyes.

"Son bitch," he said weakly.

I lifted his head.

"I'd give you fake pill. You know. Wouldn't kill."

"Sure. How else would you get laid?" I said.

"Right. Lying. … Would poison. No loose ends. Sorry. … Colonel?"

"He's looking for me. I can't stay."

"Tonight. Academy dinner. … Poison Castro water. Stop him."

"You want me to save Castro?"

"No. Want to screw Enriques. … Bastard. I knew. Thought I had time. … Was leaving tonight before he knew."

"You knew he would try to kill you?"

"No loose ends."

"Screw him."

"Right. You go. Village Cojimar. … Near beach we went. Fish boat *Alicia*. … Rendezvous for U.S. Take my passport. Money for captain. … Me. Be me."

"Be you?"

"Hermanos …"

He was gone. I did as he said, taking his passport, wallet, money, everything he had, as quickly as I could, then hurried to the director's office to see if the phone worked. It didn't. I went back to Roger. I wanted to put him and Juan in the infirmary, but if Enriques came back and didn't see them lying there, he'd know I'd been back.

Fuck it, I thought, I can't leave them there.

I picked Roger up and carried him into the infirmary. It wasn't easy. I had to put him down halfway there and drag him the rest of the way. Inside, I hoisted him up onto the examining table, then hurried back out to get Juan. I was about to pick him up when I heard an approaching engine. It was too far back to the infirmary, and also more in view of someone driving into the camp. I dove for the pool of blood where Roger had been lying. I lay face down, my arm crossed in front of my head. I watched from under my bent arm as Enriques drove back into camp, stopping farther back than he had before. He got out cautiously, gun drawn, staying behind the car door. I had the gun in my waistband, but didn't plan to use my one bullet unless it looked like he was going to come right up to me.

It was easy to read his mind. He was trying to figure out if there was any way he could know for sure whether I was dead somewhere in the woods or had somehow managed to stay alive. No loose ends. But there wasn't any way for him to know unless he was willing to wait for the fire to burn out and then look for my body in the woods. He tried to come at it as many ways as he could, but there was nothing else to be done. And what if he couldn't find a body? What if I had gotten out of the burning woods? Would that mean I got away? Or would it mean I struggled on into the cane fields beyond and now lay dead behind a row of cut stalks?

It was too much. He had to get back to Havana to kill Castro. He'd come back tomorrow and look for me then. Or send a team of his students out to scour the area for me, since he'd be busy taking over the government. But what about Roger and Juan? Should he hide them? Maybe he could figure out a way to pin their murders on me. Yes, that would work well, even if they found me alive instead of dead. Yes, he was done with the camp for now. He got back in the car and drove away.

- Seventy-Four -

I lay hardly breathing for about fifteen minutes before I got up. Juan was easier to lift than Roger. I carried him to the infirmary and put him on the examining table next to Roger. It was crowded, but they weren't about to complain. There was the chance that Enriques was playing a game and might still come back, so I kept an ear tuned for any noise outside while I very quietly went about the business of bandaging the rest of my cuts. I had learned some things from medics in the field and some more by watching the nurses when I was in the hospital, and altogether I came up with something that I could fairly say was better than half-assed.

I looked around to see if by some miracle there was a gun anywhere. There wasn't. But I did find a shirt hanging on the back of the door. It was a little too big for me and it wasn't clean, but it also wasn't covered in blood.

Evening was coming on and I had no idea when this dinner was supposed to happen. Roger had said it would be at the Academy, and I had no idea where the Academy was. I assumed it was in Havana, since I was supposed to stay with Roger while I was working there. But since the whole job thing was bullshit, for all I knew the Academy could be outside of the city or in another city entirely. Maybe it didn't exist at all. There was nothing to do except get to Havana and hope it was there.

I was all set to leave when I had one more thought. I took out my wallet and went through it for anything personal that I would want to keep. After clearing out some pictures and the card from Ed McWilliams,

I put the wallet and my Venceremos Brigade ID in Roger's pockets. I was about to add my passport, the one that Ward/Howard had given me, but I looked at the picture and hesitated. We did vaguely look like brothers, but I didn't think anyone looking at the passport would think it was a picture of Roger. There was only one thing to do. I took a sheet and covered his face and then took the gun and used it like a hammer, pounding at him as hard as I could, then took the sheet away and slipped the passport in his pocket. No one would bother to try to identify him from the picture.

I came out of the infirmary, gun ready with its single bullet. It wasn't likely he was out there waiting to ambush me, but I didn't want to find out I was wrong, either. I took one last look back into the infirmary at the two bodies. I hated to leave them there, but I couldn't wait any longer to get started. Looking at Juan, it suddenly hit me that his bike might be somewhere around. Juan had been in the workshop and I hurried over there. Sure enough, inside the door was the bike. He'd been working on it, replacing the old basket attached to the handlebars with a new one. He must have just finished when he heard the shots. His tool kit lay open in the new basket. I grabbed the bike, got on, and rode to the gate and out onto the road.

It didn't take long for the effort of pedaling to wear me down. I stopped and went into the foliage and lay down with the bike beside me, out of sight from the road. I tried to count ten minutes, cursing Roger for not having had a watch, and when the time seemed about right, I got back on the road and pedaled some more. Pedaling and resting, pedaling and resting.

Poor Juan. When he saw the gun pointed at me, had he considered letting me get shot, leaving the way open for him and Avis? But no, whatever else I was, we were comrades of the Brigade and he had to defend me. He would have been glad to know that he died trying to kill the guy who was going to try to kill Fidel. Or he would have been upset that he had failed to kill him. However it might have gone, he was dead, still a boy, a New Man, a good man, but still a boy. It made me want to get Enriques that much more.

And Roger was dead. Roger was dead. I had come to Cuba to kill him and he was supposed to kill me and I was alive and he was dead.

He had pretended to be my friend right to the end, but at least then he admitted that he was going to poison me after all. No loose ends for him or for Enriques. And I was alive and he was dead.

He wanted me trusting him, believing in him. Like training Eddie and the others to make bombs right to the last minute while he was getting ready to blow them up. He was a rotten bastard and I didn't want to start feeling sorry for him now that he was gone. It was him or me, just as it had been right from the time I met the McWilliamses. And I was alive and he was dead.

Bonded. Brothers. Hermanos. It seemed so real when he said it. Was it true? I thought he meant it. It didn't mean he wasn't going to kill me when the time came. He would call me his brother, think of me as his brother, love me like a brother, and kill me like a brother. All men are brothers; the war had taught me that. But it didn't stop us from killing each other when we had to. And in front of Enriques he had to.

But when Roger failed to kill me, when he was dying, he told me how to get away. His passport in my pocket. He said we could pass for brothers. Maybe I could fool my way past whoever was supposed to rescue him. If they didn't know Roger, they might assume I was him if I was in the fishing boat making the connection. Hermanos.

PART X
Havana

- Seventy-Five -

It was still light when I reached the city. I had a vague idea where I was from having looked out the window when I'd come in on the bus. Now I had to figure out where to find the Academy. I couldn't ask a policeman. Instead, I pulled up to the curb and asked the first guy I saw who looked like he might speak English.

Not only did he not speak English, but he eyed at me with that same suspicious look I'd seen before from the neighborhood watchers. I kept pedaling, aware of the looks I was getting as I went down the road. Not from everyone, maybe just one in ten. The other nine pretended that they didn't see me. I looked like trouble and they all had enough of that in their lives.

It was crazy. I was knocking myself out trying to save their beloved leader and all I got from them was the hairy eyeball. I liked Fidel, I really did. But Roger was right. He was a dictator and maybe the Cubans would be better off without him.

On the other hand, I could forget Castro and head to the fishing boat and get my ass out of there before Enriques tracked me down. I had the bike and I knew more or less how to get to Cojimar. It made more sense than anything else. I felt closer to free than at any time in the past several months. I started pedaling again, pushing hard.

It was getting late. I didn't know if I could make it. It suddenly dawned on me that only a few blocks farther on was the Nacional, where I'd kicked Enriques in the nuts. Beyond it was the Capri, where Anya and

Tatiana were probably still asleep. Anya and Tatiana who spoke Spanish and English as well as Russian.

I'd told Roger I'd stop Enriques. I don't know whether I meant it when I said it, and maybe saving Fidel was a mistake, but letting Enriques win seemed like a bigger mistake. And more than that, I couldn't let him make me run. I'd been running for too long. Cowboy John Lydon's words popped into my head: Even if you've got nothing but bad choices, he'd said, when it comes down to it, you'll know what to do.

- Seventy-Six -

I knocked on the door gently but got no response. I tried again, a little louder. Still nothing. The next time, I hit it hard, rapping my knuckles. I knew we had fucked their brains out and they were exhausted from their flight, but they had to hear that unless they were dead. There was noise inside and a moment later Anya opened the door.

"Vronsky," she said. "Back for more?"

She took my hand and yanked me into the room, nearly pulling me off my feet. She steered me toward the bed, but I dug in my heels and held her back.

"Wait," I said. "I need your help."

"I need your help, too."

On the other bed, Tatiana, half asleep, raised her head.

"Where is your brother? Onegin?"

"He's dead."

They laughed.

"I mean it. He's dead. Murdered."

Tatiana sat up, suddenly wide awake. Anya released her grip on my arm and stepped back.

"This is a joke?"

"No joke. And the man who killed him wants to kill Fidel. We have to stop him."

"Kill Fidel?" said Anya. "But—"

"Listen to me—we have to stop this man. He's going to try to kill

Fidel tonight, soon, at a place called the Academy of Officer Cadets. I don't know where this place is. I don't speak Spanish. I need you to call down to the desk and ask them where this place is and how to get there. But we have to hurry. He could be putting poison in Fidel's drink right now. Please!"

Anya picked up the phone and called the desk. She spoke in Spanish. Tatiana grabbed a pad and a pen from the desk and put them down in front of Anya. I couldn't believe how cool they were, snapping into action from the dreamy sensuality of their warm beds. I would feel safe on any plane where they were the stewardesses.

Anya scribbled as she listened, then put down the phone. She gave me the note with the name of the street where the Academy was located and directions, written in English. So cool. I glanced at the notes quickly. The Academy was only a few blocks away.

"Great," I said. "I love you both."

I turned to the door.

"Wait," said Anya. "What else can we do?"

"Pray, comrades. Pray for Fidel."

- Seventy-Seven -

It was a ten-minute ride to the Academy. I wasn't exactly sure what I'd do when I got there. I only hoped that Fidel was still alive. If he was dead then Enriques had won and I would turn around and head for the boat. I didn't want to run, but I didn't want to end up in a Cuban jail, far worse, I guessed, than winding up in a U.S. jail.

The Academy was a brick building four stories high. It looked like nothing less than PS 48, my elementary school in Bensonhurst. There were lights shining from the windows on the first floor, but the other floors were dark. As I pedaled toward the entrance, I could see two guards in front. I slowed as got closer, wondering if they were always there or just there for Fidel, or if Enriques had taken the precaution of stationing them there in case I showed up.

I pulled the bike up to the side of the entrance. The two guards began walking toward me, saying something in Spanish that I assumed was "Hey, buddy, you can't park there." I drew the gun out from my belt and they stopped where they were. I gestured for them to drop their guns on the ground. They hesitated then obeyed. I gestured again for them to head down the street.

"Get going," I said.

They just stood there.

"Get lost," I shouted, and gestured again.

They still didn't move. I tried to remember any Spanish word that meant run or go or anything like it. One of them took a step forward. I fired my last bullet at his feet.

"*Vamos!*" I said, raising the gun as if to fire right at them. I took a step forward and shouted again.

"Scram! Vamoose!"

I realized I was talking cowboy movie talk and hoped it wasn't jargon made up in Hollywood that actually meant nothing. Whether it did or not, the gun in my hand meant something. They turned and ran down the street.

"Vamoose!" I shouted after them, then I picked up their guns just as the door opened and two more guards came out. I pointed the guns at them. They dropped theirs and headed down the street after the first two guards.

I dashed inside, locking the door behind me. The place was lit up, with chandeliers along the corridor that stretched left and right from the entrance. But I was focused on the double doors directly in front of me. Loud applause came from inside. I ducked low and opened one of them just enough to look inside.

It was the dining hall where I might have been eating for free if anything Roger had said to me had been true. The tables were lined up perpendicular to the doors. There might have been a couple of hundred young guys in uniform at the tables, all standing and applauding. When they sat down, I could see the dais at the other end of the hall opposite the doors. Castro was standing at the middle, his bodyguards standing behind him. Seated to his right was Enriques, looking up admiringly at the man he was planning to kill.

As the applause subsided, Castro began speaking. I didn't know if he was just starting his speech or if the applause had interrupted him at some notable line and he was picking up where he'd left off. It was all so sane and reasonable, the great commanding figure of Fidel, the fresh-faced worshipful cadets in their sharp uniforms, the bright light of the ornate chandeliers.

Everything seemed right except Enriques. He picked up the glass of water in front of his own place setting and drank from it, never taking his eyes off Castro. As he put the glass down, I could see his free hand come up from behind the table and pass over the glass. Then he raised it to his lips, still gazing up at Castro. The glass never touched his mouth. After pretending to drink, he put the glass down again, but not in front of his own setting. Instead, he placed it next to the glass in front of Castro.

He kept his hand on the glass for a moment, then shifted his fingers to the other glass and picked it up and drank, this time for real, then put that glass down in front of his place. He had completed the switch. The poison was in place.

Castro hit another one of his applause lines. The cadets began to clap and stand up. As they did, Castro reached down for his glass. I pushed the doors open and ran down the aisle between the tables directly toward him. I should have asked the girls how to say *poison* in Spanish. Or *danger*. Or "*Don't drink that.*"

All I could do was shout, "No! No!"

Enriques was on his feet.

"Stop him!"

Drawing their guns, Castro's bodyguards jumped in front of their boss while the cadets along the row where I was turned and grabbed at me. Clearly, I was some kind of dangerous lunatic. I didn't care. I could see between the bodyguards that Castro had paused and put the glass down. He was staring at me, trying to remember why I looked familiar. Then I knew what I had to say.

"Rincon caliente! Rincon caliente!"

He remembered. In Spanish he ordered the cadets to release me and his bodyguards to step back. Enriques jabbered something to Castro, gesturing at me. I had the feeling he was trying to pin the rap on me, although there was nothing to indicate that there was any rap to be pinned. The glass still sat on the table like a ticking bomb. I grabbed the gun from my belt. Cadets jumped away from me. Castro drew back. His bodyguards, who had relaxed, thrust themselves forward as they reached for their guns again.

Enriques reached for his gun. Before he could get it out, I threw my gun at the glass. I was close enough so that I could hardly miss. The gun didn't break the glass, but it did knock it off the table.

"Agua poison!" I said, sounding like Tarzan talking to Jane, and pointing at Enriques as the nearest cadets pounced on me again. I only stayed on my feet because there were as many cadets pushing me forward as there were pushing me back.

I was hoping that *poison* was the same in Spanish as it was in English. I found out later that it wasn't, but fortunately Castro's English was much better than my Spanish. He looked at the glass and he looked at Enriques standing next to him, gun in hand. I think Enriques would have fired at me as soon as he drew, but the cadets who had jumped me blocked his shot. Now he looked at Castro and it wasn't hard to see that he was thinking that this was the moment for him to act. But he hesitated, I think intimidated by Fidel's size—not just his physical size, but the way he seemed to swell with authority at the idea that that authority could be challenged.

And in that moment of hesitancy he was lost because sirens started screaming. The sound was piercing and seemed to come from everywhere. A voice came over a loudspeaker. I didn't know what it said, but I was pretty sure I heard "*bomba*." A panic set in as the cadets began racing for the exits. I got swept up in the crowd. As I got close to a side exit, I was able to look back to the dais. Castro was gone, but Enriques was still standing there, gun in hand, hanging at his side, as Castro's bodyguards closed in on him. As I shoved my way through the exit, I thought I heard a shot, but with the shouting and sirens it was hard to say for sure.

The exit went directly out onto the street. Most of the cadets stopped as soon as they were across the street from their school, but I kept going, turning the nearest corner and moving away as quickly as I could, once again trying not to run. I had only gone a few yards when I saw the girls. I headed to them and the three of us turned down an alley and kept going until we were another block away.

"What happened?" said Anya.

"He's okay. Fidel lives! We got there in time."

The girls jumped up and down, squealing with delight, hugged each other and me, and we all kissed.

"Come on," I said. "We should move. There might be a bomb in the building."

"Don't worry," said Anya. "There is no bomb."

"No bomb," echoed Tatiana. They laughed.

"How do you know?"

"We called the police," said Tatiana. "We told them about the bomb."

"You told them?"

"Like in America," said Tatiana. "Like American school."

"What?"

"An American told us. You call in bomb when you not ready for test. Good joke, yes?"

- Seventy-Eight -

The girls wanted me to come back to the hotel with them. But I explained that I had no idea who might be looking for me, and anyway, I had a ride to catch. They were upset and kept asking if I could give them at least an hour. As tempting as the request was, and as much as I thought Roger would have done it, I was too far gone to take the chance.

I did go back with them to the hotel, where I was able to get a taxi. Before I left, I asked them to do one more thing: call the police and tell them about the bodies at the camp. We kissed goodbye and I gave them the phone number at the commune and told them they could always reach me that way. I didn't really know if that was true, but I couldn't think of any alternative. They wrote their names down and their addresses in Russia so I could write to them, and reminded me that I could reach them through Aeroflot, too. As I left I hoped I would see them again. We had had sex but I didn't know them and I wanted to. They were fantastic human beings with great hearts, capable of heroic acts and I wanted to know them.

The taxi took me to the waterfront in Cojimar. I found my way to the *Alicia*. A voice from on board challenged me as I got alongside the boat. I said I was Roger.

"Come aboard," said the voice. There was only one man on the boat. His face was so weathered, he could have been anywhere between forty and sixty. He flashed a light on my face.

"*Usted no es* Roger."

"Sí," I said. I reached for the passport. I heard the click of the hammer on his gun and put my hands up.

"*Un momento, por favor,*" I said and slowly, very slowly, using two fingers, I took out Roger's passport and, more importantly, the wads of bills Roger had had in his pocket. The captain looked at the picture and at my face and took the money.

"*Usted es* Roger."

He handed me a beat-up old hat and a short jacket that smelled of fish, and pointed to a corner in the back of the boat where I could settle in. He stowed the money inside his own jacket and proceeded to take the boat out.

I slept. I woke with my host shaking my shoulder with one hand while holding his other hand over my mouth. He put a finger to his lips, signaling for me not to speak. The night was clear and the sky bright with stars that outshone the quarter moon hanging low on the horizon. The captain pointed out past the stern of the boat. I looked but there was nothing to see. As my head came clear of sleep, I could hear the sound of an engine idling low. The captain flashed his light in a signal in that direction. A series of flashes came back at us. The captain nodded to me. This was our rendezvous.

He took the boat around to where we had seen the light, and now we could see the outline of the boat, about the same size as ours, against the starry horizon. The captain idled the engine, got out a pike, and pulled the two unlighted boats together, then signaled for me to cross over. I gave him a wave of thanks and vaulted from one boat to the other. As soon as I was off his boat, he put his engine back in gear and took off at top speed into the dark.

A familiar voice said, "Jeez, Roger, about time. Been waiting here over an hour."

A tall figure loomed up in the dark.

"Is it done?" he said.

"Oh, it's done."

"Roger?"

"And out."

Gordon was a foot away. I swung as hard as I could and caught him on the temple. He staggered. I swung again, an uppercut, and hit him in the jaw. He fell against the side of the boat. I grabbed him quick and swung him up and over the side. Just like in the movies, he shouted "Help!" as he hit the water.

I spotted a life preserver against the back of the cabin, pulled it free, and tossed it over the side, then went back into the cabin and found a light switch. A flashlight was lying on a table. I turned it on and went back out. He was still screaming for help and was easy to spot. He had the life preserver.

"Hang on," I said.

I untied a raft at the back of the boat and sent it over the side, shining the light until he reached it.

"You'd better paddle away. I'm starting the engine."

"Cardinale, you motherfucker."

"Would you like me to shoot a hole in the raft?"

"Fuck you!"

"Back away, asshole."

I went to the cabin and looked over the controls. Just like the ones on the fishing boats in Sheepshead Bay. I started the engine up. Looking out the window, I spotted the Dipper and the North Star. I went back to the rail of the boat to make sure Gordon had moved off. He had.

"So long, sucker!" I said and went back to the controls. I put the boat in gear, and, following the stars, began cruising north by northwest toward what I hoped would be Key West.

Locking the wheel, I looked around the cabin. I found a bottle of whiskey and a pack of cigarettes. Things were looking up. I settled in behind the wheel and let my thoughts roam.

One word floated to the top.

Venceremos.

PART XI
The States

- Seventy-Nine -

My mother was shocked when I showed up late one night, since she'd been told I was dead. Also, I'd grown a beard so I'd look more like Roger's passport picture, and that freaked her out. I kept it simple, saying I'd switched clothes with someone and he got killed. But I reminded her I was still wanted, so she had better not let anyone know I'd come back.

I was glad I got to see my father, as wasted away as he was. My mother hadn't told him that I was dead, figuring he had enough on his plate. But he was still surprised to see me. I fed him the story about how being a deserter was all a cover for me to go on a secret mission for the government. He seemed to buy it. I was his hero again.

I got to spend a week with my dad before he died. I stayed by his side almost the whole time. We pretended he was going to get better. We made plans to go out to Shea. Sometimes, when he was a little out of it, he talked as if I was still in Canada.

"I'll come up to Montreal," he said. "Take the train. We'll go see the Expos. Come up for a Mets game."

"I'd like that."

"I went to Montreal once."

"You did? I didn't know that."

"Before the war. A bunch of guys from the neighborhood would go up to the mountains to ride horses. One year, we took a few extra days and went to Canada. To Montreal. They talk French there."

"That's right."

"We had a great time. Ate French food."

"Well, maybe we'll get to do that together."

"You bet. But don't tell your mother. She hates French food."

- Eighty -

I couldn't go to the funeral. I didn't even go out of the house once I got there, and avoided any contact with the old friends of his that stopped by to visit, although there weren't that many. No one really wanted to see him the way he was. My mother had plenty of support from family and friends, and she hadn't expected me to be there anyway, so it wasn't so bad that she couldn't lean on me.

After he was gone, I stayed on a couple of days so the house wouldn't be completely empty for her. But then it was time to go.

"Where are you going?" she wanted to know.

"I'm not sure," I said. "Probably back to Canada. I'll write you and we'll figure out a way to meet up somewhere soon."

"Why can't you stay? If everything is okay with the Army, you should be able to stay."

"Ma, I only told Daddy it was okay. It's really not, remember?"

"Oh, right."

I left at night. I thought about heading into Manhattan and tracking down Walter, but having to tell him the whole story and then answer all his questions seemed like more than I could deal with. I only wanted to tell the story once and it wasn't to him.

I got a late bus out of Port Authority. When we stopped in Pittsburgh for a break, I called Ed McWilliams to tell him Roger was dead. He already knew.

"Howard told me," he said. "Look, I'm sorry it didn't work out about the pardon. You understand we thought that was legitimate. We thought it was all legitimate. We were used, too, you know."

"Of course. You couldn't know." He could and probably did, I thought, but why argue?

"If there is anything else I can do … Do you need any money?"

"Sure. But I don't think there's any way you can get it to me that I could trust."

"You don't trust me?"

"Let's just say I don't trust your friends."

We left it there. Any more and I would have started saying mean things about his wife.

Before the bus left, I found a post office and sent a package off to Wildflower at the commune. I had managed to keep a few hundred dollars of the cash Howard had given me in St. John, and I wanted to pay her back, plus a little more, for the money she'd given me. I wished I had enough to send some to John Lydon and some to Tish just for having been there when I needed them. Maybe someday I'd be able to do something for them. I hoped so.

- Eighty-One -

I got to Milwaukee the next afternoon. I got her address out of the phone book, over on the East Side near Brady Street, where the hippies were remaking the old Polish neighborhood. I found a bookstore and bought a copy of the Castaneda book I'd been reading in Cuba. There was a coffee shop on the corner near her building, and I got a table where I could watch the entrance while pretending to read. They didn't seem to mind my sitting there as long as there was no crowd and I kept ordering coffee and something to eat every couple of hours.

When dinnertime came, I ate there, and then I left for a while so they could have the table for other customers. I walked around, but not so far that I couldn't keep an eye on her building.

When the dinner rush was over, I went back in and resumed my vigil.

"You waiting for someone?" said the waitress.

"Yeah, but I don't know when she's getting home."

"I hope she makes it by ten. That's when we close."

She did. She walked right past the shop window. I was caught by surprise, somehow expecting that I would see her coming the other way. I threw some tip money down on the table, grabbed my stuff, and raced out after her. She was almost to her door.

I called to her. She stopped and looked back. At first she didn't recognize me because of the beard and because of thinking I was dead.

"I'm alive," I said.

She stood still, staring at me. I went up to her. She didn't move, just kept staring.

"I'm alive. It was Roger who got killed."

I took her in my arms and kissed her. She put her arms around my neck and kissed me back. We looked at each other. She had tears in her eyes.

"Sugar, sugar," I said.

"Honey, honey," she answered.

- Eighty-Two -

I knew he would show up sooner or later. I'd gotten a job washing dishes through the union Avis worked for, and was learning to be a short-order cook. One night, I stepped out into the alley behind the kitchen on a break, and had just lit a cigarette when I saw him standing on the edge of the circle of light from a bare bulb over the exit door.

"Hey, Roger," he said as he stepped into the light.

"Howard. You look well. Come to arrest me?"

"Nah. We dropped all that 'wanted' stuff."

"I kind of figured, since I'm still walking around."

"Yeah. It was, you know, just part of the game."

"Right. So, how's Gordon?"

"Prospering. He's become a naval hero for his extraordinary seamanship, managing to steer that little raft all the way to Florida."

"Too bad. I was hoping the sharks would get him."

"Nah. Sharks knew better than to mess with Gordon. He's a little peeved with you, though. Says you sucker-punched him."

"I did. I'd do it again, too."

"That's why I thought to leave him back at HQ. Oh, by the way, regards from Miss More."

"Mine back to her. So are we going to continue this chit-chat, or have you got something real to say?"

"You should have let us get Castro. That was a mistake."

"Enriques was a bigger mistake."

"Not for us."

"Well, what's done is done. Anything else?"

"Not really, just wanted to let you know we're keeping tabs."

"What about Roger? Did he have any family?"

"Not really. An ex-wife from a bunch of years ago, but she wouldn't care."

"Do you care?"

"Frankly, he was becoming a bore. You did us a favor."

"I didn't do it. Enriques did."

"Whatever."

"Anything else?"

"Nothing for now."

He walked out of the circle of light. I could see his outline as he went down the alley toward the street.

"What about later?" I said.

He spoke without turning.

"You never know. You got skills, kid. We like skills."

He faded into the night.

Praise for *Venceremos*

A tale of hunger—for revenge, for love, for meaning, for a better life—told with intensity by a writer who was there to witness the turmoil, confusion, hope, and humor of the 60s. A fiction with one foot in history and the other in the unresolved present-day conflicts of American society.
—ELLEN SORRIN, Director, The George Balanchine Trust

How great to have someone finally capture the real idealism and urgency of the '60s and understand the complex seductions of Castro's Cuba—then tell it all as a thrilling romantic adventure story.
—LINDA WINER, Theater Critic and Arts Columnist

Howard Waxman creates a sense of time and place as vivid as the characters living it. The voice of Jay Cardinale is as honest and anguished as American Literature has seen in a good long while. Venceremos is a compelling, lightning fast read of the highest order, the work of an extraordinary talent.
—STANLEY HOFFMAN, author of *Solomon's Temple*